DOTTED
LINES

Essential Prose Series 222

Guernica Editions Inc. acknowledges the support of the Canada Council
for the Arts and the Ontario Arts Council. The Ontario Arts Council
is an agency of the Government of Ontario.

We acknowledge the financial support of the Government of Canada.

DOTTED LINES

STEPHANIE CESCA

GUERNICA
EDITIONS
TORONTO · CHICAGO · BUFFALO · LANCASTER (U.K.)
2024

Guernica Founder: Antonio D'Alfonso

Michael Mirolla, general editor
Julie Roorda, editor
David Moratto, interior and cover designer

Guernica Editions Inc.
1241 Marble Rock Rd., Gananoque, ON K7G 2V4
2250 Military Road, Tonawanda, N.Y. 14150-6000 U.S.A.
www.guernicaeditions.com

Distributors:
Independent Publishers Group (IPG)
600 North Pulaski Road, Chicago IL 60624
University of Toronto Press Distribution (UTP)
5201 Dufferin Street, Toronto (ON), Canada M3H 5T8

First edition.
Printed in Canada.

Legal Deposit—Third Quarter
Library of Congress Catalog Card Number: 2024930296
Library and Archives Canada Cataloguing in Publication
Title: Dotted lines / Stephanie Cesca.
Names: Cesca, Stephanie, author.
Series: Essential prose series ; 222.
Description: First edition. | Series statement: Essential prose series ; 222
Identifiers: Canadiana (print) 20240286758 | Canadiana (ebook)
20240286766 | ISBN 9781771839051 (softcover) |
ISBN 9781771839068 (EPUB)
Subjects: LCGFT: Novels.
Classification: LCC PS8605.E86 D67 2024 | DDC C813/.6—dc23

For Ben, Theo & Katie

CONTENTS

❖❖❖

CHAPTER ONE

———◦◇◦———

DAVE

September 1983

A RAY OF green light hit the wall of my bedroom, numbers flashing together with the beat of the buzzer.

5:15 a.m. Time to get up.

I looked over at my mother beside me on the mattress; she was face-down in the pillow. Her dark brown hair fell around her shoulders, long enough that it spilled onto the carpeted floor, which was different shades of beige depending on where the stains were.

I leaned over to hit the off button and then gently nudged her. "Mom . . . Mom. It's morning."

She rolled around before answering. "It's too early," she said, her voice muffled by the pillow.

I elbowed her again, this time harder, and she rolled over so that her back was up against me. "I hate mornings," she said. "I don't want to go to work."

It was Saturday, which meant her shift at Sunny's started at six. The diner was owned not by a Sunny but by an Eleanor, a woman in her sixties who wore green eyeliner and smelled like cigarettes. Her sunken eyes and wrinkled face carried a constant frown that scared

1

the customers despite her attempts to smile. At least she tried.

Mom slowly sat up, tucking her feet under her thighs in a cross-legged position on the mattress. She rolled her head up and down, then left, twisting herself so she finally faced me.

"Are you coming in today?"

"I don't know," I said. "Maybe."

"Don't stay home alone again," she said. "Besides, I might need you for something."

I sat up beside her on the mattress. I thought of the television set, whose dials were still broken, and the empty fridge. "Okay," I said.

We climbed out of bed and made breakfast—coffee for Mom, milk and cereal for me—then brushed our teeth and got dressed. We left the house at 5:50 a.m., so we had to hurry to make it to the restaurant four blocks away.

"We're late again," Mom said as we jogged down the street. "El's gonna kill me—she's been in a real pissy mood lately."

As soon as we got there, Mom threw on her hairnet, tied up her apron and showed me to my usual seat. "Get your books out," she said. "I'll bring you some juice as soon as I get a minute."

"Why do you have to wear that thing?" I asked. The brown net looked like a shower cap she'd forgotten to take off before coming to work.

"It's beautiful, isn't it?" Mom said, putting one hand behind her head as if she was posing for a photo.

"But Eleanor doesn't make the other waitresses wear that."

"Yeah, well, I guess Eleanor must really like me," she said before walking away.

I reached into my knapsack and pulled out my fun for the morning: a box of broken crayons and a Care Bears colouring book Mom found at the doctor's office. I opened it up to a picture that hadn't already been scribbled on: a set of smiling bears playing on a floating cloud.

I looked up after a couple of minutes and noticed there was already a customer in the restaurant—a man who was there every weekend. Because Mom had always referred to the regular customers by their orders instead of their names, I knew him as "Hold the Bacon." He seemed quiet and even younger than my mom. But he had warm and friendly eyes and, though he didn't say much, he liked to smile a lot.

Mom had never appeared to pay much attention to him, so I was surprised when, after the morning rush, I found them both standing over me at my table.

"Melanie, I want you to meet someone. This is Dave."

I was busy working on a page with Love-a-Lot and Tenderheart, so I looked up for only a second. "Mom," I said, "can we leave now?"

"Melanie," she said. "Me and Dave—and you—are going to be spending a bit more time together, sweetheart. We may even be staying over at his place for a while."

I looked up and saw him standing there, a tall guy with light brown hair wearing a jean jacket and a Blue Jays baseball cap. He kept smiling but didn't say anything. I started to colour again.

"So, sweetie . . . would that be okay with you?"

I didn't care. I figured he'd be gone in a few weeks like the rest of Mom's boyfriends. "Sure," I said.

Dave knelt beside me so we were face to face. His eyes were clear and green, and he smelled like coffee and that pine tree-smelling stuff men splashed on their faces after they shaved.

"Melanie, your mom tells me you're in Grade Two. That makes you what—six?"

"Not six," I said. "*Seven*."

"Oh yes, that's right. She also tells me that you really like dogs. I've got two of them at home—they're both puppies. I think you'll really like them."

"I like Golden Retrievers," I said. "And Dalmatians."

"Well, I've got two Border Collies. They're baby brothers, actually. I think you guys will get along."

Dave stood up as Eleanor approached, her heavily lined eyes noticing that Mom had taken off her hairnet.

"Abby, I need this table so if you wouldn't *mind*," she said. "And—please—could you get those crayon marks out?"

Eleanor marched off as Mom's face went flush, a line of red that started at her neck and worked its way up. "Come on, Mel, let's move over here," Mom said, her eyebrows squished together. I stood up as she wiped the table, rubbing the parts marked by green and pink crayon.

Dave touched Mom's elbow to get her attention, but she kept her eyes lowered. "I'm going to get going, but I'll come back to pick you guys up at two?"

Mom shook her head. "Probably better if you meet me back at my house," she said. "I don't want to give El any other reason to be mad at me."

Dave nodded and pecked Mom on the cheek. "It was good meeting you, Melanie. Bye for now." He waved before leaving the restaurant with a newspaper tucked under his arm.

Mom led me to another table at the back, careful to avoid talking to me for the rest of her shift. When she was finally finished, she grabbed me by the arm and hurried me through the back door.

"Dumb bitch," she said as soon as we were in the parking lot, stuffing her hairnet into her purse. "I've been there for a whole year and she still treats me like a dog. She's so bloody rude. No wonder business is slow."

She continued like this the entire walk back, repeating herself until we arrived home to find Dave's pickup in the driveway.

"Hey there," he said. "Thought you could use a hand getting your things together."

I waited for Mom to answer, then realized he was speaking to me. Dave approached us with his hands in his pockets, joining us as we climbed the front steps to the house. Mom's keys jangled as she pulled them out of her purse and tried opening the door. Dave and I stood there as she twisted the key back and forth in the lock. The door wouldn't open.

"Sometimes this stupid thing gets stuck," Mom said. "Here, let me try."

Mom moved out of the way so Dave could take over. He grabbed the handle with both hands and pressed one of his shoulders up against the door, putting enough pressure on it to swing open.

"Ta da!" Dave held his arm out so we could go first. "After you."

Once inside the four small rooms—the kitchen, den, bedroom and bath, all in the same cracked and peeling green paint—Dave could see there wasn't a lot to take with us. "I've got some boxes in the back of the truck," he said. "Not sure how many we'll need."

Mom and I had been there only a few months, and all we had to show for it was a few dishes, a dirty mattress, a broken blender and a Diana Ross poster taped to the wall of the bedroom. Still, we visited each room, packing up our things and putting them by the front door so that Dave could pile everything in the truck. The broken television came with the place, so we left it there.

"Well, we're off," Dave said. He gave me a wink as Mom locked the front door before joining us in the truck.

"Goodbye, lovely house!" Mom waved as we backed out of the driveway.

I looked at her, wondering if she'd really miss this place. She'd forgotten about the others so quickly. "Goodbye, house!" I repeated, kicking my feet up against the air vent. I waved my hand back and forth, staring not at the house but at Dave.

"Melanie, you'll have your own room where we're going," he said. "I don't think you'll miss your house one bit."

Dave's promise took my imagination to a faraway place with green grass and a swing set, so I was surprised when we pulled into the driveway of another brown brick house around the corner in Richmond Hill, our plain and boring town near Toronto.

"We're here!" Dave said as we were greeted by the barks of two black and white puppies chained to the front porch. He opened the door and led me out by hand, leaving my mother alone in the truck. "Melanie, I want you to meet Dougie and Luke Skywalker. Dougie's the smaller one and Luke's got the patch of white behind his ear here. These are my very special dogs."

I stood at the foot of the front porch as both animals barked at our feet.

"They're young pups, so they're a bit excited. They'll stop barking once they get to know you." He turned around and motioned for my mother to join us.

Dave took me on a tour so that I could get acquainted with things. He kept using that expression—"let's get acquainted with this" or "why don't you acquaint yourself with that." I didn't understand what he meant, but he seemed excited to show me his stuff, so I followed him from room to room.

The basement was empty except for two dog cages and a pool table, and the kitchen was small with not much room to sit. But Dave had a TV with a VCR and a large bathroom with a working tub.

"Your mom's been here before," Dave said. "She even helped me paint your room one day while you were at school."

"Can I see it?"

Dave took me by the hand and led me to a bedroom whose walls were a pale yellow. It had a small bed with pink bed sheets, a nightstand with a lamp and a dresser. "Well, here it is. This'll be your room. Sorry, we didn't have time to get you a desk."

"I don't need a desk," I said. "I like to do my artwork on the floor."

"Well, that makes things easier, doesn't it?" he said. "There's one other thing I want to show you."

Dave led me down the hall and out to the back deck where my mother was seated, her eyes shut and her face lifted toward the sun. Leaning up against the back of the house was a bright purple bike. The seat was a glossy white and attached to the handlebars was a set of sparkly streamers.

"This is for you, Melanie. This is a gift from me and your mother."

I looked at the shiny frame, its pink and purple streamers shimmering in the afternoon light. I had watched other girls riding their bikes on the street before, pink and red ones with baskets on the front and stickers all over. This one, though, was the prettiest I'd ever seen. I looked at Mom to make sure it was really mine.

"Can I put glitter glue on the seat so it matches?" I asked.

"If it's okay with Dave it's okay with me."

"Of course," Dave said, holding one of the handlebars while patting the seat. "Did you want to take it for a ride right now?"

The bike didn't have training wheels, so I thought about what to say. "Can I try it a bit later? I want to watch TV now."

Dave took his hand off the handlebar, placing the bike back up against the brick wall. "You bet, kiddo," he said. "We'll leave this for you right where you found it. This is your bike, Melanie—and your home. I want you to be happy here."

* * *

I decided to keep my new bike on the front porch. I wheeled it around the side of the house and up the front steps, pulling it carefully as Dave coached me from the lawn.

"Turn left a bit. Careful." I flipped up the kickstand and placed it on an angle, presenting it as if it was on display at a store. "Looks beautiful," Dave said, his thumb pressed to his finger to give me the okay symbol. "Just what this old house needed—a bit of sparkle."

The brown house with no upstairs was plain and simple, a rectangular box that looked like a school portable. It was small but adequate, plain but practical. It was the nicest home I'd ever lived in and, yet, I knew it was going to take some time getting used to it. The cold tap in the bathroom sink, for example, didn't work, so I had to brush my teeth with warm water. If I left the tap running, or didn't brush fast enough, the water would get too hot to rinse my mouth.

Mom and Dave's work hours meant we weren't together a lot. Dave's shift as supervisor at an airplane parts factory started early afternoon, so he didn't get home until after I was asleep. Mom, on the other hand, worked the breakfast shift Tuesdays to Saturdays, and had to go to bed early if she wanted to be on time. Not that she ever went to bed early or was ever on time.

Things, though, eventually became less strange, and I had a routine. For one, I didn't have to wake up at the same time as my mother any longer. And no more hanging out at the diner, where I had to ignore Eleanor's dirty looks as I took up a table, drinking her juice.

The biggest surprise, though, was the best: I had someone to walk me to school. Dave never asked if I wanted company, and probably didn't even know that

I'd already been walking by myself since I was six—the only one in my class to do so. He knocked on my bedroom door that first Monday morning, only two days after we moved in, and assumed he'd join me.

"Cock-a-doodle-doo, kiddo. Your mom's having a sleep-in, but it's time for you to get up."

The truth was I'd already been awake for an hour, watching a spider climb the wall of my bedroom. But I greeted Dave with a fake yawn to make him think he woke me up. I got out of bed, put on my pair of jean overalls and went to the kitchen.

"Morning," he said.

"Morning."

"I'm making eggs ... scrambled."

"Thanks. I don't feel like toast."

"Understood."

Dave tilted the pan sideways and slid the eggs onto a plate. He put the food in front of me and poured a glass of juice.

"So," he said, "how do you like school this year so far?"

"It's good."

"Good," he said. "Good is good. Do you have any favourite subjects?"

"Art class is my favourite. I like to colour and draw. And reading, too. The teacher says I'm a fast reader."

"Well, we'll have to get you some new books, won't we?"

"Mom says books belong in the library. But I do need some new art things."

"We'll have to get you some of those then."

Dave rounded up the dogs as I finished my breakfast, putting them on their leashes before heading outside. I joined him on the front porch, taking a minute to look at my bike, which was still in display mode.

"She's looking a bit bored," Dave said, his hand resting on one of the handlebars. "You may need to take it for a ride after school."

"Yeah," I said, noticing we were both wearing light blue jean jackets. "Maybe later."

The four of us started off on our path toward the schoolyard, the leashes between Dougie and Luke Skywalker tangling along the way. Dave pointed to some of the houses, telling me about the neighbours he knew: "Greg lives there. Alone now after his mother died," he said, pointing to another brown brick house. The shingles on the roof were weathered and tired-looking, and one of the yellow window shutters was crookedly hanging off the hinge. "And Linda's over there," he said of the plain house with white siding and brown door. "With her two kids. Nice kids, a bit older than you. She puts on a pretty scary house for Halloween."

Dave kept walking and pointed to what he said was his favourite house in the neighbourhood. "Not because it's the biggest or the fanciest," he said, slowing down in front of it. "But because it has character."

The white brick home had a wraparound porch, baby blue shutters and a front door to match. Bright blue flowers filled its outdoor garden, making it stand out from the plainer homes that reminded me of mud.

"It looks like a fancy gingerbread house," I said.

Dave nodded his head in appreciation. "You've got a point there, kiddo."

We turned the corner and heard the sound of kids grow louder as we approached the school. The bell rang just as we got to the yard. "Have a good day," Dave said as I left his side. "The pups will be waiting for you at home."

I waved goodbye and skipped toward the school, joining the rest of my class as they shuffled through the door in single file.

I really thought that would be the first and only time he'd take me to school. But Dave's company continued, and he knocked on my door the next day so we could have breakfast and head out. "The dogs," he said as we got ready to leave the house. "They need their morning walk, right?"

We were halfway out the door that morning when we saw a young girl standing at the foot of our driveway, facing the house.

Dave waved. "Hi, Stacey," he said.

She was a redhead, like me, but her face was full of freckles. She waved back at Dave. She'd been looking at my bike.

Dave led me down the driveway to introduce us. Though we were the same age, she went to the local Catholic school. "Stacey lives in that house," Dave said, pointing diagonally to another bungalow, this one ranch-style, across the street.

"Hi," I said.

"Hi," she said, already turning around to return to her driveway, where a woman and boy were getting into the car.

"She's nice," Dave said as the car drove away. "You guys should be friends."

"Yeah," I said. "Maybe."

As we walked to school that morning, I asked Dave if he could help me with two things with the bike. First,

I wanted to put glitter glue on the seat and, second, I wanted to learn how to ride it. Dave nodded at my requests and didn't say anything further. I thought he forgot about it, but that Saturday when I woke up, I heard him leave the house, start his truck and pull out of the driveway. I wondered where he was going, and thought it was strange that he'd leave without saying anything, but he came back inside two minutes later.

"Ready to rock, Melanie. Put your shoes on after you've eaten breakfast and I'll meet you out front."

I didn't bother with breakfast and went outside to find my bike on the driveway. The pickup truck was parked on the street; we had the full driveway to ourselves. Dave helped me up on the seat and then grabbed hold of the handlebars, making sure I didn't topple over. I pedalled slowly at first as Dave kept pace beside me, holding the bike steady. I rode up and down the driveway so that I could get the hang of things. After a couple of dozen times, Dave suggested we try the sidewalk so that I could pick up the pace. I sat on the seat with one foot on the pedal, the other on the pavement. Dave made sure to hold the seat behind me so I wouldn't fall.

"Let's do this, Melanie!" he shouted in encouragement as he pushed the bike forward. I started to pedal, feeling the power in my legs as the bike wobbled and then steadied under Dave's hand. I picked up speed, seeing the streamers flapping in the wind for the first time.

"Wow, we're going fast!" I said, my heart fluttering in my chest. Dave didn't say anything so I turned my head quickly to discover he was fifty feet behind me, waving his arms in the air in celebration. I had been on my own and didn't know it. I could do it. I could ride my bike.

Dave shouted "Woo hoo!" as I hit the brakes, turned around and did it all over again, meeting him at the point he had set me free.

"You did it, Melanie—congratulations! Fastest learner I ever met in my life."

I gripped the handlebars and smiled with pride.

To celebrate my achievement, Dave rounded up the dogs and we walked over to Bargain Harold's on Yonge Street. I strolled up and down the aisles as Dave waited outside with Luke and Dougie, who were busy sniffing the concrete barriers that lined each parking space. I circled the store, visiting each aisle until I found what I was looking for. In the school supply section, beside the pipe cleaners and popsicle sticks, was the most perfect tube of glitter glue. I read the description on the label: incandescent pink and purple with flecks of white and silver.

It wasn't long until Stacey asked me if she could borrow my bike. I wasn't surprised; I could feel her stare as I pedalled up and down the street, a dazzling display of streamers shimmering beside me. I'd zip past her house, the fire hydrant, the broken-down Chevrolet, looping back a hundred times, a thousand. She waited and watched.

It was a Sunday before dinner when Stacey approached me on the driveway. "My mom said I could ride your bike if it was okay with you," she said.

I had spent the past two hours riding around and was about to go inside. "I guess," I said. "Will you be back soon?"

"Yeah, like, five minutes."

I skipped dinner and waited on the steps of the front porch with Dougie and Luke Skywalker for an hour for her to return. It was getting dark. I counted: fifty-seven cars went by. But no Stacey. I went inside, poured myself a glass of milk, took a gulp, spilled some on my shirt and put the glass back on the counter. For later.

I went back outside, pushing the screen door open, forgetting to close it, hurrying down the front steps, waiting at the end of the driveway, seeing nothing, walking back up to the porch, standing in the spot where the bike used to be, holding the railing with one hand, brushing over the same rusty patch with my fingers. Eventually, Mom came out.

"What are you doing?"

"Waiting for Stacey."

"Well, hurry up," she said, before closing the screen door and going back inside.

I started pacing. I really wanted my bike back. It was the first thing Dave had given me. It was the only special thing that I owned. I couldn't lose it when I'd just learned to ride it.

It was after seven and already dark when I finally heard the pedalling motions come to a halt at the foot of the driveway. I stared at Stacey as she hopped off the bike, the click-click-clicking of the chain rotating over and over again. Even though I was angry, I was relieved to see her back.

"I'm here," she said as she walked toward the porch, placing the bike on the grass a few feet away from me. "This bike's a bit bumpy. Anyway, my mom's going to get mad at me so I should get back."

Stacey turned around and ran home, cutting through the lawn as a shortcut. My eyes widened as I bent over; one of the streamers was missing. A few short strands poked out of the left bar. I put my hand where the streamer had been—an amputated arm with an ugly stub.

Luke Skywalker sniffed the back tire as I propped the bike up, dragging it up the steps. I put it back in its usual place, taking a minute to stare at it under the porch light. The shiny purple bike looked lopsided, like a dog with only one floppy ear. Now it was just like everything else: broken, cracked and needing repairs.

After that, Stacey didn't say hi to me anymore. Instead, she met my gaze with a head turned in the opposite direction. I became angrier each time I saw her, and narrowed my eyes as I stared at her freckles. It must not have bothered her because, less than two weeks later, I noticed something else. I'd always kept my bike propped up with the help of the kickstand, its front tire pointed left and turned slightly on an angle. But one afternoon I found it leaning up against the rail of the porch, the kickstand not extended.

I thought of Stacey and my face went prickly; I wanted to get revenge. I told Dave about it and asked him what to do. Dave wanted me to be kind. "Don't get all upset, kiddo. Try asking if it was her."

But I didn't have to. Later that afternoon, as she was getting into the back of her mom's car, I saw the evidence on the back of her jeans: pink and purple glitter glue with flecks of white and silver.

* * *

Dave left me home alone one Saturday morning and came back two hours later in a different vehicle. I heard it before I saw it, the howls of rock music mixed with the hum of an unfamiliar engine pulling into the driveway.

I was on the floor of the living room, watching my usual series of *Scooby-Doo* and *Inspector Gadget*, when he got back. I popped my head over the couch to see him in the driver's seat, not in the usual pickup truck but in a van I'd never seen before. I watched him jump out of the vehicle, double up on the steps of the porch and push on the front door, forgetting he'd locked it. I heard him fumble for his keys as I turned back toward the television, not wanting to miss the commercial that had started for the marshmallow cereal I liked. A few seconds later, the door swung open. Dave shouted my name toward the side of the house as if I was in my bedroom. I waved from my place on the carpeted floor, catching his attention.

"I'm right here," I said.

"Oh, hi. You hungry? I have an idea."

I wasn't, but Dave still made me turn off the TV and change out of my pyjamas. He took my hand as we walked out the front door, pulling me down the front steps.

"You like it?" I looked out. It was a big, white, boxy van, the kind that construction workers use. "It's a surprise, Melanie. For your mom."

"Mom doesn't drive," I said. "I like the pickup truck better."

"I know," Dave said, pausing for a second. "But now we have more space for things."

"Like what?"

"Well, for you. And the dogs. And now we won't have to put our groceries in the back of the pick-up anymore. Didn't that drive you crazy, bringing home wet groceries?"

"I guess."

"Well, come take a look."

Dave opened the passenger door and motioned me with his arm to get in. I played dumb until he did it again. "Hop in, Melanie, hop in." I took hold of the inside of the door and used it to help me climb into the seat, exaggerating the step so it looked harder than it was. The inside was empty. It smelled like plastic. Thankfully, there were two extra seats in the back so I wouldn't have to squeeze in between Mom and Dave anymore. Dave came in through the driver's side and put the keys in the ignition, the rock music blaring at full volume. He winced, turned it down, waited for me to shut my door and then put the van in reverse.

"Where are we going?" I asked him.

"Thought we could head over to the diner and get some lunch."

I thought of Eleanor and her beige-tiled restaurant with the dirty bathrooms, the smell of frying bacon mixed with cleaning solution, burnt toast and waxy crayons. I hadn't been there in weeks, since the day we'd moved in with Dave.

We pulled into the parking lot and Dave got out of his seat, coming around the side of the van and opening my door as if he was a chauffeur.

"Mademoiselle," he said, holding his arm out. I placed my hand in his and jumped out of the vehicle. We walked over to the front door of the diner, trying to catch a glimpse of Mom through the windows. Eleanor greeted us at the doorway, at first mistaking us for ordinary customers, her smile vanishing the second she realized who we were.

"Abby's in the kitchen," she said in her usual bitter tone, her back already facing us.

Mom came a few minutes later, smoothing her apron as she approached us at the front door. "Hi," she said. "Wasn't expecting you." The bags under her eyes were bigger than usual, the lines around her mouth slightly grooved.

"We were hungry," Dave said. "Also, we wanted to show you something ... whenever you're not busy."

"Oh? Okay, have a seat."

Mom came back five minutes later to pour Dave coffee and take our orders. "Eleanor's on a tear today," she said, filling his mug to the brim. "The till was short a hundred and fifty bucks yesterday and she keeps bringing it up every five minutes. I feel like telling her to just come out and say it."

"Ignore her," Dave said.

"Oh, I don't care," she said, grabbing two clean glasses from the next table and putting them onto ours. "I've learned to let her be." Mom looked over her shoulder, making sure that Eleanor was still out of earshot. "She'll be wishing she was nicer to me sooner than she thinks. Anyway, what was it that you wanted to show me?"

"Dave bought a new truck," I said, blurting it out.

Mom's eyes widened as she turned toward Dave. "You did?"

"No, not a truck," Dave said. "It's a surprise. I bought a ... surprise. We wanted to show you."

Mom turned her head toward the window, squinting her eyes as she tried to figure out which one of the junk boxes in the dumpy parking lot of the rundown strip mall belonged to her. A bit of coffee splashed up from the pot she was holding and onto the floor beside her feet.

"What did you get?" she said. "Is it nice?"

"It's a Chevy. New. Very nice and spacious. You'll see."

"Is it here?" She twisted her neck further to get a better view.

"It's the white one," I said.

Her neck stopped moving as her gaze fixated on one particular place in the parking lot. "You got a ... van?"

"It's beautiful, Abby. I think you'll really like it—"

"You got a van for our family? Without asking me?"

Mom's eyes got really small, almost as if she was squinting from the sun. She was shaking. I could tell by the way her hand was clutching the coffee pot that she wasn't pretending. Mom didn't wait long enough for him to answer and stormed off toward the back of the restaurant.

"Shit!" Dave said.

I tried to take a sip of water but remembered my glass was empty. Eleanor walked by and I asked her if she could fill it up. She turned away without saying anything and didn't come back.

After about ten minutes, Mom returned to the table with our pancakes, her eyes red and swollen. Dave didn't say anything. We ate our pancakes in silence and Dave paid the bill. Nobody filled our water glasses. Dave tried to get Mom's attention a couple of times, but she seemed busy with the other customers. We left the restaurant a few minutes later. Dave waved goodbye, but Mom ignored us.

* * *

I was in my bedroom a few hours later when I heard the signs of fighting: low voices and slammed fists. I didn't want to leave my room but eventually Mom asked me to come to dinner. There was no food in sight, so I asked her what we were having. "There's cereal in the cupboard," she said as she left the kitchen. The van wasn't in the driveway.

The next morning I went into the kitchen to find Mom sitting at the table in her housecoat, drinking coffee and reading the weekly flyers. Dave was at the sink doing dishes. He turned off the tap and dried his hands as soon as he heard me. There was no sign of their fight from the day before.

"Hi, Melanie, good morning," Dave said. "We want to talk to you."

His tone was serious; I'd never heard him speak like that. I looked to my mother for clues, but she ignored me. And, then, it hit me: I was in trouble for spilling the beans about the van. I felt a flash of anger and wondered how my mother could sit there so quietly when I was about to get punished for something that wasn't my fault.

Dave pulled out one of the kitchen chairs as an invitation for me to sit, so I did. Mom kept reading the flyer until he motioned for her to put it down. I sat there and waited for someone to speak. There was a long period of silence as Mom and Dave stared at one another, waiting for the other person.

I knew I was in trouble, but no one was saying anything. I felt around the back of my head and patted my hair, which felt nice and smooth. Suddenly, I felt something different: a shorter strand, sticking out at the top of my head, a bit rougher than the others, like it had speed bumps on it. I closed my eyes and pulled it really fast, so fast that I almost didn't feel it. I wanted to find another one, to do it again. But Dave broke the silence.

"Melanie, your mother wants to tell you something."

I looked over at Mom, who kept looking at Dave, who kept waiting for her to speak. She shook her head slightly, slowly, a gesture meant for Dave but also obvious to me. Dave, blinking, turned back toward me.

"Melanie," he said, pausing before the next sentence. "You're going to be a big sister." He paused again, waiting for a reaction. I said nothing. "Your mom's having a baby."

My mother sat there with an empty coffee mug on her lap and a blank expression. She should have been excited, but she looked so tired—her eyes were puffy, her lips thin. I tried to remember how old she was, but couldn't. Sometimes it felt like she could never be happy.

She didn't say anything so I turned back to Dave: "Do I have to give up my bedroom?"

Dave released his hands, which had been pressed together on his lap. "Melanie, we're going to do even better than that. Not only will you have your own room, but we're all going to move into a bigger and better house."

"But I just moved here."

"I know, but it will be for the best."

I waited for my mom to say something, to react, but she gave me nothing: no hug, no smile, not even a raised eyebrow. I turned toward her and asked if I could have some cereal, at which point she got up from her chair and went to the bathroom. Dave put some Lucky Charms in a bowl and placed it in front of me.

I thought about my yellow room, the front porch, the way I'd organized my crayons in separate plastic cups. I had just gotten settled. I didn't want to move again. I also didn't want to be a big sister.

Dave sat and watched me as I ate my breakfast, scooping up the parts with the marshmallows first. "I'm sorry about yesterday," he said.

"Aren't you mad at me? For telling Mom about the van."

"Mad at you? More like mad at myself. I shouldn't have surprised your mom like that. We should have talked about it first."

"It's just a car."

"A van, actually."

"Is Mom mad at me, then?" I asked.

"Not at all—your mother adores you."

I dragged my spoon along the bottom of the bowl. "Sometimes she doesn't act like it."

"Melanie, you have to understand, your mom grew up in a house where it wasn't happy all of the time. She moved out when she was very, very young. She may be a tricky person sometimes, but it doesn't mean she doesn't care."

"She ran away from home?" I asked in disbelief. I didn't know.

"Well, not exactly—she was eighteen. The point is your mom loves you very much. She talks about you all the time."

I took in what he said. I wasn't sure what I was supposed to say, so I just said, "Okay."

"And we're going to keep it—the van. We're going to make it work with the baby. Are you happy about being a sister?"

"I guess ... not really."

"Things will change once the baby's here, Mel Belle. You'll see. You'll love it to pieces. I can't wait to see you guys together."

I finished my bowl of cereal, leaving a few frosted oats floating in a shallow pool of sugary milk.

"I want it to be a boy. I don't want to have to share my things if it's a girl," I said.

Dave patted my head as he left the kitchen. "Well, we'll see."

CHAPTER TWO

———⋘◆⋙———

THE STUFFED ELEPHANT

February 1984

TO PREPARE FOR the baby, Mom and I went shopping. Dave was the one who insisted. We needed everything —a crib, a playpen, a high chair, new clothes. I asked my mother what she did with all my old things and she shrugged.

"We didn't have much, Mel. I really don't remember."

Dave drove us to the mall on a Saturday afternoon after Mom's shift ended, pulling up in front of the outside entrance of Kmart. He put on his blinkers and hopped out of the van, coming around the side to open the door for Mom. As I stepped out onto the curb, Dave slid me a ten-dollar bill, tucking it into my coat pocket.

"I want you to use this money to buy the baby a special gift," he said. "It's a gift from you and only you. I want you to choose it."

"Okay," I said. "Why?"

"It will always be a reminder that you are its sister. A keepsake ... meaning it will be kept for a long time. Know what I mean?"

"I guess so. What should I get, a book? No—a lamp."

Dave laughed. "Up to you, kiddo. But try to think of something that the baby would like."

"Okay."

Mom was already through the doors and in the store, so I gave Dave a high-five and ran after her before she disappeared into the Saturday crowds. Mom wanted to look for a new scarf, but agreed to get the baby items first if we promised to hurry.

"Let's not be here all day," she said.

I followed her as she walked by the racks, picking up a few items that were displayed on hangers.

"You like this?" She waved a sailor suit with blue pants and a striped sweater. Even from several feet away, I could see the crooked stitching. "It's not really for a newborn," she said before I could answer, placing the outfit back on the rack. "The thing is it's hard to pick anything out when you don't know what you're having. I'd love to know what it is before it's born. I don't want everything to be yellow—I hate that colour."

"That's the colour you painted my room," I said.

She looked toward the ceiling, as if she couldn't remember. "Clothes and walls are different. Anyway, I need coffee. We done here?"

"I'm going to choose a gift for when the baby's born. As long as it's under ten dollars."

"Knock yourself out," she said, already walking away. "I'll wait for you by the front cashier."

I left the racks of clothing and headed down the first aisle, where I was greeted by a wall of baby blankets, bedding and towels. I thought of what Dave had said—a keepsake. My hand brushed along the front of the shelves as I walked beside them, not seeing anything that caught my eye. I made a U-turn so that I could enter the next aisle. Here everything was plastic: toys, games and activities. I picked up a block set and shook the box, hearing the pieces of plastic tapping against each other. No, I thought, placing it back on the shelf. Not special enough. I passed by some books, a plastic bunny—no good. I continued walking, approaching a section of stuffed animals on display: bears, giraffes, bunnies, all facing the aisle with blank stares. I stopped and picked one up, a stuffed cow, medium brown with a set of smiling white teeth stitched onto its face. I put it back, its face-side down, and picked up the one next to it, a pale grey elephant, perfect for a boy or girl. I squeezed its body with both hands, feeling the fur in between my fingers, petting the soft hairs with my thumbs. I brought the stuffed elephant to the front register, paying the cashier with the ten-dollar bill Dave gave me. I walked out of the store to find my mother admiring the display window of a shoe store.

"There you are," she said. "All done?"

"Yeah. I got a stuffed toy." I pulled the elephant out of the plastic bag.

"Cute," she said. Her eyes turned back toward the window. "Let's do something else now. I'm starved."

I followed her lead as she made her way to the food court and headed for the coffee stand. She ordered a carrot muffin and a large Irish cream coffee with milk and sugar, and then paid the cashier. She looked down at me. "Did you want something, too?"

I shook my head. "I ate with Dave already."

She ignored me as she looked at the drinks on display. "And a chocolate milk for my daughter!" she yelled over to the cashier. "I forgot to order a chocolate milk." The cashier nodded and grabbed one out of the refrigerator. "Sorry, Melanie," Mom said as she searched her purse for change. "I think this pregnancy's making me crazy."

I didn't feel like chocolate milk but knew Mom felt bad, so when the cashier handed me the carton, I opened it up and drank it. Mom took her coffee and muffin and we started walking again. "So," I said. "Did you want to go back to Kmart?"

Mom let out a sigh through her nose, her mouth full of muffin. "Sure," she said. "We shouldn't go home empty-handed."

We eyed the shops as we passed them by: the Laura Secord, a jewellery store, a place that sold house stuff. "Seriously," Mom said, looking at a punch bowl. "Who needs that crap?"

As we kept walking, we saw a children's boutique with a royal blue sign in the front. A fancy crib and rocking chair were on display in the window, showing off beautiful baby blankets and bed sheets in bright whites and warm creams.

"Here." I pointed. "Let's go in here."

Mom shuffled behind me, following as I led her into the store.

"This is good," I said, holding up a fuzzy blanket, a beige checkered pattern with a satin trim.

"Nice but not practical," Mom said, barely looking at it.

We moved to the furniture section, where three baby cribs were on display, each in a different shade of wood.

Mom turned over a tag on one of the nearby dressers to reveal its price.

"This is over the top," she said. "Forget it."

"Do you want to look at the clothes?"

My mother swung around to face me, her chin sticking out. "Aren't you seeing what I'm seeing, Melanie? This is a fancy boutique. What are you thinking? That Dave is Daddy Warbucks?"

"But Dave dropped us off here," I said, feeling my cheeks go red. Another woman and girl were shopping a few feet from us. The woman was holding a set of bed sheets, but her eyes were focused on the floor as she tried to pretend she wasn't listening.

"Yes, but we can't take advantage of him, either. We haven't gone rags to riches."

I stood there, watching the little girl sit on one of the rocking chairs. "You don't have to be so grumpy."

She was worked up now—I could tell by the way her eyes were squinting. "You think it's easy being pregnant, Melanie? Hmm? Well, it's not. It's not easy being pregnant and it's not easy being a mother. And *this*," she said, motioning her hands around the store, "is not normal. Think anyone sent me to the mall to buy things when I was expecting you?"

I knew I should have kept my mouth shut, but I was so mad and embarrassed. I took a deep breath and said something that surprised even myself: "I don't even know who my dad is, so how would I know?"

My mother flinched. "Don't get smart."

"I'm ... I'm *not*," I said. At this point, the woman and girl were not even pretending to be minding their own business. I wanted to die. I wanted to run away.

But, mostly, I wanted to show my mom that I planned to have my own baby one day—and that I'd be a better parent than she was.

"When I grow up, I'm going to be a mom, too. I'm going to have one daughter and we're going to have a happy family and we're going to be really normal."

"Is that so?"

"Yeah, and we're going to go on vacations and cook really nice dinners and we're even going to have a swimming pool. And I'm never going to be tired and grumpy, either."

"Wow, I hope that's the case, but guess what, Melanie? Sometimes life has a different plan for us. You don't always get to choose."

"Well, I will," I said. "And I choose to get married, have a baby and be the best mom in the world."

At this she let out a little laugh. It was her way of making me feel bad while still getting the last word. "Sounds like the only thing you're forgetting are your glass slippers and your pumpkin carriage. You just better find a nice, rich man, Melanie. Anyway, I'm tired of this store."

I shrugged my shoulders. "Do you want to go back to the other store?" I asked her.

Mom rolled her eyes. "Sure, I mean, where else are we going to go?"

We left the store in silence and went back to where I bought the stuffed elephant. This time Mom was the leader, and I followed her as she marched up and down the aisles, picking up a few items hanging on the racks.

"This one's nice," she said, holding a white sleeper by its hanger. "We'll need pyjamas."

She picked up the same outfit in a larger size, this one in red. She kept walking, looking at a few things and putting them back. Lifting a white blanket off a shelf, she said, "We'll need one of these, too." With the three items hanging off her arm, she went to the cash and paid for them. I followed her as she walked back into the main part of the mall to find a payphone.

Dave came fifteen minutes later, picking us up in the same spot where he'd dropped us off. "That's all you got?" he asked, looking at the one bag Mom was holding.

"Things were too expensive. Ridiculous," she said as she got into the van. "We should get a used crib or something. And I can come back for more clothes when the sales are on."

Dave turned to me as I slid into my seat in the back, shutting the door behind me.

"What about you, kiddo? Any luck?"

I pulled the grey elephant out of the plastic bag to show him. "A stuffed toy," I said. "I want to give it to the baby as soon as it's born."

"Sounds like a great plan."

Mom stared out of the van's window as if she had something interesting to look at. Dave stared at her but didn't say anything, pulling out of the parking lot instead.

* * *

The final months of Mom's pregnancy were exhausting to watch. Although she kept her shifts at the diner until the end, putting all of her tips in her glass Mason jars, she gave up on her chores at home. All she did was go from the TV to fridge to bed.

As the months went by, it was not her body that changed the most but her face. The first thing was her hair got darker. I think her eye sockets went deeper back in her head, too. No matter how long she slept, she always looked tired. Also, Mom didn't go to all of her doctors' appointments, something that made Dave furious. She would either forget or she did it on purpose. With her, you never knew.

Her belly, though, got really big and round, something that attracted a lot of looks and comments from strangers. When Mom was six months, a lady on the bus patted her belly and said, "Oh, how lovely." Mom jerked away from the stranger, wrapping her coat around her body to try to hide the baby.

By nine months, it seemed like all Mom did was sigh in discomfort. I don't think she was sleeping much. Most nights, Dave had to move to the couch so that he wouldn't be bothered by her tossing and turning.

I don't know how she went to work. I'm pretty sure Eleanor wasn't happy to keep her. At the end of her last day, at the very end of her pregnancy, Mom left the diner without saying goodbye. Angry that Eleanor had never said anything about the baby, Mom walked out with a big package of tin foil stuffed in her purse.

"Good riddance," she said as she opened the door to the van, where Dave and I had been waiting to take her home. I think she knew she would never go back.

Dave leaned over and gave her a peck on her cheek. "We should celebrate," he said as he pulled out of the parking lot, his arm hanging out the window.

"Yeah, let's go to Vegas. Or dancing—I'm really up for that," Mom said, laughing.

"No, I'm serious," he said. "It's the end of an era for you. Let's go to dinner. Or see a movie—or something. Let's mark the occasion."

"I already have plans. Tonight I'm counting my Mason jars."

Mom's jars lined the top of her dresser in her bedroom, and were the only things in the house I wasn't allowed to touch. The jars were always her first stop as soon as she got home from Sunny's—she went there even before she took her coat off.

Although I couldn't touch anything, Mom did let me watch her count her money when she came home from work each Saturday. She'd take off her black server's apron with the three deep pockets as soon as she entered her bedroom. The centre pocket was where she kept her notepad and pen for taking down orders and the side pockets were for her tips. She'd take out the money and count it slowly, placing it all in the glass until it reached the top.

The jars were filled with quarters, dimes, nickels, pennies, but also a lot of one-, two- and even five-dollar bills. Since we'd moved in with Dave, Mom didn't need to use her tip money for rent or groceries, so she'd been saving every penny. In total, she had eighteen jars—two for each month of pregnancy.

While she'd gone to the trouble of counting her money after each workday, she never bothered to write anything down. The overall number was a mystery. But now that her time at Sunny's had come to an end, she was ready to find out what her final amount was.

Once we pulled into the driveway, I followed Mom into the house and toward her bedroom, assuming she'd let me watch like other times. But as soon as we reached the door to her room, she turned around.

"Not this time, Melanie," she said. "I need peace and quiet."

"Come on, Mom, why not? I can help you."

"No. No distractions. Can't I ever have a minute?"

"It's not fair," I said. "I've been helping every weekend."

Mom put her hands behind her hips and bent backwards, stretching her muscles. "God, Melanie, can't you just ..." Her eyes rolled. She sighed. Then she took a deep breath and started again. "Listen ... kiddo ... next time, okay?"

Kiddo.

I didn't say anything as she opened the door to her room and shut it behind her, leaving me alone in the hallway. Our discussion was over. Dave and I took the dogs for a walk, heading to the Mill Pond and back to give her enough time. We got home forty minutes later, but Mom was still in her bedroom, the door still shut. She came out after another hour, sitting down with me and Dave at the kitchen table as we played a game of Twenty-One.

"So, did you count your money?" I asked. I thought of the game at the school fair where everyone had to guess how many jellybeans were in a container. I'd submitted my guess: 1,349, but heard that someone in an older grade had won. I never learned how many jellybeans were in that jar.

Mom got up from the table and opened the pantry door, taking a deep breath and exhaling loudly as she examined the shelves. "There you go again, Melanie. You must think we're rich? You know, when I was your age, I already had my first job," she said, closing the pantry door without taking anything out.

"Don't mind her," Dave said as she left us for the living room. He picked up his next card: a seven of hearts. "Yes!" he said with a fist pump. "A lucky seven. Twenty-one even. I win."

"Yeah, you win," I said, hesitating before I asked my next question. "Dave ... do you like your job? Making parts for airplanes?"

"I do, kiddo. Time flies when I'm there—hardy har har."

"So, what do you make? The wings? Or the engine?" I had given up on the card game.

"Nothing that exciting, Melanie—we make the parts that help let the plane breathe, you know?"

"Do you get free tickets to see the planes you work on?"

Dave threw his head back and let out a deep laugh. "Don't I wish. Actually, I've never even been on a plane."

I didn't believe him. I shook my head. "No way."

"It's true."

"You make airplanes and you've never even flown before?"

"I guess I've never thought of it that way before—but, yes, that's a fact."

"Wow," I said, still surprised. "Dave, do you think I should get a job? I don't want to eat all of your food. I can help pay for things that way."

Dave's face turned serious. "You're not getting a job, Melanie—you're too busy being a kid."

"But Mom said—"

"Never mind your mom," he said, leaning toward me so that he could switch to a whisper. "Sometimes people say things that they don't really mean."

CHAPTER THREE

MOTHER'S DAY

May 1984

JESSE WAS BORN on Mother's Day, a week before my eighth birthday.

Because I had no other family to stay with, Dave asked our neighbour Becky if I could stay with her for a few days while he and Mom were at the hospital. I didn't know her well, but Dave had been her neighbour for years. Mom said she felt comfortable about the situation because Becky had two boys of her own. The dogs, though, had to stay with Dave's friend from work.

Dave helped me pack my overnight bag a month before the baby came, saying we needed to be ready just in case.

"Just in case what?" I asked.

"Just in case the baby comes."

"But you know it's coming," I said.

This made him laugh. I packed my clothes and toothbrush and also the stuffed elephant I'd bought, waiting for the moment I'd have to leave home. Dave kept saying the baby was going to arrive any minute now while Mom kept complaining that it was never going to happen. When the time did eventually come, Dave swung the door of my room open so quickly that it hit the wall and bounced back shut. "Your mom and I are going to the hospital," he said behind the closed door.

Dave shooed me along as soon as I climbed out of bed, telling me over and over again that we had to move it. I grabbed my overnight bag and went into the living room where I saw my mother sitting on the couch. Her hands were on her belly, but other than that she seemed calm. Dave, though, was running around the house half-speaking to himself.

"Where are my keys?" he shouted.

"They're in your hands," I said.

"Who left the back door open?" Dave wanted to know.

"You did," Mom said.

Finally, he turned to me: "Let's go, let's go Melanie, out the door!"

Dave picked up my bag with his right arm and lifted me up in his left so that my feet were dangling a foot off the ground. He raced out of the house and over to the neighbour's, ringing the bell three times. The door swung open and there was Becky. Her dark hair was long and loose and she was wearing a tropical print T-shirt and jeans. Her brown eyes were big and round, almost perfect circles.

"Hiya, Melanie. Come on in."

Dave dropped me to my feet, swung around and ran back home. "Thanks for taking her, Beck!" he shouted.

Becky put her arm around me and led me inside the house, which was much larger than it had appeared from the outside. The rooms were clean and organized.

I smelled coffee and heard the familiar sounds of Sunday morning cartoons. Both of her boys were already awake, shirtless and sitting on the floor of their living room as they watched television. Chris was nine with skinny legs, dirty blond hair and a patch of bruises on his knees. Michael had similar features but was two years younger, with darker skin and a shorter head of hair that ended in a rat's tail.

"Boys, Melanie's here. Melanie's come to stay with us."

They ignored me as they stared at the TV. "Boys!" Becky said in a louder voice, close to shouting. "Say hi to Melanie."

"Hi Melanie," they both said together, their heads never turning away from the TV.

"Hi," I said, wishing the baby was already born so that I could go home.

Becky led me to the kitchen, where she sat me down at the table. "You're here for a couple of days so I really hope you make yourself at home. Did you have breakfast yet? What can I make you?"

She looked at me with a warm smile. She must have been close in age to my mother, but she moved quickly and was busy a lot. She seemed to like having things in order. I wondered for a moment if boys were the answer. I wished at that moment that Mom could give me a brother.

Becky sliced me an orange and popped two frozen waffles into the toaster, asking me how school was going and if I liked my teacher. "I guess," I told her in between mouthfuls, waiting for her to ask a new question. Eventually, I finished eating and she ran out of things to say, so she walked over to the living room and turned off the television, asking Chris and Michael if they could take me downstairs to play. Chris—the older one—ran to his bedroom to put on a T-shirt first, meeting me and his brother downstairs in the basement. There, another television sat in a wall unit whose shelves were filled with toys and games.

"We don't have any girl toys," Michael said.

"I like boys' things, too," I said.

Chris reached up to the top shelf, pulling down a stack of boxes. "We have Monopoly, playing cards, Operation."

I shrugged my shoulders, pretending like I didn't care even though I hated Monopoly. "Anything, I guess."

"I want to play Operation," Michael said. "Let's see who kills the patient first."

Chris opened the box and pulled out the game—a cardboard operating table with a cartooned patient lying on it. The patient's body was pocked with holes filled with tiny pieces of plastic that needed to be removed with tweezers. Chris decided he would go first. He winced his eyes, focusing carefully as he squeezed a set of spareribs, plucking it out of the hole without touching the metal edges.

"Yes!" he said, handing the metal tool to his brother. "Beat that."

Michael leaned in closely with the tweezers in his right hand, his face only a few inches away from the board. With the metal pincers inside the tiny hole, he plucked the funny bone up and out, pulling it away before it could make contact. "Ha ha!" he said, making a face at his brother. "Suck it, Chris."

He handed me the tweezers. I scrunched my nose as I focused on the broken heart near the centre of the board. My right hand shook as I squeezed the tool, making the end as small as possible. Once inside, I released the pressure so I could grab the heart. But as I did this, my hand shook and the tweezers touched the metal edge of the opening. The patient's nose buzzed loudly and flashed bright red. Failure. I was out.

"Ha!" Mike said, rolling on his side and laughing hysterically. "Girls suck!"

"That was your fault," I said. It wasn't true, but I was angry that I'd agreed to play. "You moved the board."

"No, I didn't," Mike said. "You suck. And so does the baby, who's not even your real family. It's only your half-sibling." I sat there in silence, staring at the plastic heart that remained inside the patient's cartoon body. "The baby's your half-family and your dad's not even your dad, so you're not really related to anyone."

"Shut up, Mikey," Chris said. "Mom's going to get mad. Let's put this away." Chris yanked the operating table off the floor and stuffed it back into its box.

Later that day Becky called us to lunch outside in the backyard. "I hope you like peanut butter," she said.

We sat out back on the picnic table, which overlooked our yard next door. Through the chain-link fence I could see our deck with lawn chairs but no table. The green grass looked yellow because there were so many dandelions. I sat down beside Becky and across from Chris and Michael, who seemed quieter than they'd been that morning. Becky told us to start eating and stood back up, saying she needed to grab something from inside. I was the first to take a bite out of my sandwich, something that made both boys burst into laughter. I looked around and down at my lap, wondering what could be so funny. And then I saw it through the layers of sliced bread: green grass mashed into the peanut butter. I spat out my mouthful, which made the boys laugh even harder. Michael fell off the bench of the picnic table, clutching his belly with both hands as he rolled around on the lawn.

The laughter continued until Becky came to the table with plastic cups and a jug of lemonade. I followed her eyes as she looked at my plate and noticed the blades of grass sticking out of the peanut butter. She put the lemonade and glasses down in the centre of the table, took my plate away and went back into the house. The boys grew quiet as their mom came back out a few minutes later. Becky was carrying another peanut butter sandwich for me, but this time it had a stack of Oreo cookies.

Michael's mouth hung open as Becky stared at him, her fists clenched on her hips. I looked down at the plate in front of me. Ignoring the sandwich, I picked up an Oreo and placed the entire thing in my mouth. I devoured the first one, the second and then the third as Michael and Chris watched in silence. Once the cookies were done, we all ate our sandwiches together.

Over the next several hours, I watched Becky and her husband Ron. They were busy doing laundry, busy helping their boys with homework, busy cooking dinner. Neither of them ever sat down. I asked Becky if she liked being a mom. "It's a lot of cleaning things and family chores," I said.

Without hesitating she looked at me and said, "Best job in the world."

The phone rang later that night while I was brushing my teeth. Becky knocked on the bathroom door even though it was halfway open. "Melanie, there's a phone call for you."

I walked down to the kitchen and picked up the receiver.

"Is that you, kiddo?"

"Hello?"

"Melanie, your sister's here. Her name's Jessica and she's beautiful. Your mom says hi."

"Can I talk to her?"

"She's not with me right now, Mel Belle—she's tired and with the baby. But your sister is absolutely beautiful."

"Can I give her the stuffed elephant?"

"Of course. As soon as we get home. She'll be so glad to meet you."

I went to bed that night thinking about the baby and wondering what she looked like. But I was also thinking about Mom. I wondered if she'd be more tired, if she'd love the baby more than me. I felt like I'd hardly seen her since we'd moved in with Dave. I was sorry for thinking she was a bad mom sometimes. I just wanted her to be happy.

Dave and Mom got home not the next morning but the morning after. Becky called me to the living room window as soon as they pulled into our driveway next door. I ran outside, waving at Mom seated in the passenger seat. Even from outside of the van I could see a change. Her face was white and her eyes were puffed up and swollen, almost like they were disappearing inside her head.

Dave hopped out of the van and brought me around the side, where he opened the door so I could see the baby. She was in her car seat, covered by a pink blanket, in one of the bucket seats in the back. Her tiny face was a perfect circle, her skin redder than I expected. I leaned in closer and noticed her hair was blonde—so different from me, a redhead, and my mother, whose hair was dark.

I could feel Becky standing over my shoulder, trying to get a good look. "She's beautiful, Abby. Congratulations."

My mom gave a weak smile. "Thanks."

I climbed into the van, skipped over my seat and crouched down beside my new sister. "She's so cute," I said. "Can we bring her inside?"

Dave had parked the car as close to the house as possible so Mom wouldn't have to walk far. "Stay with the baby for a minute, kiddo," he said as he opened the passenger door, extending his hand to help Mom out.

"I'm okay, I can walk," she told him, grabbing hold of the side door and stepping down herself.

Dave jogged to the house, unlocking the front door with his key and holding it open as he waited for Mom to pass through. Mom made her way up the front steps, ignoring Dave as she went inside. He left the door of the house open and ran back down to us. As he approached the van, I turned back toward the baby, watching the pink fleece around her face rise and fall with each breath.

"She's still alive," I said.

"That's excellent," he said.

Dave instructed me to grab the duffle bag as he took hold of the car seat. He waited for me to hop out of the van and then shut the door behind us. "And don't forget to get your overnight bag from Becky's."

I did as he asked, bringing Mom's bag to the front porch and gathering my things from next door. Once I was home, I looked inside my bag so that I could give the baby her special gift. But the stuffed elephant wasn't there. I ransacked my room, looking under the bed and opening all my drawers. Although I remembered packing it in my bag for Becky's, I didn't remember seeing it during my time there. I searched everywhere but came up empty handed. Later, I found Mom lying on the couch.

"Have you seen the stuffed toy I bought for the baby?" I asked.

She didn't move or open her eyes. "What stuffed toy?"

"The elephant I got at the mall, remember?"

"Sorry," Mom said.

Thinking the toy must have been left at Becky's, I got Dave to call her to see if she could find it. She promised to do a thorough check of the house. I answered the phone when she got back to us forty-five minutes later.

"Hi, love. I searched up and down. I can't find it anywhere," she said. I felt a lump rise in my throat. "I'll keep my eyes open in case it shows up while I'm cleaning. It might pop up somewhere."

I thanked Becky and hung up the phone.

* * *

Mom went into hibernation as soon as Jesse was born. She cried a lot, almost as much as the baby. She didn't like to leave her room. Sometimes, she locked herself in the bathroom for a long time. When I did see her, her hair and clothes were a mess, and her eyes were swollen and full of red lines. I never saw her eat; she stopped having dinner with us at night.

I know being pregnant was hard on her. Dave reminded me of that all the time. But the birth of the baby made things even worse. Mom tried breastfeeding, something she did with me to "save a few bucks." But Jesse fussed and cried instead of taking in milk.

"I don't understand why it's so hard this time," Mom said to Dave between sobs. "Melanie was an angel. I didn't even need the nurse's help with her."

She gave up after a week.

The baby's constant crying was more than Mom could handle. Jesse wailed a lot, especially around dinnertime. Mom would hold her and rock her back and forth, patting her back, rubbing her tummy, but Jesse cried straight until she fell asleep around nine. It seemed like someone was always awake, no matter what time of night. Dougie and Luke Skywalker started sleeping in the basement.

"I don't understand what's wrong with her," Mom said to Dave one morning. "Why does she cry so much?"

Dave rubbed his eyes and shrugged his shoulders. "I don't know."

The next week he took the baby to the doctor and got some drops to settle her stomach. I asked him what was wrong with her. "Nothing's wrong, kiddo. Jesse just cries a bit more than some other babies. The doctor thinks she might have a bit of a sore tummy sometimes. She'll grow out of it, you'll see."

Mom and Dave argued even more than the baby cried. They fought about Jesse's sleep schedule, the bottles, her doctor's appointments, the laundry, the house. Sometimes the arguing would keep me up at night. "God, I hate you!" Mom told Dave. Dave grew quiet.

One morning I woke up to find no clean clothes to wear. No underwear, no socks. I opened all my dresser drawers, finding that each one was empty. I put on the same clothes I had been wearing the day before, which were still on the bedroom floor.

Even though he'd been helping her all along, Dave decided to take over the night duties to give Mom a chance to catch her breath. Dave said this was better than having both of them up and tired.

With Dave up most of the nights, he'd try to sleep in as much as he could in the mornings. So I was back to walking to school by myself. I'd follow the same route every day: east three blocks, turning left at the house with the "Welcome Friends" garden sign on the front lawn, north for a longer stretch and then back west for one block. I always took my time on the walk home from school, knowing that Mom would be there alone with the baby. But when I'd return Dougie and Luke Skywalker would wag their tails and lick my face, and I would feel guilty for wanting to stay away.

With Dave in charge at night, things settled down a bit. The baby still cried, but at least she was the only one. Still, Dave's eyes were creased around the edges and he had these lines around his mouth that made it look like he was frowning. I could tell he couldn't last much longer.

As the weeks went on, Dave decided that we needed to change our situation as soon as possible. The house was too small, he said. The walls were too thin. Dave felt we needed to move right away. "We could use a fresh start," he said. "We need a separate room for the baby."

Mom didn't even bother to shrug her shoulders. And why would she care? For us, houses were never the beginning of anything—they were things you had to leave in the end.

Dave asked me for help in finding a new place. "Your mom's pretty busy with everything, Mel Belle. So maybe we can check out some places together and show her the ones we like the best."

I agreed to help, but Dave liked the first one so much he decided that was the one. The home was what Dave called a sidesplit and it was on a dead-end street one block east from where we were. With three bedrooms, it was bigger than the bungalow, but it wasn't much nicer. The ceilings were lined and cracking, the windows were old and draughty and the basement was dark and stinky. There was only one bathroom.

Dave, though, circled the home during our tour, touching the walls of each room, admiring the view from the living room as if it didn't look out on another ugly sidesplit. "Yep," he said, his arm leaning up against the wall. "This is real nice."

He told Mom about it later that day while she was feeding the baby.

"Maybe," she said while letting out a yawn.

But Dave wouldn't let it go. He reminded Mom every five minutes that we needed three bedrooms. When that didn't work, he just said, "Come on, Abby."

Mom finally agreed to see it. The next Saturday, we pulled up to the sidesplit in our white van.

"The street's nice and quiet," Mom said, noticing the dead end.

"Sure is," Dave said, sounding encouraged.

Dave opened the side door and pulled Jesse out, carrying her in his arms.

"This way," he said as he led Mom up the front steps. We walked through the house in five minutes, Mom not saying much as she checked out the kitchen, the laundry room, the bathroom. Dave kept saying the same thing over and over again: "Now you have to see this," as if it was more than just a washer and dryer. Jesse started to fuss before we had a chance to see the backyard, so Mom said she wanted to go home even though the baby was in Dave's arms. Dave didn't argue, and instead led us back to the driveway. Once we were all seated with our belts on, he put his keys in the ignition but didn't start the van.

"So," he said, looking at Mom. "What do you think?"

Mom looked out the window toward the neighbour's maple. "I don't like the walls of the main bedroom. So seventies," she said of the floral wallpaper with its multiple shades of yellow, green and orange.

Dave nodded in agreement. "We can change that eventually. But other than that, do you think you could see us there?"

Mom stared at the tree and scratched the left side of her head before giving Dave the answer he wanted to hear. "If you think it's the right thing to do."

Buying the house took two long months. Every time something happened—like signing papers or getting the keys—Dave would look at Mom and say, "Now we're in trouble." Mom tried to smile when he said this, but by the third time she turned the other way, pretending the baby needed something. Dave looked at me and shrugged his shoulders. "Oh well," he said. "Moving is stressful."

We moved in on the first of October, a cold day interrupted by a rainstorm that meant we couldn't move until lunch. Dave hired two guys with a truck and everything felt organized. Dishes were wrapped in newspaper to prevent them from breaking and all the boxes and furniture had a label with the room clearly marked—front room, basement, kitchen—to make everything easy. Even still, my bed frame broke. The guys Dave hired slipped on the ramp leading up to the truck, dropping the frame, which cracked in three. Knowing it was too damaged to fix, Dave asked them to take it to the garbage dump at the end of the day. Without a bed, I had to sleep on the old pullout couch for a few weeks until we got something new. The sofa was dusty rose, with patterned armrests and a pancake-flat mattress that was hard to pull out. It smelled like basement, but I didn't complain. It was still better than sleeping on a mattress on the floor.

The first night in the new house I lay on the pullout and stared at the ceiling, which was so lined and peeling I thought it would crack open and crash down on me in my sleep. The room was draughty, the wind slipping through the invisible spaces along the window frames.

The new house was supposed to give us a fresh start —it was a chance to try things over with the baby. But as soon as we moved in, it was obvious that nothing would change. Dave needed to start getting some sleep, so Mom took over the nighttime feeds again. The baby was sleeping more and crying less. The screaming fits that started at dinner and went on for hours had stopped for the most part. It should have been easier. But Mom still had to feed the baby at least twice a night. She'd get up the first time, usually around midnight, and would have trouble falling back asleep. Most nights I'd wake up to the sound of the bathroom faucet or a kitchen chair being dragged along the floor.

When I did see Mom, it was usually in the afternoons when I got home from school. I'd open the front door to find Jesse crying in her playpen and Mom slouched on the sofa in front of the television, her clothes wrinkly and her hair so long it brushed the top of her bum. If I wanted a snack, I'd have to make it myself. Dinners were usually canned tuna, boxed soup or milk and cereal. Mom would tell me what to make and I would make it. Sometimes I'd prepare enough for Dave.

We got through the holidays. The snow started later that year, in mid-January, and continued for a long time. The front porch got buried a few times. Dave tried to shovel it every morning. But it was useless trying to keep up with it. By the end of February, he gave up.

"Who cares?" Mom said. "I never leave the house anyway."

Jesse started crawling in January, which was even worse than the snow. Not only did we have to follow her around everywhere, but we had to guard against three separate staircases that cut through the centre of the house. Mom got mad at Dave for buying a sidesplit. "What were you thinking?" she said, her hands hanging beside her in tight fists. Eventually, Dave removed the wall of pillows Mom had built around the foot of each staircase and put up some gates.

It was around April when I noticed something strange about Mom. Sticking out of the back of her head was a knot that looked like a bird's nest. Over the next two weeks, it grew to the size of an orange. Holding a wide-toothed comb, Dave tried to help her brush it out as he sat next to her on the ledge of the bathtub one evening, her hair doused in conditioner. Mom kept saying "Fuck" as Dave pulled the comb, trying to weave it through. The knot, though, was even worse than it looked. Dave gave up when Mom finally burst into tears, begging him to just cut it off. He grabbed the kitchen scissors, doing his best to cut it out. But it left such a big hole he had no choice but to keep going, chopping off her long hair to above her shoulders. It was the first time I'd ever seen her with short hair. Mom looked in the mirror and cried at what she saw. She didn't blame Dave, but still threw him out of the bathroom, locking herself in there for the next hour. I eventually had to pee so I knocked on the door as quietly as possible, saying "Mom?" so she'd know it was me. She kept crying and didn't answer, so Dave told me to go in the backyard, which I did.

The next afternoon I saw her with her new hairstyle, her face framed by a head wrap I'd never seen before. "You look pretty," I said even though I didn't like it.

"Yeah right," she said while pouring herself a cup of tea.

The fighting picked up again as we got closer to Jesse's first birthday. Dave wanted a party. But Mom said no. They argued about this several times, with Dave insisting that they talk in the basement. They went down all three sets of stairs and closed the door behind them so that I wouldn't hear the yelling. But of course I heard everything. And of course I blamed my mother.

Eventually, they didn't bother going downstairs and had their fights wherever they happened to be—in the bathroom, in the kitchen, in the living room with me and the baby.

"You're being ridiculous," Dave said. "Selfish."

"Go to hell," she shouted. "You couldn't care less about what I want, how I'm feeling."

"I've had to put up with so much over the past year. Everything, so far, has been about you—your moods, your laziness. Well, guess what? I'm not giving in on this. We're having a party, whether you like it or not."

"Fuck you," she said. Mom marched upstairs, came down with her purse and stormed out of the house, slamming the door behind her.

Jesse and I were in front of the television when Mom left the house. There was a commercial on for a bathroom cleaner, with the announcer using the word sparkly several times. Dave sat next to us for at least ten minutes without saying anything. He was staring at the TV set, but I could tell he wasn't paying attention. Not knowing what to do, I finally waved my hand in front of his face. He blinked for a second, turned toward me and said: "Let's go out for dinner. Burgers or something."

He put Jesse in his arms and carried her to the van as I followed. Dave reversed out of the driveway and headed east. "Who's hungry?" he asked as we drove down the street. I didn't answer. We turned right onto Yonge, heading south through the old part of town as we approached Major Mackenzie Drive. I looked out the window, to my left, at Fantastia. The dance club with the naked ladies. It wasn't dark yet, but the fancy sign outside was already on, saying hi to everyone with fluorescent pink. I turned my head right, looking out at the community centre and the church, when I noticed someone at the bus shelter. It was a woman wearing a head wrap of some kind that was blowing in the wind.

It looked like Mom from the profile, but we drove by so quickly I couldn't be sure. I was about to say something to Dave, to tell him to stop. Then I thought, no, better not to. Better to let Mom calm down.

We got to the Steer Inn, put in our order at the front and took our seats in one of the orange leather booths. There were no high chairs, so Dave put Jesse in his lap. Once the food was ready, we took turns breaking off bits of our cheeseburgers to share with her. She squealed until I finally gave in and let her grab hold of my milkshake, but as soon as I did she dropped it on the floor, spilling most of it. Dave got up to tell somebody what happened and a bald man from the kitchen came out with a bucket and a mop.

I thought of Mom as we sat there, what she looked like in the bus shelter, the dirt from the road splattered on the glass. Where was she going? She had no brothers or sisters, and she didn't talk to her parents. I'd never even met them. She had a few friends from a while ago —another waitress from the diner, a woman I sort of remembered from several houses ago—but it had been so long since we'd seen anyone. I tried looking again as we drove the same way home, trying not to let Dave know what I was up to as I turned my neck toward the window. But the bus shelter was empty as we zoomed past. We pulled into the driveway of our house a few minutes later, the lights still off.

As soon as he put Jesse to bed, Dave planted himself in front of the living room window in the old armchair. Each time a car went by, which wasn't that often on a dead end, he jumped to his feet, his nose turned up as if he was sniffing something in the air.

"Mom doesn't even drive," I said.

"I know. But she could turn up in a taxi."

"She'll call you first—you'll see."

An hour later and Dave was still sitting in the armchair with one leg crossed over the other. I flipped from channel to channel with one hand and patted the back of my head with the other. Every time I found a strand of hair that felt shorter than the other, I'd yank it out. Eventually, I got tired and went to bed.

I woke up the next morning sure I'd find Mom back home. But when I tiptoed to her room the bed was empty. I went downstairs to find Dave asleep on the couch in his clothes from the night before. I touched his shoulder as gently as possible, but he jolted to life and blinked four times.

"Everything okay?" he asked.

I could tell he was still half-asleep. "I guess. Did Mom come home?"

"I don't think so, kiddo."

That afternoon, Dave was waiting for me outside of school with Jesse, Dougie and Luke Skywalker. He was sitting on the curb, rocking the stroller back and forth with his foot, and didn't notice me until the dogs pulled at their leashes, excited to see me.

"Hi," I said, petting the top of Luke's head. "How come you're here? I've been walking home by myself lately."

"I know," he said, standing up and shaking his left leg as if it had fallen asleep. "I stayed home today so I figured I'd come and meet you. You don't mind, do you?"

I wouldn't have minded, except I knew he should have been at work.

"Where's Mom?" I asked.

"I don't know."

I pushed the carriage along the usual route as Dave made his way through the crowd of kids with the dogs. Luke and Dougie liked to dart after the bikes that rode past us, so Dave kept both hands wrapped around the leashes.

"How was your day today?" Dave asked.

I thought of Vince, who tripped me at recess when the yard supervisor wasn't looking, and Mrs. Clark, who paired me with the dumbest kid in class for our math project. "I don't know. Fine."

Dave put Jesse in front of the TV as soon as we got home and asked me to keep an eye on her while he prepared dinner. I listened to him swear under his breath in the kitchen as he tried to find his way through the cabinets. "Bloody mess," he said.

After hearing a stack of pots crash, I joined Dave in the kitchen to keep him company. He spent the next twenty minutes organizing the drawers, throwing out most of the Tupperware before starting on dinner. I watched him as he opened the door to the fridge, tapping his foot and staring inside for several minutes. He went back and forth—from pantry to fridge, fridge to pantry—at least five times. Finally, he grabbed a can of tomato soup with alphabet bits off one of the pantry shelves, opened it up and dumped it into a pot.

"Hope you girls don't mind," he said, more to himself.

After dinner Dave said I could skip my bath if I got myself to bed on my own. I did as he said and put on my pyjamas. It must have been earlier than usual because I lay awake for what felt like hours, listening through the opening in my bedroom window as another family had a backyard barbecue. It was still light out and I could feel the warmth of the setting sun trying to break through the blinds. The smell of charcoal and sizzling beef poured in, and I realized at that moment how much I hated tomato soup. I tried to think of all the meals Mom usually made, but my only memories involving her and food had to do with the diner or a box of cereal.

I lay on my bed and stared at the light fixture on my ceiling, crying as I overheard a small child laugh at something, a woman asking someone named Jim to bring out the ketchup and a dog panting as it ran through the grass. I felt embarrassed by the hot, angry tears running down my face, and prayed Dave couldn't hear. But a few minutes later, he opened the door to my room with a strange expression on his face.

Dave didn't say anything at first. He sat at the foot of my bed, his shoulders slumped, staring at the wall. "I'm sorry, Mel," he said as I wiped the tears from my cheeks. "I don't know what to tell you."

He was acting as if she'd never come home.

Nothing seemed right, not even at school. About a week after Mom left, Mrs. Clark asked me to stay in class one morning when everyone went outside for recess. Mrs. Clark had grey hair, but it was confusing because her face didn't seem that old. She pulled out one of the kids' chairs at the desk beside me and sat down so we were face to face.

"Melanie," she said, "Is everything okay with you?"

"Yes," I said, lying. "I just have a headache."

"A headache?"

"Yes, kind of."

She looked at me and nodded, looking perfectly comfortable in the orange plastic chair even though it was too low and too small. "Do you think the headache is maybe being caused by something going on? Maybe something at home?"

I wanted to tell her, but I didn't know how to say it: my mom's gone, my mom's in a fight, my mom ran away from home. And then the words came out all by themselves: "My mom left home and I'm not sure when she's coming back. She left me with my stepdad." He wasn't really my stepdad, but I didn't know what else to call him.

"I see."

"Did anyone tell you?" I asked. "I mean, how come you know?"

"Melanie, there's been a change in you. You've hardly said a word in days. You look very tired and rundown. You're not doing your artwork anymore. You wouldn't even help the other students paint the banner for the fair."

"Sorry."

"No," she said, waving her hand to show that she didn't want me to say that. "There's nothing to be sorry about. I understand it's a hard thing you're going through."

"Yeah," I said. I picked at one of my fingernails and hoped the conversation could end.

"Besides your mom being gone, is everything else okay at home? What I'm asking is . . . do you feel safe?"

"Yes," I said. I'd already told her what happened, so why wouldn't she leave me alone? I wanted her to stop asking me questions.

Mrs. Clark turned her head to one side. "Do the other students know about this?"

She knew just as well as I did that I didn't have a lot of friends. Since I moved around so much, I didn't make them easily. "No," I said. "They don't."

"Maybe that's for the best. Unless you care to share that—it's really up to you."

"I don't want to talk about it anymore."

Dave must have felt the same way because he didn't even bring up Mom's name for the next while. Instead, he called his boss at the plant and asked for some more time off. From there, he took over all the household duties: doing the laundry, cooking the meals and caring for Jess.

Dave told me not to worry. "Everything will be a-okay, Melanie. I just need a few days to figure things out."

I wanted to believe him. I really did. But I knew just as well as he did that figuring things out was going to take a lot more than that.

CHAPTER FOUR

———◦◦◦◦◦——

REMINDERS

June 1985

ONE MORNING A few weeks after Mom left, there was a knock at the door. The dogs ran to the entryway but didn't bark; they recognized the smell. Dave was changing Jesse's diaper so yelled out to see if I could get it.

I opened the door to find our old neighbour in a purple jogging suit, her hair tied up in a ponytail. She had a box of cleaning supplies at her feet and was carrying three trays of frozen food in her arms.

"Here, love, take this," Becky said before I had a chance to say hello. "Put them in the freezer or they'll start to thaw."

She marched into the house and got down to work: washing dishes, folding laundry, cleaning bottles. I stayed by her side so I could help. "Grab me the dustpan," she said. "Go fetch a couple of garbage bags."

The house looked a lot worse before it got better. Becky pulled everything out of the fridge and cupboards to do a spring cleaning. She organized all our shelves, throwing out several garbage bags of empty cereal boxes and old food, including a glass jar where the mould grew up and over the sides like a waterfall. The smelliest thing, though, was a small bag of rotten potatoes. Even though she was wearing rubber gloves, Becky still used a knife to lift the bag out of the lazy Susan and into the trash. Juices of rotting flesh dripped onto the floor.

I plugged my nose. "That's gross," I said.

"That's more than gross, love."

Once the kitchen was cleaned and organized, we moved on to Jesse's room. We took everything out of her dresser drawers, where clean clothes had been mixed with dirty ones. We even found a dirty diaper. Once everything was back in order, Becky asked if I could make labels for Jesse's drawers so that we'd know where to find things. I decided to make them purple, just like Becky's jogging suit.

As we worked, Dave went to the grocery store and did a full shop, stocking up on diapers, dog food and frozen pizzas. He came home and lined the walls of the pantry with boxes and cans, making sure to organize the freezer and showing me where everything was. It was late afternoon by the time everything was in order. Jesse was napping, so Dave got out two bottles of beer from the fridge and handed one to Becky. It was nice outside, the air warm and flowery, so they sat side by side on the front steps of the porch. I didn't join them but parked myself on the living room couch beside an open window so I could listen. They stayed there for a long time, close to an hour. Dave did most of the talking. He spoke for so long, but he was so quiet—even when I sat still and stopped breathing, I couldn't make out what he was saying. Becky asked a lot of questions but even she was too hard to understand. I heard her say one thing and maybe it was the only thing that mattered. "She'll come back," she said. "You'll see."

Life was less chaotic after that. Dave hired Becky to be Jesse's babysitter, and switched to the day shift at the plant. He dropped Jesse off at Becky's every morning at seven and picked her up every afternoon. He also registered me for summer camp. But this meant I was on my own again in the mornings. I had to set my own alarm clock, get ready by myself and wait for the bus to pick me up.

Dave made me promise to follow all the rules Mom had put in place when she used to leave me alone: no leaving the house, no answering the door and never telling anyone who called that I was there all by myself. It worked out for several weeks until the Tuesday morning in July when there were flashing lights and ambulance sirens outside. Dave and Jesse had already left for the day, and I was home getting ready for camp when I heard a commotion. I looked out of the window in Dave's bedroom and saw a bunch of firefighters shouting orders at each other outside the house across the street.

At the end of the driveway were three fire trucks, an ambulance and a police cruiser. A fireman was in the driveway with a woman in a green housecoat. She was pacing back and forth and shouting the same thing over and over again: "I told him!" At one point she lunged at the garage but tripped and fell on her side. A fireman tried to help her up, but she wouldn't move. I tried to remember who lived in the grey brick house with the brown shutters but couldn't. The woman didn't look familiar to me. I stood there, in Dave's room, not moving.

My pants and feet were wet, but I didn't know why. The police put up a tarp at the front of the house across the street, covering the garage. I ran to the bathroom, locked the door and pulled a bunch of hair out of my head.

I don't know how long I was in there, but later that morning the phone rang. Several times. I didn't want to leave the bathroom, so I let it ring, over and over again. And then I heard knocking at the door, which I didn't answer. A little while later, I heard the front door of the house open.

"Melanie?"

It was Dave. I let myself out of the bathroom and came downstairs.

"I got a call from the camp that you didn't get on the bus this morning," he said. "Have you been upstairs this whole time?"

I nodded and threw my arms around him, feeling relieved and also terrified by what I didn't know. "Were you scared by all the fire trucks?"

"What happened?"

"I'm not sure. I think there may have been an accident of some kind."

After that, Dave made me stay with Becky in the mornings. He said I could keep all my favourite cereal there and that Chris and Mike would even let me take turns picking what to watch on TV.

A few days later at Becky's, both brothers were sitting with me on the couch watching television when Mike said, "We know what happened to your neighbour—did your Dad tell you?"

"Yes," I said, lying.

Mike ignored me, wanting to tell the story anyway.

"Someone killed themself in the garage," he said. "A high school student. I heard my mom tell my dad that he hung himself. So he must have climbed on top of a ladder, put a rope around his neck and jumped. He left a note saying he hated his mom. The ambulance came too late."

I felt my face go numb.

"Did you know him?" Mike asked me.

I shook my head.

"I heard he was, like, the most popular kid. He played on all the sports teams and even had a girlfriend."

"I saw him all the time," I said, still lying. "He was really weird."

Later that night, after Dave picked me and Jesse up, I asked him about the boy who killed himself. Dave told me he didn't know the family, that he didn't know what happened, but that the police came and said it was a suicide.

"Is it true that it's his mom's fault?" I asked.

"I don't know."

While I'd barely noticed the grey brick house before, from then on it became the only thing I saw each time I stepped outside. I'd try to keep my eyes on my feet as I made my way to Dave's van in the morning so that I didn't have to look at it. When we'd pull into the driveway, I'd put my hands over my face.

A few weeks later, Dave, Jesse and I were getting into the van to do our groceries when a moving truck pulled into the house's driveway.

"That's strange," Dave said as he put on his seatbelt. "I didn't notice a For Sale sign or anything."

We sat there and waited as the truck backed up, making a beeping sound as it reversed toward the garage that had been tarped up that morning. Once the truck was parked, two men jumped out and opened the front door of the house with a key. We sat there for a long time, watching them move a bunch of things out of the home—a table, a bed, some boxes, a lamp. Through the open door I could see the inside walls of the hallway and its floral peach wallpaper. It was such a pretty print, but it made me feel so sad.

Eventually Dave stopped watching through his rearview mirror and revved the engine to life. "Sometimes," he said, reversing the van, "you just need a fresh start."

Although he didn't say her name, he made me think of Mom.

* * *

It was clear as the weeks went on that Mom wasn't coming back.

We hardly spoke about her, but there were reminders everywhere. Half of Dave's closet was still full of her clothes. The cupboard under the bathroom sink had all her things—a plastic bin with hair ties, safety pins and old bottles of nail polish. The basement had a box we brought over that Mom hadn't even unpacked. I asked Dave if we could sort through it. I think, deep down, I wanted to find a clue about why she left or where she'd gone. But Dave didn't want to touch it. "Not yet, kiddo," he said. So we left everything untouched.

I thought of her belongings—the pink and blue floral dress she wore with the brown suede belt, her favourite silver moon-shaped earrings, her coffee mug with the red geese on it. I wondered what, if anything, she took with her. It was possible she started a new life with all new possessions, things that wouldn't remind her of the family she left behind.

At the end of the summer, on a sunny Sunday morning, Dave said he wanted me to attend a family meeting while Jesse was napping. He summoned me to the kitchen, put on a pot of coffee, poured me a glass of chocolate milk and sat down at the table.

"We need to find your mother," he said with his hands pressed together like he was in prayer. "I feel like we haven't tried hard enough to find her. I've made a few calls to the diner, your old neighbours, but it hasn't gotten me anywhere. Truth is, I feel like we haven't done much to get her home. We can't just sit around and hope that she'll walk through that door." He pointed at the front door of the house and I turned around to look at it, as if expecting to see Mom there at that moment.

"So, what now?" I asked.

"Melanie, do you know anyone else we could reach? Did your mom have anyone special you remember, someone she might be staying with?"

"Like who?"

"Like, any special friends? Even an old boyfriend?"

"Mom had lots of boyfriends."

Dave sat up straight when I said this. "She did? Do you know how to reach any of them? Can you remember their names?"

I thought back to our old houses. "I remember two ... one was named Allan and he worked at a gas station,

and the other guy I can't remember what his name was.
I think maybe Steve."

"Okay, and Allan, do you know his last name?"

I shook my head.

"Do you remember which gas station he worked at?"

I shook my head again; I'd never been there. "Sorry."

"It's okay." Dave sighed and rubbed his forehead.
"There are other options, but I wanted to talk to you
first. When was the last time you spoke to someone in
your family?"

I wondered if he meant what I thought he meant: I
wondered if he wanted me to leave.

"What do you mean?" I asked him.

Dave cleared his throat. "What I mean is—is there
anyone else in your family we could reach out to? A rela-
tive I don't know about? Maybe even … your dad?"

I sat there quietly. Secretly relieved. Secretly excited
that I didn't have to leave my home.

Dave looked at me. "Melanie?" He wanted an answer.

I thought of what to say. My dad had always been a
mystery. Mom never talked about him and the few
times I asked, she said he was too immature to raise a
kid. I frowned at Dave. "I don't know who my dad is."

"It's okay," he said.

As for other family members, I knew I had grandparents—I had faded memories of my mother talking
about growing up in Manitoba—but Mom had never
taken me there and they had never visited. "What about
my grandparents? They live far away though."

"I'm not sure we should call your grandmother. I
doubt she'd know where your mom is."

"I guess. But maybe she does know?"

"I don't know, kiddo." He scratched the top of his head. "Your mom, from what I understand, hasn't spoken to her parents in years ... you already know how she left home when she was young."

"But maybe they know where Mom could have gone. Maybe they have a clue. Maybe they can help us." We at least needed to try.

"I don't think I should call them, Melanie. Your mom had a bad childhood ... a bad, very bad relationship with her dad."

"We can pretend we're the police," I said.

"No."

"Okay, let me call. I'll just say hello and ask if they know anything. Just to see if they can help."

Dave leaned back in his chair and rubbed the top of his head with both hands. Without saying anything, he picked up the phone and dialled zero. After a few seconds, he asked for all listings of either William or Irene Forsythe in a town I'd never heard of. "Actually, make that all of Manitoba," he said.

Dave stood up and grabbed a pen and newspaper flyer off the counter. After a few minutes of waiting, he scribbled something down. Then he said thanks and hung up the phone.

"There are two possibilities," Dave said. "You ready?"

I nodded.

Dave held onto the base of the phone as he passed me the receiver. Holding the flyer in one hand, he slowly dialled the number and then put his head up against mine so he could hear. The phone rang five times; I was about to hang up when someone answered.

"Hello?" A lady's voice.

"Hello, this is Melanie Forsythe and I'm calling to speak to William and Irene Forsythe."

"Bill's dead. Who's that again?"

"It's Melanie Forsythe and I'm calling about a family situation. A situation involving ... a family member."

"What do you mean?"

"A family member named Abigail Forsythe."

The woman paused before answering. "Abby doesn't live here."

I cleared my throat as Dave leaned in closer, pressing his shoulder up against mine. "This is Abby's daughter, Melanie. My name is Melanie Forsythe. My mom left home—my home—after a fight—well, just an argument really. A bad argument, I guess—it wasn't a real fight or anything. As in a fistfight. Anyway, this was a little while ago and now we are looking for her and wondering if you could maybe please offer your suggestions to find her. Or clues. We're looking for clues. Clues would be good." All I could hear was the sound of Dave's breathing as I waited for an answer. I wondered if I'd spoken too quickly.

"I think you have the wrong number." And then she hung up.

I sat there for a few seconds, replaying the scene in my head as the dial tone rang in my ear. Dave pulled the receiver away and returned it to its base.

"Do you think we should try the second number?" I said.

Dave rubbed the top of his head again. "I don't think so."

Two weeks later, Dave, Jesse and I came home from dinner at Swiss Chalet to find the light on in the upstairs hallway. "That's strange," Dave said. "I usually only leave the living room light on when we're out."

He put Jesse in her playpen and walked upstairs with his jacket and shoes still on. Hugging the side of the hallway, I followed close behind him, afraid with every step that a robber was going to jump out.

Dave passed Jesse's room first and poked his head inside. "Hello?" he said. He turned on the lights and stepped back, moving to the other side of the hallway where his bedroom was. He switched on the lights to his room and stepped inside. "All good here. Your room next, Mel."

I did as he said but let him go first. Again, he walked in the room and flipped the switch. Everything looked okay. "I guess we're in the clear," he said. I followed Dave as he walked back to his bedroom, but as he reached out to turn off the light he froze.

"Melanie," he said. I stood beside him and watched as he stared at the dresser.

Mom's Mason jars were missing.

Dave didn't move; his mouth hung open.

"Were we robbed?" I asked. Dave moved to the dresser, opening each drawer, touching all the clothes.

"Your mother was here," he said.

I shook my head. I didn't believe him. "We were robbed!" I shouted. "You need to call the police."

Dave walked over to the closet and opened the door. He tugged at the hangers, pulling dresses and shirts to the floor as he looked at everything inside. "Some of your mother's things are missing. The Mason jars are all gone and her drawers are half-empty."

"But it could have been someone else," I said. "An intruder—a *thief*."

Dave sat down on the edge of his bed. "Every day I opened the door to that closet and noticed your mother's yellow dress. She loved that dress—she wore it all the time. And now it's missing."

"A robber took it."

"It wasn't a robber, Melanie. Your mother came to collect her things."

I felt something climb my chest and then grab my throat. I couldn't hold back any longer; hot, angry tears poured out of my face.

Dave's eyes widened. "I'm sorry, Melanie. I'm sorry you have to go through this. But you need to understand—you have to understand—this isn't about you or your sister. When you have a baby, life gets tough. Some people get really sad even though it's a happy time. I think your mom just couldn't handle it all. She just couldn't handle it."

"But she could have said goodbye," I said, wiping my nose with my sleeve. "She could have said goodbye in a nice way."

Dave looked over at the dresser. Circles of dust outlined where the jars had been. "I don't know what to tell you, Mel Belle," he said. "I'm just as surprised as you are."

CHAPTER FIVE

THE CABIN IN
THE WOODS

June 1987

ONE NIGHT AFTER dinner, Dave brought up the idea of going on vacation.

"You mean like Disneyland?" I asked.

"Sort of," he said. "I was actually thinking of going somewhere a bit closer to home. You know I don't fly much."

I'd never been on vacation before, so I had no idea what he had in mind. But a few days later, Dave asked me to pack my things—enough for three sleeps away from home.

"And bring a swimsuit."

I packed exactly three pairs of pyjamas and one swimsuit and gave my bag to Dave, who was busy pulling things together for our trip. On the front porch of our house was a folded-up tent, two duffel bags, a pile of pillows, a box full of groceries, five jugs of water and three sleeping bags with the tags still on.

"Where are we going?" I asked him.

"It's a surprise," he said. "A nice one."

He packed up the van, placing the big objects in first and then tucking the jugs of water and sleeping bags in the corners. We all climbed in as soon as he was done—first Jesse, followed by me, Dougie, Luke Skywalker and Dave. The van was so full that Dave said he couldn't see in the rearview mirror.

"Let's pray for good weather and good times!" he said as he reversed out of our driveway.

Dave turned up the music full blast, the rock station blaring and his arm hanging out of the window. Jesse plugged both ears but didn't complain. This was the happiest we'd seen him since Mom left two years earlier.

We were on the road for close to three hours, listening to rock until we finally lost reception as Dave took us farther and farther north. Once we got off the highway, we drove for about an hour on a winding road, which eventually led to a narrow gravel trail. By the time we pulled up to the tiny green cabin overlooking the grey lake, the tree cover was so dense I thought it was nighttime.

"We're here," Dave said, poking his head out of the window to get a better look.

I wasn't sure if we should get out of the van. "Are there bears here, Dave?"

"Don't know," he said. "Maybe." Dave got out first and took a quick walk around the property to survey the area. "Looks good, girls." He gave us the thumbs-up sign. "Not a bear in sight. Just a lot of black flies." Jesse and I followed him up to the cabin to check out the front porch, and then down to the water, where there was a dock, a canoe and a paddleboat. Dave seemed pleased. "This place is great. We're going to have lots of fun here, girls."

He should have held his judgment until we went inside. After finding the key to the door hidden in one of the floorboards of the porch, we let ourselves in.

"Okay," Dave said with fake cheer. "Cute and cozy it is."

The cabin was tiny, barely bigger than Dave's bedroom at home, but had no bed—just a lumpy pull-out couch with a damp mattress. Daddy-long-legs dotted the walls and ceiling, and there was no kitchen—period. The place was so dark that even the dogs stayed on the porch. I plugged my nose as I walked into the bathroom. A toilet with a wall-mounted sink was inside what should have been a broom closet.

"No shower," I said.

"I think I saw a hose somewhere outside," Dave said. "Let's keep our fingers crossed for sunshine." He left the pillows and sleeping bags outside but brought in the duffel bags and groceries. "I thought there'd at least be a fridge."

There was one dresser to store our things. Dave grabbed my bag and started to put away my pyjamas. "Melanie, where are your clothes?"

"They're in the bag."

"But you only have pyjamas and a bathing suit."

"That's what you said to bring."

"No, I said you needed clothes for our stay. There's nothing here."

"You told me to bring a bathing suit and clothes for three sleeps, so I did!"

Dave put the pyjamas and bathing suit away. "Well, we'll try to make the best of it," he said, shutting the dresser drawer.

It was close to dinnertime, so Dave asked me and Jesse to wait on the porch while he prepared something to eat. A few minutes later he brought out apple slices, a box of crackers and buttered slices of bread.

"Crackers!" Jesse squealed.

"That's the right attitude, kiddo," he said to her.

I took an apple slice and looked out at the lake, its dark grey ripples lapping at the dock. The closest neighbour was anyone's guess; we couldn't see or hear anything, and the stillness of the water showed no signs of nearby swimmers or boaters.

"Tomorrow's going to be a beautiful day," Dave said.

He must have jinxed us because I woke up in the middle of the night to the sound of rain batting at the windows. Jesse and I shared the sofa bed while Dave was in his sleeping bag on the floor. I sat up to make sure I knew where I was. It was the blackest black I'd ever seen. I felt around me, finding Jesse's small, warm body, the damp mattress underneath us. Although I couldn't see him, I heard Dave's snores from the floor. After a few minutes, I fell back asleep. It was still raining when I woke up hours later. Jesse was still beside me, but Dave's sleeping bag was empty. Probably with the dogs. I stayed in bed, playing connect-the-dots with the spiders on the ceiling. Dave came in a few minutes later, leaving Luke and Dougie outside.

"Rise and shine," he whispered, noticing Jesse was still asleep.

I gave him a wave as he took out some food. Dave held up a box of Twinkies with one hand while the other was in a thumbs-up position. He shrugged his shoulders as if to say 'Okay?'

"I don't care," I whisper-shouted.

He nodded, tucking the box of Twinkies into his armpit so that he could grab two apples and a knife with one hand and a jug of water and three plastic cups with the other.

"Meet you outside," he whisper-shouted back.

Jesse must have heard because she started to stir, her eyes still closed.

"I want Daddy," she said, kneeing my back.

"Then go outside," I said, rolling out of bed.

I went out to meet Dave, who was busy placing apple slices on the wooden handrail of the porch, skin sides down.

"Morning," he said, not looking up as he lined the slices in a neat row. Did you have a good sleep?"

"Okay, I guess." The rain had slowed to a faint drizzle. The trees around us were lush and green, still wet from the overnight soak, and the lake was coated in a thick layer of fog, almost like a frosted cake. "What time is it?"

"Just after eight," he said, swatting at a bug.

I took a slice of apple from the middle of the row, leaving an extra wide gap between the pieces. Dave took a slice from the end of the line and placed it where I'd left the extra space, restoring order to his arrangement. Dougie and Luke Skywalker sniffed around the cabin, making sure to stop every few feet to mark their territory. I took another apple slice, this time from the end of the row.

"So," I said. "What are we going to do today?"

Dave looked out at the lake, rubbing his chin with the hand holding the knife.

"Well, I was thinking we could take the boat out on the lake, do some exploring. Or maybe hike around the property a bit, see what we can find."

"What if we find bears?"

"Well, that would be a problem," he said, pausing for a second to reconsider that as a possibility. He rested the knife on top of the handrail and went back to rubbing the bottom of his chin, which was stubbly from not shaving.

"Let's start with the boat. It'll be nice to be out on the water."

The door swung open and we both looked over to see Jesse, who was dragging her pillow behind her.

"Good morning, Sunshine!" Dave said, swooping down to lift her up in his arms. Jesse tucked her head into his armpit and her thumb into her mouth as the pillow dangled from her other hand. "Jesse, what do you think about going on a little boat ride in the water?"

"No."

"But, sweetie, it will be so fun to …"

"No!" Jesse squealed, squirming out of his arms and kicking her legs out. As she did this, one of her legs hit the top of the handrail, swiping half the row of apple slices off the ledge and into the mud.

Dave sighed and placed her back down on the porch. "Let's have some breakfast, then."

We ate the remaining apple slices and Twinkies in silence as the rain finally stopped. Dougie and Luke Skywalker took a break from exploring and were stretched out on what little space was left of the porch. I looked at Dave as he stood leaning up against the front of the cabin, eating a Twinkie. His face seemed lighter than usual, as if the first night in the woods had erased the hard edges. Once we were done breakfast, Dave spent forty-five minutes trying to get Jesse dressed into her clothes, but—because I had to stay in my pyjamas—she refused to change as well.

"You need to change, Jesse," he said.

"No!" she shouted.

"I'm your father," Dave said, his voice unsteady. "You have to listen to me."

"No! I'm wearing pyjamas like Melanie!"

"Fine!" he finally yelled, slamming his fist on the dresser. "Stay in your bloody pyjamas!"

Jesse looked down at her nightgown, lifting up the skirted edge as if it was an apron.

"They're not bloody!" she screamed.

Once Dave had calmed down, he put the dogs inside the cabin and we headed down to the water.

"All right, girls, look how beautiful this is. We just don't have this at home."

Off to the side of the dock was a grassy shoreline where we found a green canoe, parked upside down, and a beat-up paddle boat. Jesse's eyes brightened at the sight of the boat, whose orange shell and white underbelly made me think of Creamsicles.

"Paddle boat, paddle boat, paddle boat!" she yelled as she climbed inside.

"Jesse, let's get the boat into the water first and then you can sit in it," Dave said. Jesse ignored Dave as she sat in the driver's seat, clutching the wheel with both hands as she pretended to steer.

"Fun stuff, right?" Dave said as he took her hand. But Jesse refused to budge. When Dave pulled harder, she kicked and screamed. Dave let go instead of trying to fight it.

"Melanie, please grab the other side so we can carry this over to the water."

Dave's side lifted up, but the boat was so heavy my side stayed planted in the ground. Realizing he was on his own, he dragged the paddle boat with Jesse inside as she still pretended to steer. He gave a fist-pump in the air as soon as he reached the water, the boat bobbing and swaying. We jumped in, first me and then Dave, with Jesse on his lap. But as soon as we did, the boat started to veer back toward land.

"Let's go Melanie!" he shouted as Jesse giggled. "Pedal, pedal, pedal!"

Dave twirled his feet as quickly as possible but was limited by Jesse on his lap. Even though I was trying as hard as I could, the boat seemed to stay in one place.

"Keep pedalling!" Dave shouted.

Finally, we started to make some headway. "Let's go that way," Dave said, pointing left.

The water was calm and dark, lined with a lot of greenery and the occasional dock. Jesse squirmed as Dave tried to move his legs to propel the boat forward. Eventually, she climbed over him and sat on the bench behind the bucket seats.

Once we got farther out, we realized the tiny lake was connected to a larger chain. "We could explore for days," I said. "And then maybe go down a waterfall."

"Maybe," Dave said. "But I wouldn't wish for it."

He was fascinated as we went farther and farther into the maze of water, pointing each time he'd see something—a rock, a loon, a weeping willow. We'd been exploring for half an hour when Jesse started to fuss.

"We should probably head back, Mel Belle."

We turned around, making an extra-wide U to return to the cabin, but after a few minutes, we felt like we were somewhere we hadn't been before.

"I don't remember the lake being this narrow," Dave said. "Did we take a turn and not realize it?"

We went back in the other direction, this time pedalling for about ten minutes. But Dave seemed only more confused. I had no idea where we were or what direction we had taken; everything looked the same to me no matter where we went. Jesse began to cry loudly. Dave rested the bottom of his chin between his thumb and finger as if he was in thinking mode. I could tell he was getting worried.

"Dave, are we lost?"

He looked straight ahead, squinting. "Maybe," he said. He turned around, I guess to get his bearings, but he shook his head. "Let's sit and wait for someone," he said, mostly to himself.

Jesse continued to cry, waving her arms and kicking the back of my seat over and over again. "I want to go home!" she yelled.

Dave ignored her as he sat there looking straight ahead, still thinking. "I wish there were other boats around," he said.

We'd passed only a couple of docks and there didn't appear to be much activity on the lake. Jesse cried for what seemed like forever as Dave and I sat there, waiting for something to happen.

"Maybe we should try calling out for help," he said.

Dave stood up, the paddleboat swaying gently, and cupped his hands to his mouth.

"Hello!" he yelled. "We're lost and need help!" This, though, made Jesse cry even louder. Dave sat back down. A nearby tree rustled. "Shit," Dave said.

Jesse cried for several more minutes until she started to run out of steam. Her face was red and sticky with tears and sweat and I could tell she was tired. "I want to go home," she said.

"Let's try pedalling in this direction, Mel Belle," Dave said. "We might recognize something."

We started pedaling again, turning a corner I wasn't sure we'd seen before.

"This might be it," he said.

The lake was a bit wider at this point. I didn't recognize anything, but Dave insisted that we keep on pushing. We went on for another couple of minutes until he suddenly stopped. "Do you hear that?"

I looked at him and waited. And then I heard it. Dogs barking.

"Keep going," he said.

The barking got louder until we saw it—a dock. Dave went into high gear, pedaling his feet like a madman who hadn't seen land in days. Despite his efforts, the boat moved slowly as it approached the T-shaped float of old wooden planks. We climbed out and were greeted by two large Golden Retrievers who wagged their tails as they circled our feet and sniffed our privates.

"Look at these guys," Dave said, patting one of them on the head. "So friendly, too. They must know we're dog people."

The cottage on the property was wide and low, with a barely sloped roof and a wall full of windows. I tried to see if there was anyone inside, but the light hit the windows in such a way that I could only see reflections of the lake.

"I think someone's home," Dave said. "Let's try not to scare them."

He led the way in the front as Jesse, the two Golden Retrievers and I followed in a V shape, the five of us like a flock of geese. Dave switched to his tiptoes as he left the dock for land, slowly making his way up the arched patch of spotted grass that reached the back deck. As soon as we got there, Dave raised his right hand and motioned for us to stop.

"What's wrong?" I asked.

He didn't say anything as he continued to look ahead. I followed his gaze into one of the windows. From this angle the light had shifted, so I could now see inside the main living room, where a man and a woman were standing on opposite sides of the room. The woman was yelling, making motions with her hands and arms, though I couldn't make out what she was saying. The man would listen, then start to shout back so they'd be yelling over each other at the same time.

Dave leaned over to pick up Jesse and then slowly waved at the couple with his other hand. At first, they didn't notice, but Dave swung his arm back and forth more rapidly. The couple both looked toward the window at the same time, startled to see three strangers observing what had been a private moment. Dave used his free hand to point over at the boat, which didn't do much to explain that we were lost. The couple came out of their cottage.

The woman was tall and brunette, about the same age as Mom, and was wearing a pink floral dress and flip-flops. The man must have been at least ten years older, though his hair didn't have any grey. I wondered if they were married.

"Hi there," Dave said, a bit too enthusiastically. "Sorry to disturb you like this, but I've been in a boat with my girls for quite some time and I'm afraid we're lost. I was wondering if you could help us out."

"Oh my goodness, of course," the woman said, looking at Jesse. Her voice was deeper than expected, and now that she was closer I could see that her eyes were red and swollen from crying. She approached Jesse and Dave first, touching Jesse's leg before asking, "What's your name?"

Jesse tugged away, putting her head into Dave's shoulder. "I'm thirsty," she said.

The woman smiled. "Very nice to meet you, Thirsty. My name's Donna. Maybe you'd like a glass of water?"

"That'd be great," Dave said.

The woman went back into the cottage as the man walked toward us. He introduced himself as Eddie and explained that he and his wife were both teachers and liked to spend most of their summers here. Dave told him how we'd gotten lost and credited the dogs for helping us find their cottage.

"Max and Gus are the best there is," Eddie said, patting one of the dogs' heads. "This is the second time they've been able to help someone on the water."

"What happened?" I asked him.

"Oh, they're great dogs," Eddie continued. "Best there is."

I waited for him to go on, but it was Dave who spoke next. "The girls love dogs. We have two ourselves."

"Nice ... nice," the man said.

Dave tried to put Jesse down on her feet, but she wrapped her arms around his neck, refusing to budge. Eddie smiled at Jesse, but she turned further into Dave's shoulder to hide her face.

"Sorry if you heard any of that," Eddie said, motioning toward the living room where he and Donna had been fighting.

"Not at all," Dave said.

"Things haven't been easy," Eddie said.

Dave stood there and didn't say anything.

"We lost our son last summer."

Dave looked down toward the ground. "I'm sorry," he said.

"I appreciate it. He was our only child."

I wanted to tell the man that we'd lost our mother, but I knew Dave wouldn't like that, so I didn't say anything.

"So, who do *you* look like?" Eddie said, poking Jesse's arm. "Do you look like your mommy or your daddy?"

"Daddy," Jesse said as she buried her face further into Dave.

The man chuckled and then looked at me. "And, wow, you sure take after your dad, don't you?"

I eyed Dave, wondering if he was going to correct him. Dave gave me a quick wink. "I have two beautiful girls, that's for sure."

Donna came out with a map and some water, so that gave us something new to talk about. Eddie and Dave looked over it together and were able to figure out where our cabin was. Eddie insisted on taking us back in his motorboat. He and Dave tied the paddle boat behind us so that we could bring it back to the cabin. Eddie put on a hat and sunglasses and said, "Climb in!"

We all did so as Donna stood on the dock with the dogs and waved goodbye. Eddie pulled away in what felt like slow-motion and kept that same pace the entire way back, puttering along the chain of lakes. Eventually, we recognized the tiny green cabin and Eddie steered the boat toward the dock.

"Thanks for your help," Dave said, shaking Eddie's hand.

"My pleasure."

"Bye!" Jesse waved as we jumped off the boat.

Once we were inside the cabin, Dave whipped up a quick lunch of jam sandwiches and apple sauce and then put Jesse down for a nap.

"Let's hang out on the front porch," he said to me as he grabbed two cans of ginger ale.

I followed Dave to the front steps, where we both sat down. Dougie and Luke darted around the bushes, sniffing and searching for something unknown.

"Well, that was fun," Dave said, making a face to show his sarcasm. A hissing sound escaped from each can as he opened them up and passed one to me.

"Yeah," I said. "I feel kind of tired now."

"Me too," Dave said. "We'll try to take it easy for the rest of the day."

I took a sip of warm ginger ale and wondered what Eddie and Donna's cottage was like inside. I imagined an oversized television and several spare rooms with comfortable beds and chairs.

"Do you think we can go back to that couple's cottage?" I asked Dave.

"Oh, I don't think so, Mel Belle. They've already helped us out quite a bit."

"Their place is much better than the cabin," I said. "Like, it's probably even bigger than our house at home."

"Yes, it looked very nice."

"Dave," I said, not sure if I should ask the next question. It was something that had been bugging me, something I'd been wondering since Eddie told us about his son. "Those people—now that they don't have any children, does that mean they're not parents anymore?"

Dave stared out at the lake and took a sip of his ginger ale. "Well, I don't know, Melanie," he said. "Hadn't really thought about it."

"I guess I'm just wondering. If your child is gone, how can you still be a parent?"

Dave considered this for a moment. "Well, once you're a parent, I think you're always a parent—no matter what. I'm not sure it's something that goes away. Know what I mean?"

"I guess," I said, taking another sip of ginger ale. "And what about me?"

Dave turned to look at me. "What about you?"

"Can I be a daughter if I don't have any parents?"

At this, Dave put his arm around me, tucked my head into his chest and looked back toward the lake. "You're *my* daughter," he said, rubbing the side of my shoulder. "And you always will be."

It was nice of him, but it wasn't what I wanted. What he needed to say, what I had to hear, was that Mom was coming home.

CHAPTER SIX

———◦◇◦———

THE PINEAPPLE
DOORKNOCKER

October 1987

WITH MOM STILL out of the picture, I could tell Dave was trying to get his life back together. For one, he started eating healthy. Every time we sat down to dinner, we had to have a salad first. "Greens, greens, they're good for your heart. The more you eat, the more you—"

"Wrong food," I said.

Then one Saturday morning, he dragged me and Jesse to the mall so he could buy himself a new pair of running shoes, sleek red and blue ones with high-performance cushions built into them.

"These are beauties!" he said as he kicked off his old shoes at the cash register so he could wear his new ones home.

"I want a pair, too," I said.

"Sorry, kiddo," Dave said. "These are a gift to myself—for something special."

"What's that?" I asked, wondering if we'd be going on another vacation.

"You'll never guess," he said as he raised his eyebrows.

I waited for an answer, watching for the eyebrows to drop.

"I joined a running club."

I imagined Dave wearing short shorts and a windbreaker while running along the side of the road in one of those groups that always seemed to annoy drivers. He was right; I never would have guessed.

"Why running?" I asked. To be honest, it sounded boring.

"I don't know, I just thought it'd be fun to get together with some other parents in the neighbourhood and exercise for a bit."

I understood this to mean he needed a break from me and Jess. And I couldn't really blame him.

The next Saturday, Dave was wearing his new sneakers as he stood over my bed to wake me up. "Rise and shine," he said. "I've got a hot date in thirty minutes."

"Date?" I asked.

"My running group. We meet at eight sharp."

Wearing his fancy new sneakers, Dave ushered us into the van so he could drive us to someone else's house.

"Where are we going?" I asked as he drove north on Yonge.

"The home of one of the other running guys. His name's Dave, too."

"Why are we going there?"

"His wife Marla agreed to watch you and your sister Saturday mornings so we can train. At least until the spring. They've got a son too so you may make a new friend."

"I don't want a new friend. Why can't we just go to Becky's?"

"You guys spend enough time there as it is," he said. "Becky has her own life and her own family."

Dave drove for a few more minutes before turning left into a well-to-do area of big homes and luxury cars. Tall evergreens stood on each side of the road and some of the properties were gated. I turned my head as I tried to see if anyone had a swimming pool.

"Wow, people live here?" I asked.

"It's a nice neighbourhood," Dave said.

We pulled into the driveway of a big red brick home with a three-car garage and a walkway lined with yellow flowers. Dave took Jesse by the hand and led her to the house as I followed. There was not one front door but two. Black, shiny and really tall, almost as tall as our own home. Mounted on one of them was a giant gold pineapple doorknocker. Dave leaned over, lifted it with one hand and gave the great big house such a gentle knock that I was surprised when the door swung open a few seconds later.

"Twenty-seven more weeks till race day!"

The other Dave was beaming as he stood in the doorway with his hands on his hips and his socks pulled up to his knees.

"Wasn't sure if I was too early," Dave said. "Or if your family was still asleep."

"Oh, don't worry about them," the other Dave said. "Come in! Come in, girls. Marla's getting up now and she'll want to make you some breakfast."

We stepped into the foyer, a grand marble room with soaring ceilings and a cascading staircase. Greeting all visitors were two life-size statues of large dogs in painted ceramic. Each one was designed in such detail they even had their own ceramic nametags: Marcus and Maze. I studied the black spots painted on their bodies and noticed they even had ceramic tongues in their mouths. Dalmatians, I thought. It was the perfect house.

At that moment a blonde-haired woman wearing a silky coral robe came down the spiral staircase, the slit in her gown showcasing her legs with each step. Her matching slippers were made of feathers and even had a little heel.

"Good morning," she said as she approached us in the entryway. Our Dave stood there stupidly and, instead of saying hello, gave Marla an army salute with his right hand, something I'd never seen him do before.

"You must be Melanie and Jordan," she said as she came down the final steps.

Jesse squinted. "I'm Jesse," she said.

"That's right," Marla said.

Marla's robe swept the beige-swirled marble floor behind her as she shooed us toward the back of the house. "Come in, come in, come in," she said, motioning her hands to keep us moving.

The two Daves left to meet the others as the ladies made our way to the kitchen. Something smelled bad as soon as we entered the room. Dirty dishes spilled out and over the sink, empty wine bottles littered the countertop and an overfull garbage bag leaned up against a wall.

"Sorry," Marla said. "The cleaning lady doesn't come until Monday."

She opened the fridge. "There's milk in here somewhere. Do you girls like toast and jam?"

Jesse and I stood frozen, not sure if we should sit.

"Yes, please," Jesse said.

"Yes please—so adorable," Marla said as she crouched down toward Jesse. "You are as cute as a button." Jesse turned toward me to hide her face in my side. Marla tried to straighten back up but had to place her hand on the tiled floor to regain her balance.

"Woopsie!" she said, laughing. "It's so early it still feels like last night."

Marla made us toast and poured us milk, removing enough of the mess from the table so we could sit down. Jess started to eat, gulping the milk in between mouthfuls.

"So, what do you girls want to do while you're here?" Marla asked. "You can watch TV, you can play video games. We've got games and toys somewhere. You can also play outside."

"I don't want to," Jesse said.

I felt my face turn red with embarrassment. "She doesn't like the cold," I said.

"Is it cold out?" Marla said, turning toward the window. She thought about it for a second. "Well, I guess it is."

"A little bit," I said quietly, ashamed I'd said anything.

"We also have an indoor pool you girls could swim in."

I'd heard of houses with swimming pools but never an indoor one. Not even on *Lifestyles of the Rich and Famous*. Jesse must have been just as excited as I was because her eyes got really big and bright. "There's an inside pool?" she asked.

"Yes, there is. Want to see it?"

We finished our toast as quickly as possible and then followed Marla's coral robe as it flowed through the hall and down to the basement. The main rec room had all the things Dave would have loved—a gitoni table, a mini bar and even its own movie theatre.

"This is big!" Jesse said. "It's like a big ship."

"You can have all the fun you like," Marla said. "The pool's just right over here."

She led us over to the next room, which was enormous, maybe even bigger than our entire house. In the centre was a large rectangular pool lit up with emerald green lights. Each side was lined with white plastic lounge chairs and the walls were decorated with green mosaic tiles. I had no idea something like this could exist inside someone's house.

"Lovelies, here you are. There are towels in the side bathroom."

Jesse looked at me as if to say, "What now?"

"We didn't bring our swimsuits," I said to Marla, my voice sounding smaller than I'd wanted.

"Oh. But you girls can go in your underwear. No one will be down here. There's lots of privacy."

"Okay," I said.

Jesse and I stood there for a moment. I breathed in deeply but didn't detect the smell of chlorine.

"So, we're all set. Do you girls mind if I go back upstairs then? You can keep yourselves busy swimming?"

"Yes," I said, nodding.

With that, the coral robe swung around and flowed back toward the staircase.

"I want to go in," Jesse said.

"Me too. But Dave may get mad."

"I want to go in!"

I took Jesse's hand and led her to the edge of the pool, where I took off my socks, rolled up my pants and dipped my feet in. The shock of the temperature made me suck in my breath. Jesse joined me at the edge of the pool and did the same.

"It's cold!" she yelled. "I want Daddy."

"It's like an icy lake," I said. "A lake inside a house."

We pulled our feet out of the water, put our socks back on and decided to explore the rest of the basement. Jesse walked into the rec room and started opening all the cupboards under the bar. I heard the clinking of glass bottles so ran over and pulled her away before she broke something.

"Don't touch that, Jess," I said. "We're going to get in trouble."

I took Jesse by the hand and plopped her into one of the leather seats in the theatre room. I found four separate remote controls, so it took me a while to figure out how to turn everything on. Once I did, I let Jesse pick the movie: *Annie*. We were about halfway through when a boy walked in. He had light brown hair, wasn't that tall, but I could tell he was a teenager.

"Who are you?" he asked.

"We're with Dave."

"What do you mean?"

"Our dad's in the running club."

"What club?"

"The club where our dads run."

"Oh," he said. "Who's your dad?"

"Dave."

"My dad's Dave," he said.

"Yeah, they have the same name."

"Oh," he said. "I'm Jason."

"I'm Melanie. This is Jesse. My sister."

"Hi."

"We're watching *Annie*," Jesse said.

"Oh. Does my mom know you're here?"

Jesse shrugged her shoulders.

"Oh," he said. "Have fun."

"Bye!" Jesse shouted.

Jason turned and walked away. I cringed as I thought about the way my voice sounded. We watched another few minutes of the movie before Jesse got bored, deciding she wanted to see the rest of the basement again. I tried getting her to sit back down, but she insisted on opening every door and exploring every room.

"This house is big," she said.

"Stop touching everything."

She became braver as she pressed on with her search. She rifled through everything and made several new discoveries: the games room, a guest bedroom, a wine cellar. I put my foot in front of her as she tried to mount the staircase back to the main floor.

"Stop it," I said. "You're going to get us in trouble."

She scurried past my foot and ran up the steps, ignoring my warnings and forcing me to chase her. Once she reached the main level, she decided to keep going up, circling around to the front entryway and climbing the steps leading to the bedrooms.

"No, no, no! Jesse—*don't*. I'm serious."

She ignored my pleas despite my hushed, angry tones and made her way to the top, defiantly opening the first door she found on the left. "Towels!" she said as she slammed the door shut, turning around to try the next one.

I grabbed her arm as she crossed my path, but she slipped out of my grip, opened the next door in her path and darted inside.

"Come on!" I said.

I heard her running around, opening and closing drawers. Afraid that someone else was inside, I knocked on the door gently and popped my head inside the room.

"Hello?"

No one answered. In the centre of the room was a wrought iron bed flanked by wooden night tables and matching side lamps. Across from the bed was a large armoire, its double doors flung open. I guessed from the lack of contents inside that this was a guest room. Jesse was nowhere in sight. I started to head toward the door to what was either a bathroom or a closet when Jesse burst through it and tried to run past me. I grabbed her arm securely this time, tackling her to the carpeted floor to keep her from wriggling away.

"Stop it!" I said. "I'm going to tell Dad and you're going to be in so much trouble."

I marched out of the room clutching her arm when the door to another room at the opposite side of the hallway swung open. Jason stared at us as I tried to drag Jesse back downstairs.

"Hey," he said. "What are you guys up to?"

"Sorry. It's my sister—she's trying to explore all the rooms. We're going to go back downstairs now."

"No, it's okay," he said. "Did you want to hang out here?"

Jesse made a face at me as if to say, "*See?*"

"I guess," I said. "If you don't mind? I think she's getting bored."

"Yeah," he said. "I'm bored, too."

"Is this your room?" I asked him as I approached the door. Jesse had already ducked underneath his arm to go inside.

"Yeah," he said. "Smallest one in the house. Because it's the furthest away from my parents."

I looked at Jason carefully, studying his heart-shaped face, light brown hair and slightly crooked smile. "How old are you?" I asked him.

"Seventeen in December. You?"

"I'm eleven," I said before correcting myself: "Eleven and a half."

"That sucks that you have to watch your sister."

"I know. She keeps misbehaving."

Jason turned his head back into his bedroom. "You can come in if you want. I'm just listening to music."

I walked inside to find a pie-shaped room with dark green walls, plaid linen and several pillows bearing the Union Jack. A ghetto blaster sat on a desk and was playing a Bon Jovi song I knew Dave liked. Despite its decent size, the room's irregular shape made it feel cramped and uncomfortable.

"Neat room," I said. "It's very decorated."

"Thanks," he said. "My mom hired someone."

Jesse was kneeling on the floor opening the drawers to his desk. "Don't do that," I said. "It's not your house."

"It's okay," he said, turning to Jess. "You can touch my things—as long as you promise not to make too much of a mess."

She ignored both of us and took out a stack of CDs that had been wedged into one of the drawers.

"So, where's your mom?" I asked him, sitting down beside Jesse on the carpeted floor.

He walked to the stereo, turning the volume down a bit. "Probably tired and sleeping. Mom and Dad were at a party last night. I got to stay home alone until Dad got home."

"Oh," I said. "I'm sorry."

"Why are you sorry?" he said. "Being home alone is awesome."

"Oh," I said. "That's what I meant." I felt my face go red.

"So, where's *your* mom?" Jason asked. "Like, why do you have to stay here while our dads are out?"

I had no idea how to answer that question. I didn't know what to say.

"She died."

Now it was Jason's face that turned red.

"Sorry," he said. "That sucks."

"Um, I don't really like to talk about it," I said, praying that Jesse didn't expose me.

Luckily, she was still busy making a mess of things. After finishing with the CDs, she found another drawer stuffed with papers and binders. She started to pull everything out in a hurry, as if she knew someone was going to put an end to her fun. I was about to start yelling at her when we heard Jason's Dave call out to us.

"Hello, girls? You up there?"

I grabbed Jesse's arm, but she pulled it away. "We've got to go," I said. I was using the most mature voice I could muster, but I really wanted to grab her by the hair. "Now—*please*."

Jesse tried to open another drawer, so I stood up and scooped her up by looping my arms around her torso. She shrieked in protest and kicked her legs against my shins.

"Bye," Jason said as I carried her out of the bedroom, her legs still fluttering. "I guess I'll see you next time."

CHAPTER SEVEN

SHARON, LOIS & BRAM

April 1989

DAVE AND I were doing the groceries when he dropped a bombshell in front of the bananas.

"So, Melanie, I wanted to let you know that I've met a new friend ... A female friend, I guess you could call her. It's someone I met right here in the grocery store actually."

"Oh," I said as I pushed the cart with Jesse in it. I could feel him watching me, searching for a reaction. I was shocked but didn't want him to think I was upset—even though I was. "Do you, like, go to the movies and stuff?"

Dave chuckled. "Not exactly. Just coffee once or twice. But it's hard to see her when I'm either working or at home with you girls. So I was thinking—hoping, actually—that she could maybe come by the house one time."

"Oh," I said. "Sure. I mean, I don't mind."

I did mind. Whoever it was, it wasn't Mom. And I mostly, positively, did not want anyone moving in the house with us.

Dave organized an introduction the next afternoon while we were preparing dinner. The doorbell didn't even ring. I heard the dogs barking and suddenly Dave was leading a woman by the elbow into the kitchen, where I was folding paper napkins.

"Melanie," Dave said. He was smiling like an idiot. "This is Rona."

I looked at her, a small woman with shoulder-length blonde hair and tortoise-shell eyeglasses. Nice. Pretty. But too short for Dave.

"Hi," I said.

"Hi, Melanie," Rona said while holding a large plastic bag in her arms. "I brought something for you and your sister."

"Oh," I said, unsure if I should take the bag from her. "Thank you."

"Jesse's up in her bedroom," Dave said. "I'll go grab her right now." He turned around and left me and Rona alone in the kitchen.

"So," Rona said, not missing a beat. "Dave tells me that you're in Grade Seven."

"Yeah," I answered. I didn't know what else to say.

"That's nice. What's your favourite subject?"

"Art."

"Is that a subject or an activity?"

"I don't know. Both, I guess."

"Oh, very nice."

I wondered where Dave was. "What about you?" I asked.

"Mmm?"

"In school. What was your favourite subject?"

"Math."

"That's a hard subject."

"It's actually very easy if you learn all the rules and then follow them."

I wrinkled my nose. "So, are you a mathematician?"

Rona laughed. "Sort of. I'm an accountant."

"Sounds interesting." It didn't sound interesting at all. I looked over my shoulder to see if Dave was coming back.

"I also have a lot of hobbies. I play squash at the country club—have you ever played squash before?"

"Um, I'd have to ask Dave."

Thankfully, Dave rescued me from the conversation by returning to the kitchen with Jesse. Rona crouched down so they were at eye level. "Hi Jesse," Rona said. "I brought you a gift—did you want to see what it was?"

Jesse nodded, at which point Rona handed her the large plastic bag. She pulled out a mermaid puzzle set. Dave nodded at Jesse, giving her the signal to say thanks.

"Thank you," Jesse said.

"My pleasure," Rona said. "There's something else in there for your sister."

Jesse pulled out the next item: a pink box with a Barbie doll. Barbie was wearing a shimmery turquoise dress and had that artificial smile plastered on her face. Her eyes were blue and vacant. I looked at Rona, wondering if there was a mistake. I was about to turn thirteen and hadn't played with a doll in years.

"Hope you like it, Melanie," Rona said.

"Oh, thanks," I said, taking the package from Jesse. I looked at Dave who was nodding with another stupid grin on his face.

Rona became a regular fixture after that. I tried to ignore her, but she came over every Tuesday and Saturday with several grocery bags for us. "Here," she'd say, throwing me a box of crackers. "For you and your sister." Occasionally, she'd put a box of popsicles in the freezer. "I used to love these," she said. "But don't eat them all at once."

I slowly warmed up to her, especially when it appeared she would not be moving in.

Jesse followed her everywhere. "Roada," she liked to remind us, was good at everything. When Dave made dinner, Jesse would eat half then push the plate away. "Roada's mac 'n cheese is better," she said. If I sat down to do some colouring with her, she'd shrug at my finished page. "Roada colours the nicest."

One Saturday morning in June, a couple of months after they started dating, Dave took me and Jess to the convenience store to buy milk and lottery tickets when I noticed Dave eyeing the bouquets of flowers displayed on the sidewalk.

"These would be nice for Rona, no?" he said. He leaned over to pick up a modest bunch of black-eyed Susans.

Jesse wrinkled her nose when she saw the batch. "No, Daddy, those are no good." She reached down toward the rows of flowers in green and yellow plastic buckets and picked out a large bouquet of pale pink roses, their stems long and thorny.

"These ones," she said, using both hands to lift the bouquet. Dave let out an exaggerated gasp when he saw the price tag, then laughed to himself and brought the flowers to the cash.

"These can be a gift from you guys," he said.

"Is it Roada's birthday?" Jesse asked.

"It's not her birthday," Dave said. "I thought it would be nice to get her something special."

Later that afternoon, when Rona knocked at the front door, Jesse wouldn't let Dave open it until she had the flowers in her arms, sprawled out as if she was holding a baby.

"Here, Roada, these are for you."

She bent over to smell the flowers in Jesse's arms and gave her a hug. "Oh, sweetie, these are beautiful. Thank you."

"Thank you, Roada."

I heard Dave chuckle to himself in the next room. "Roada," he repeated.

Rona made dinner for us that night: grilled steak and mixed vegetables. We sat out on the table in the back as the dogs drooled at our feet, waiting for us to throw them a fatty piece of meat too difficult to chew. From the outside we probably looked like an ordinary family enjoying a quiet Saturday at home. Our relationships may not have been normal but, for the first time in a long time, it felt like I had a real family.

I wondered what Mom would have thought of Rona. There was a part of me that believed Dave had chosen Rona because she was so different. While Mom strolled, Rona scurried. Mom's long and messy hair matched her loose and shabby clothing. But Rona always looked like she was going somewhere special. Her hair was never out of place and her clothes looked expensive. She even had multiple pairs of sunglasses in designer names that Dave couldn't pronounce.

I'm sure Mom would have rolled her eyes at Rona's fancy taste, her daybook for appointments, her love of reading. I imagined Mom's reaction: *"Does she think she's a member of the royal family?"* The thought of it made me sad. But, mostly, it made me feel guilty because I wanted to be like Rona, too. I wanted to wear nice clothes and get a good job and have an exercise schedule and be on time for things. I wanted to be the kind of organized and successful person my mom could never be.

Naturally, everyone thought Rona was our mother: the cashier at the grocery store, the secretary at the doctor's office, even one of the teachers at school. At first, I felt proud. But Rona was never shy about setting the record straight. "Nope, wish I could say they're mine, but they're not."

Jesse, though, started to get clingy. At night, she whined and begged. She wanted Roada to give her a bath. She wanted Roada to tuck her in.

"Sweetie," Dave said, "Rona needs to be in her own house sometimes. She needs time to work and do things." But Jesse would only shriek and kick the sheets off her bed.

One night after one of Jesse's tantrums, I found Dave sitting outside on the front steps, a bottle of beer in his hand and his shoulders slouched.

"Jesse's still not asleep," I said. "She keeps talking and everything."

"Yeah."

"What's wrong with her?" I asked.

"What's wrong with her is that she needs a mother."

"So ... are you and Rona going to get married?" I was afraid to hear the answer. I wasn't even sure what I wanted.

Dave took a gulp of his beer and swallowed. "No, we're not. She doesn't want to."

I stared at him to see if he meant what he said. "Why not? Why wouldn't she?"

"She says she likes things as they are. She wants her own space. And she's busy at work."

I was back to not liking her. "Does Jesse know? That she doesn't want to ... you know."

"Course not. Anyway, things are not all bad. Rona adores you girls, and we see her every week. We're lucky to have her."

"I'm sorry, Dave."

"It's okay, kiddo."

* * *

To give Dave a hand, Rona chaperoned Jesse every Saturday morning to ballet class, a series of lessons that was supposed to prepare her and the other girls for an end-of-season recital. For that, the dance academy rented out the auditorium of a local community college, where dancers from Jesse's age all the way up to high school would perform for their friends and family.

Jesse and her group, the youngest of the dancers, had been assigned to perform in a traditional pale pink leotard with matching tutu, an outfit she wore nearly every day for the three weeks leading up to the recital. "I'm a fairy princess," she said about a hundred times a day, twirling in her tulle.

The bodysuit had a large grape juice stain because Jesse had insisted on eating dinner in it. Rona had done her best to get it out, but a faded purple blob the size of an orange stubbornly remained on the front. Amazingly, Jesse did not behave like it was the end of the world

—maybe because Rona had assured her it would be fine. "Nobody in the audience will see it," she'd said.

The morning of the dance recital, Rona pulled up to the house and rang the doorbell. I opened the door a minute later to find Rona crouched down, combing her fingers through the grass.

"Why are you down there?" I asked.

"Take a look," she said as she pointed toward the window.

A bird had struck the front window of the house, splattering its innards on the glass and falling to its death on the front lawn.

"Gross," I said. "Dave will have to clean it."

"Poor little birdie," Rona said.

I went inside to call Dave, but as soon as I opened the door Dougie and Luke bolted outside to greet Rona. They must have picked up the scent immediately because they shoved their noses in the grass and tussled for first dibs. Dougie outsmarted Luke by distracting him with a quick spin and then dived for the bird. He paraded his win as he walked up and down the driveway, the dead bird clenched between his teeth. Luke was left to sniff the remains on the lawn as Rona called for Dave to come quick. Dave opened the front door to see what was going on, but as soon as he did Dougie bolted around the house and into the backyard with the bird still in his mouth. Rona ran after him with Dave following her, still unclear about what was going on.

"Oh my God! Dave, get it out! Get it out of his mouth!"

We all ran out back to find Dougie on the grass, the dead bird lying between his paws.

"Oh, man," Dave said. "What happened?"

"The bird hit the front window," Rona said. "He had it in his mouth."

Dave tried to call Dougie back into the house, but he wouldn't listen. Every time he approached, Dougie grabbed the bird and took it to a different part of the backyard. Dave started to chase him, but the dog kept running around in circles to evade capture.

"Damn dog!" Dave shouted, looking down at his watch. "We're going to be late for the recital."

Rona went inside the house and returned with a plastic container of leftover barbeque from the night before. She walked around the backyard and waved the plastic container in the air. She then placed it on the deck beside the sliding door. Rona went back inside the kitchen and waited with the door still open as Dougie approached the meat to take a sniff. When he did, Rona leaned down to grab his collar and yanked him inside the kitchen.

"You're brilliant!" Dave shouted from the lawn.

Rona rolled her eyes but still smiled. After the dogs were secure indoors, Dave put a plastic bag around each of his hands, picked up the bird with one bag and put it inside the other.

"Let me get rid of this and then we need to get going," he said. "We've got to hustle."

We all piled into Rona's car with Jesse sitting beside me, her feet up against the back of the passenger seat.

"We're going to be late," Rona told Dave as he pulled out of the driveway. Dave didn't say anything as he looked at his watch again, but he started driving more aggressively than usual.

"We'll make up for it on the road," he said.

We pulled up to the theatre over half an hour later, which Dave called ridiculous because of all the traffic. He stopped the car in front of the main doors so that Rona and Jesse could jump out and get a head start.

"We'll meet you ladies inside," Dave said. "Good luck, Jessica!"

We parked Rona's car and made our way to the auditorium, where parents, siblings and other dancers were crammed in to see nearly twenty performances. The lights were already dim and the dance school director had wrapped up her introduction when Dave and I found a section of empty seats toward the back. We took our places as the lights went out and a hush came over the auditorium. It was show time.

Thirteen little girls in matching pink tutus shuffled onto the stage in single file as members of the audience chuckled at the sight. The music started—*Swan Lake*, what else—and the ballerinas all moved in what was intended unison but ended up being something less organized. The audience giggled as the group of girls danced on their toes, their arms up and down.

Dave leaned into me. "This is Jesse's performance, right?" he whispered. I nodded. "I don't see her," he said. I didn't see her either. Dave shifted in his seat. "I wonder what's going on."

The ballerinas became less coordinated as the song continued. Half of them were doing one thing while the other half did something else. One of the girls stopped dancing altogether and stood motionless in the front row. When it ended, the crowd erupted into applause. Dave got up from his seat. I followed him through the aisle and down the main hallway where the change rooms were. We saw Rona first and then Jesse, who was twirling around in her costume.

"She had to go pee and then it took us a while to find her troupe, who was already on stage," Rona said. "I didn't know. I didn't know we were first up."

Dave crouched down to Jesse so they could be eye level. "Honey, I'm so sorry we missed your dance. I'm sorry, sweetie." Jesse didn't say anything but kept spinning in circles until she became so dizzy that she bounced off the wall. "Jesse?" She continued to twirl until Dave took her by the hand. "Here, let's go get you an ice cream."

Dave drove around to three separate ice cream shops, but nothing was open until the afternoon. Finally, we went through the McDonald's drive-through and got three vanilla cones. Rona didn't want one. Jesse licked hers slowly, so half of it melted on the front of her Danskin, forming somewhat of a collage with the grape juice stain.

Nobody said much during the ride home, but as we were turning onto our street Jesse looked out the window.

"It's because of the bird," she said.

"What do you mean?" Dave asked.

"That we missed my dancing. It's the bird's fault. It wasn't Roada."

"I know," he said.

To make up for missing the recital, Dave and Rona bought tickets to a Sharon, Lois and Bram concert. They got me a seat too even though it was a little kids' show. It was the last place on earth I wanted to be.

The morning of the concert, Dave knocked on my bedroom door while I was still sleeping and told me to get out of my pyjamas. "*Now*, Melanie—I mean it. We're not going to be late this time."

I rolled out of bed and put on pants and a sweat top, grabbing a baseball cap so I could hide my face in public. Jesse skipped her way to Rona's car while singing the theme song from *Sesame Street*.

"It's the wrong song," I said. "We're not going to see Big Bird."

Jesse ignored me and sang most of the way downtown. Dave complained about the price of parking while Rona maneuvered her car into a tight space, backing into it so she wouldn't have to reverse later on.

We got to the auditorium with time to spare, and waited at the door for fifteen minutes with a throng of other small children and their also-impatient parents. We filed through a line to show our tickets then walked through the doors to the concert area. Seating was unassigned so we made our way to the front, placing ourselves in the centre of the third row.

"Sweet spot," Dave said to Rona. She looked at him from the corner of her eyes and smiled.

We sat there as other families filed in steadily, filling in the seats throughout the rest of the room. Jesse started fidgeting.

"I have to go pee," she said.

Rona took Jesse's hand and led her down the hall to the nearest bathroom while Dave and I saved their seats. They came back ten minutes later, squeezing themselves in between the rows of kids with their parents and siblings. I kept the rim of my baseball hat as low as possible, worried that someone from school might be there.

After some more waiting, the show finally started. The kids clapped and squealed as the parents sighed with relief. The performers got up on stage, the guitars strumming, the energy flowing. Sharon and Lois were wearing colourful skirts as they swayed to the music. Bram smiled as he sang. I looked at Dave and sighed, rolling my eyes when I knew he was looking.

The songs continued, one after the other. Jesse jiggled on her feet and pretended to know the words. Rona elbowed Dave to get him to notice. They laughed together. At least the time was going by quickly.

Jesse took a break from dancing and was back in her seat just as Sharon, Lois and Bram started to sing "Skinnamarink." The rows of kids and parents in front of us were on their feet, clapping and singing when Jesse leaned forward. A little girl with long blonde hair was directly in front of her. Jesse hit the back of her head, then pulled her hair as hard as she could.

The little girl shrieked as her mother turned around.

"Oh my God!" the woman shouted, trying to separate her daughter's hair from Jesse's grip. Heads turned as Dave leaned toward Jesse and told her to stop. But Jesse would not let go. Sharon, Lois and Bram kept singing.

I didn't know what to do, so I grabbed hold of both of Jesse's wrists and tried to wrestle her away—"Stop, Jesse! Stop! Stop!"—until she finally did, an empty look on her face. Dave opened his mouth as if he was going to say something, but he didn't. Instead, he took Jesse by the arm and led her out of the theatre, a hundred angry parents staring at him as he shuffled between the rows. Rona and I were left standing there unsure how best to exit. Everyone was looking; their eyes felt like lasers.

"Did you see that?" someone said.

"What just happened?" said another.

Rona tapped me on the shoulder and motioned for us to leave in the opposite direction. I pulled my baseball cap as low as it could go and followed her toward the door.

Rona's heels clicked in sync with the music as we exited the building and turned left on the street. Steam escaped the manholes and we picked up speed, turning another corner. We entered the parking lot and saw Dave crouched down, his hands rested on Jesse's shoulders. Dave was speaking and Jesse was listening with her eyes lowered. As soon as Rona caught sight of this, she slowed her pace, raising her right arm to prevent me from moving ahead. I wanted to be with Dave, to give Jesse hell, to ask her why she did it, to tell her a hundred times that what she did was wrong. But Rona held her arm out.

"Give them a minute," she said.

So I waited and watched as Dave spoke and Jesse nodded. Finally, Dave stood up and gave her a pat on the back.

"Hi," Rona said as she approached them. "Everything okay?"

Dave shrugged. "Let's go get something to eat."

We got into the car and Rona put the vehicle in drive. "Where to?" she asked.

"I don't know," Dave said. "Let's get out of downtown first and then decide."

Rona pulled out of the parking lot and headed toward the highway. She changed the radio station every thirty seconds until Dave took over the dial. Jesse's chin leaned on her hand while her elbow rested on the door.

Dave had still not mentioned where he wanted to eat, so Rona drove north and pulled off the highway at our usual exit.

"So," Rona said. "Why don't we go to the egg place near your house?" She was talking about Sunny's, the crappy diner where Mom used to work. "Eggs and pancakes everyone?"

Even from the backseat, I could tell Dave was clenching his jaw.

"No," he said.

"Why not?" Rona asked.

"I don't feel like eggs."

"Okay, eat something else then? They have other things."

"No," Dave said again.

"I want pancakes," Jesse said, kicking the back of the seat. She, like Rona, had no idea about the connection to Mom.

"I want a cheeseburger," I said. "Can we go to the Steer Inn?"

"Jesse wants pancakes," Rona said. "Dave, it's been a tough day so far. Can we just go to the diner?"

"I ... I don't want to," Dave said. I couldn't understand why he just didn't tell her the truth.

"Dave," Rona said. Her tone was quick, angry. "I've had a really shitty morning here. I just want a bloody cup of coffee and some eggs and toast. Is that too much to ask for?"

She pulled into the parking lot at Sunny's a few minutes later. Dave didn't say anything, but I could tell he was in a panic. The top of his upper lip was sweaty. He kept blinking a lot.

Jesse jumped out of the car and walked to the restaurant holding hands with Rona. Dave shut the car door and followed them slowly. I stared at him to get his attention, but he just shrugged his shoulders as he opened the door and walked in.

All four of us were standing in the entryway of the restaurant when I heard a familiar voice. "Well. This is quite the surprise."

It was her. Eleanor. She was still wearing green eyeliner. Her voice was still raspy as if she'd smoked a thousand cigarettes. But her face looked older. Fatter. I thought back to the dirty looks she used to give me whenever I came to the restaurant and the way she talked down to Mom. I wanted Dave to punch her in the face.

Instead, he nodded politely. "Hello," he said. "Table for four."

"Not five?" Eleanor said. So it was going to be like this.

"Table for four," Dave said again as Rona gave him a confused look.

Eleanor put on a big dumb grin as fake as her drugstore eyelashes, grabbed four menus from the hostess stand and led us to a table in the back right beside the bathrooms.

"Your server will be right with you," she said as she placed the menus on the table.

"What was that all about?" Rona asked. Her eyes followed Eleanor, who returned to the front of the restaurant.

"Long story," Dave said, sitting down. "I used to come here a lot."

Rona hung her purse on the back of her chair. "Care to talk about it?" she asked.

"Not here," Dave said. "Let's talk later."

Our waitress came to the table, a young blonde woman I'd never seen before. I could tell Dave was as relieved as I was. "We'll order everything all at once," he said to her, trying hard to smile. "We've got a hungry group here."

As soon as the waitress had our orders, I looked around the room. It still smelled like cleaning solution and fried grease. The grout lines along the floor tiles were dark and filthy and the windows were smudged with fingerprint marks. I wondered how Mom managed to work here as long as she did.

Jesse was busy playing with the saltshaker when Rona leaned across the table.

"So, why did she attack that girl?" she whispered to Dave. "I feel like it came out of nowhere."

Dave looked at Jess, I guess to make sure she wasn't paying attention.

"She acts out from time to time," he whispered. "It's actually not ..." His voice got even lower. "It's actually not the first time."

That was news to me. I gave Dave a funny look to get his attention but he either didn't see or he ignored me.

"What do you mean?" Rona whispered, a bit louder this time.

"It's happened two other times at the playground. Also unprovoked."

"Gosh," Rona said. "Have you talked to her about it?"

Dave took a second before he answered. "Well, I tried to today by the car," he said. "I brushed it off before. But now it seems ..." He looked at Jess again. "It seems to be a pattern."

Rona was about to say something back, but the waitress arrived with the juice and coffee.

"Thanks," Dave said to the woman.

"I'm sure it's just a phase," Rona said, opening a cream container and dumping it into her mug. "My brother used to ... you know ... beat up on everyone at the park."

"I don't know," Dave said. He looked over at Jess again, who was busy playing with her straw. "But things aren't getting any easier."

Our meals arrived a few minutes later and everyone ate quickly and quietly. My pancakes didn't taste like anything, so I poured half the jug of syrup on them. Dave was the first to finish his eggs. As soon as he was done, he pulled out his wallet and waved it at the waitress to show he was ready for the bill. The woman nodded, but a few minutes later Eleanor came to our table with the cheque in hand.

"So, I guess you're paying the bill today instead of stealing from me the way Abby did."

Dave looked up from the table. "Abby didn't steal."

Eleanor put her free hand on her hip like she meant business. "Is that right? Because I remember differently. Maybe I should ask Abby's replacement what she thinks." Eleanor turned toward Rona, but Rona didn't blink.

"You know what," Dave said, tucking his wallet back into the pocket of his jeans. "We actually won't be paying today. The food wasn't great. But more importantly, the hospitality was terrible."

"You can't do that," Eleanor said, her voice so hoarse I thought she'd break out into a coughing fit.

"I can," Dave said, standing up. "And I will. Thank you, Eleanor. But we're leaving."

With that, he took Jesse's hand and led her toward the front door of the restaurant. For the second time that morning, Rona and I stood up and followed Dave's lead. I was halfway across the restaurant, almost out of earshot, when I turned around to face Eleanor for what I hoped would be the last time.

"You know, you were always really mean to my mom," I said. "And I'm sorry she had to work here."

Chapter Eight

---◦◦◦◦---

PERFECT HAIR

August 1989

I WAS IN the kitchen pouring myself a glass of orange juice when I overheard Dave on the phone. He was talking to Rona—that much was obvious by the way he kept using the word sweetheart. Dougie and Luke Skywalker were at the screen door, barking at the squirrels in the backyard, so I had to lean in to listen. Seated at the table with a notepad in his hand, Dave was going through a list of names, none of them familiar. I heard him mention the word 'party.' And then he said, "I love these reunions." He nodded his head and listened to the other end of the line.

I wanted to know what was going on. Dave had always said he was an only child. His parents were dead, both from cancer, something that happened when he was in his twenties. A picture of his mom and dad were on his nightstand. They were both wearing dark-rimmed glasses and turtleneck sweaters, Mary in blush pink and Arnold in mustard. They were smiling and looked happy. They seemed like good people. But there were never photos of any other family.

I asked Dave about it when he got off the line. "Dave," I said, clearing my throat. "Do you have another family?"

"Not that I'm aware of."

"Then why are you talking about a reunion?"

"Oh that," he said, chuckling, getting up to pour himself a cup of coffee. "I'm planning a barbeque with some of my old friends from high school. We try to get together every now and then."

"Oh," I said, embarrassed. "Sounds fun."

"Yes, it should be."

I'd never known Dave to throw a party for anyone except me and Jess. "Are you going to have a band play?" I asked. "Or can it be dress-up?"

Dave laughed while taking a sip of his coffee, making him choke and cough. "No dress-up, Melanie," he said, clearing his throat. "Can you imagine me in anything other than jeans?" He laughed again and sat back down at the table. "Melanie," he said, a bit more seriously. "I wanted to see if you ... I wanted to let you know..." I looked at him and waited for him to finish.

"What?"

Dave put his coffee mug down on the table. "Listen Mel, Rona doesn't really want this to be a kid's party. Especially when it comes to Jess—it probably wouldn't be that much fun for her. So Jess is going to stay with Becky that night. It's up to you where you'd rather be. You're more than welcome to stay here or you can go to Beck's. Just let me know."

I wasn't about to miss the first adult party I'd ever been invited to. "I want to stay here," I said.

"Sure thing, kiddo. You can meet all my old friends."

Dave and Rona spent the next two weeks planning for their backyard barbeque—buying charcoal, meat, corn, lettuce. Rona pulled the weeds out of the garden. Dave mowed the lawn. He even hauled the coolers out of the garage and sprayed them with the hose.

"How much beer should we buy?" Rona asked.

Dave shrugged. "Don't be shy. I'll drink whatever they don't."

The afternoon of the party, Dave dropped Jesse off at Becky's as I helped Rona set the table outside.

"It's buffet style," Rona explained. "We put everything out and everyone will help themselves."

I took the boxes of plastic cutlery and arranged them on the picnic table. I lined up all the forks in a neat row, followed by a line of knives.

"Looks good," Rona said. "Very symmetrical."

She took out a stack of paper napkins and placed them on the table. Using an empty water glass, she made a clockwise twisting motion until the ordinary pile turned into a fancy spiralled stack.

I watched in amazement. "So neat," I said.

"Thanks, Melanie. Would you also mind getting the kids' juice boxes out of the fridge?"

"Sure," I said, remembering what Dave had told me. "But I thought this was an adult party?"

"Oh, it is sweetheart, of course."

"But are other kids coming?"

"A few, yes."

I didn't understand. "Then why can't Jess be here?"

"It's not that Jess can't be here," Rona said, taking a step back to admire the table. "It's just that sometimes she can be . . . a bit of a distraction."

I turned toward Rona and looked at her hair. It was hot and sticky outside, but each strand on her head was perfect, tucked neatly behind her ears. Her hair looked nice. Her dress was pretty. But things didn't feel right. I went inside and didn't get the juice boxes.

It was around four in the afternoon when the doorbell rang. The first guests were a guy named Mark and his eight-year-old son. Mark was carrying a case of beer with both hands, which he put on the ground so that he could pet Dougie and Luke, whose tails wagged furiously as they examined our new houseguests.

"These are nice boys," he said. "Hey, are you Jessica?"

"I'm Melanie."

"Of course, what am I thinking," he said. "The older one. Nice to meet you."

I led him through the hallway to the kitchen and out the sliding door to the backyard, where Dave was manning the barbeque.

"Hey, buddy," Mark said. "Such a long time."

Dave smiled as he temporarily abandoned the barbeque, spatula in hand, to give Mark a bear hug. Flames flickered in between the burgers, which all competed for space on the crammed grill.

The rest of Dave's guests followed so that everybody was piled in the backyard by five o'clock. I counted thirteen adults and six kids in total. I repeated the numbers in my head so I wouldn't forget.

After we ate, two of the wives decided it would be fun to start a game of limbo. They went into the garage in search of something to play and emerged a few minutes later with Jesse's skipping rope.

"Come on!" one of the women said, gesturing to the group to try. All the men stood around with their beer bottles in their hands, not moving an inch. Someone turned up the volume on the ghetto blaster to try to get things started, but everyone stood around and waited for something to happen. After a few seconds of silence, a young woman who'd introduced herself as Carla volunteered to go first. She took off her shoes and leaned back, managing to keep her drink steady in one of her hands so that it didn't tip over. The two women holding the rope cheered her on as the men watched in silence. Stevie B's "Spring Love" blared from the speakers. Carla leaned back further as she made her approach, but just as she was about to clear it, the centre of the rope drooped and hit her chin. She straightened back up, abandoning her attempt, and Jesse's skipping rope was put away.

The guests spent the rest of the evening listening to music and roasting marshmallows on the fire pit Rona had put together using some of the old bricks piled in the garage. At one point, Dave even let me take a swig of his beer.

"Tastes like skunk," I said.

"You're not entirely wrong," he said.

One of Dave's friends, Andy, came with his two daughters, Ashley and Meghan. Both were brown-haired, dark-eyed and mysterious looking. Ashley was twelve, so closer to my age, while Meghan was nine. They carried backpacks with Velcro flaps, which they opened and closed all night, being careful to make sure I couldn't see what was inside. "Let's go try on my lipstick," Meghan told Ashley, grabbing her hand as we sat by the fire.

"Where's the bathroom?" Ashley asked me, holding her purple backpack with both of her hands.

"I can show you," I said.

She looked at Meghan, then back at me. "It's okay," she said. "Your mom already told us where it was."

She grabbed her sister's hand and off they went. I stayed by the fire. Rona and Dave were sitting beside me, their back toward the pit so they could talk to the adults on the deck. "I know," I heard Rona say. "I keep trying to find them but every time I go to the store, they're sold out."

I left Dave and Rona and went inside, where most of the kids were. I walked through the kitchen, which was a mess of empty beer cases and leftover food, past the group of kids sitting on the living room floor watching whatever made-for-TV movie was on and headed upstairs. I stopped outside the bathroom and gently knocked on the door, expecting to hear the chatter and giggles of the two sisters.

Instead, a man's voice answered. "One minute," he said. I didn't know who it was, so I went into my bedroom. A couple of minutes later, there was a knock at my door.

"Who is it?" I asked.

"It's Fred."

I didn't know who that was but I still said okay. A man with a horseshoe-shaped hairline and wire-rimmed glasses walked into the room.

"Hi," he said, sitting down on the bed. "Remember me?"

I didn't but I nodded anyway. "I was waiting for the bathroom," I explained.

"I'm all done now," he said.

There was a pause as I looked at him. I noticed a bulge under his shorts. I didn't say anything, and he kept staring at me. The silence went on for a long time, so I finally said, "Is it okay if I leave?"

He said it was okay, so I got up, left the bedroom and locked myself in the bathroom. As I sat on the ledge of the bathtub, I thought of the time Mom slapped a man in the face at the bus shelter because he said she had nice tits. I was probably only four at the time, but I remember feeling confused about what had happened until Mom sat me down and explained.

"Melanie, whatever you do, don't ever let anyone treat you badly. Do you hear me?"

I'd nodded, realizing that tits was a bad word.

"If any man ever says anything to you that is rude or if he ever—*ever*—touches you, you do as I do. You punch him really hard and you get away."

"Okay," I'd said. "I'll punch him in the head."

With Fred, though, I'd forgotten what she taught me. Instead of fighting back, I patted the back of my head and plucked several strands of hair. My fingers couldn't stop so I kept pulling strand after strand. I stayed there for so long that a pile of hair formed at my feet. Eventually, I fell asleep on the floor.

A knock at the door woke me up a while later, but I pretended I was still sleeping. "Melanie? Are you in there?" It was Dave, so I let him in. "What are you doing here?"

"I fell asleep."

"I can see that."

"Are your friends still here?"

"No, they've all gone home. Rona and I've finished cleaning up. You should get yourself to bed."

I went back to my room but didn't want to sleep where Fred had been sitting, so I grabbed my pillow and moved to the floor. Just as I was dozing off, I heard voices from downstairs. Dave and Rona were having some kind of discussion. It wasn't yelling, but it was pretty close. I picked up a few words from Rona—"stayed so late," "drank too much," "why on earth." And then finally from Dave: "couldn't even have my own daughter here." A door slammed and the discussion was over.

The next morning, Dave was preparing breakfast.

"Where's Rona?" I asked.

"She went home after the party."

"I heard you guys fighting."

"I think we were both tired and grumpy," he said. "Anyway, eat your breakfast."

He placed a piece of toast in front of me. Jesse was already home, sitting in front of a bowl of fruit at the table. "I hate peaches," she said as she threw a piece my way. It missed me, and Dave ignored her, so I took a banana and went outside on the back deck. The backyard had been cleaned up. Not including the firepit, there was no sign of any party. I took a bite out of my banana, listening to Jesse as she hummed the tune of a song I didn't recognize.

I was about to return inside when I heard the front door of the house open. By the way the keys jangled I could tell it was Rona. Dave opened the screen door and poked his head outside. "Mind taking care of your sis for a bit?" he asked. "I think I might go out for a spin."

I went inside and brought Jess into my bedroom, where she explored all of the contents of my dresser. After a half-hour, she became bored of my room and wanted to go somewhere else. I led her downstairs and plunked her in front of the television until Dave came home about half an hour later, the blood drained from his face.

"Did Rona come back?" I asked. "What happened?"

"Oh, you know," Dave said, searching for something in his pockets that he couldn't find. "At least she had the decency to say goodbye."

"You mean, you're broken up?" I wasn't surprised. Or even that unhappy. Rona was the type of person who liked to colour inside the lines. But we were the type of family that only knew how to scribble.

"I suppose we are."

"Sorry, Dave."

He sighed. "That's okay, kiddo."

"I don't know if she was a good fit, though. I hope that's okay to say." Dave didn't say anything. It was silent for a long time, so I decided to explain what I meant. "What I want to say is …" I was still thinking about how to phrase it. "What I mean is, you're a good dad. A great dad, actually. I know Rona tried hard, but I don't think she wanted to be a mom. I'm not sure she liked Jess a lot."

"She did like Jess," Dave said.

"Rona liked Jess on good days. But Jess is hard to be around sometimes."

"Being a parent is hard work, Melanie. And being a stepmom—sometimes that can be even harder. Rona's a good person. She liked you and Jesse a lot, believe me.

But I don't know if she felt like she was cut out for this. She didn't feel like she was very good at it."

"She also liked to have nice hair," I said. "You can't have perfect hair when you're a mother."

"That's very true. Remember your mom's hair?"

I thought of the tangled bird's nest Dave had to cut out. I let out a laugh but somehow my eyes started to sting. I tried not to think of her because I knew I'd start crying, but I couldn't help it. It all made me so angry. And I still missed her.

"What about you, kiddo? What kind of hair do you think you'll want? When you've finished growing up, that is."

"Whatever kind will let me have a normal family," I said. "No offence."

Dave let out a chuckle and put his arm around me. "None taken."

CHAPTER NINE

———◆———

THE BUS SHELTER

August 1990

IN THE LAST week of summer before high school started, we all got sick with the flu. Dave seemed to have it the worst; his fever was so high he couldn't stop shaking. Not able to care for Jesse, he tried to reach Becky to see if she could give us a hand. He called eight times and left two messages but couldn't reach her. "You should try again," I said. But he ignored me.

We all spent an entire day in our pyjamas, with Jesse calling out for Dave nonstop. He dragged his feet to her room but couldn't do much except tell her to drink more water. I lay on the couch, watching cheesy romance movies and Janet Jackson music videos as I drifted in and out of sleep.

By the third day, Dave got some of his energy back and slowly returned to life. Jesse bounced back as well, drinking chamomile tea and eating the cans of soup Dave prepared for her. But I remained, what Dave kept calling me, "sick as shit." At the end of the fifth day, Dave came into my room and tried to get me out of bed, but I couldn't budge.

"Come on, Melanie, at least sit up to have a sip of water."

He lifted up my arm, but it was so weak and limp it dropped back down to the mattress. Dave slid a thermometer under my tongue and told me it was one hundred and three. Finally, he lifted me up with both arms and flung me over his shoulder. "We need to take you to the hospital, Mel Belle."

Dave carried me to the back of the van and placed me on one of the dogs' blankets on the floor. "You go in the front seat," he said to Jess, who for once did as she was told.

Once we got to the hospital, Dave left me and Jess in the van for a few minutes while he ran inside to fetch a wheelchair. As Dave wheeled me into the emergency room, the cold air conditioning blasting on my shivering body, Jesse said: "You're going to die, Melanie! You're really going to die!" I would have rolled my eyes but didn't have the energy, so I slumped over in the wheelchair and waited for Dave to register me at the front desk.

The nurse looked over at me as Dave was talking. "She hasn't eaten for days ... won't drink anything either."

"I'm not sure ... we bounced back a lot sooner."

"Yes, fever ... vomiting."

A doctor came to see me a couple of hours later.

He asked me a bunch of questions while he examined me, listening to my heartbeat, looking into my ears, pressing on my stomach. I winced in pain and pulled away from the pressure. The doctor scribbled down some notes then called Dave back into the room.

"I think this is a case of appendicitis," he said.

"What's that?" Jesse said. "Is she going to die?"

"We'll need to move her into surgery as soon as we can. I suspect it's ruptured but we won't know for sure until we operate."

"I told you, Melanie!" Jesse said. "I told you you're going to die."

Ignoring her, the doctor turned to me and asked if I had any questions. I had many, but I didn't want to ask them in front of Dave and Jess, so I just said no. I was left in the room for another half-hour, dozing in and out of sleep until two nurses came to transfer me onto a gurney.

"You'll be okay, kiddo," Dave said. He kissed my forehead as a nurse tucked a sheet around my sides. "I'm glad I brought you in. I thought you had the flu like the rest of us."

As the nurses wheeled me toward the elevator, I could hear Jesse shouting from down the hall: "You're dead, Melanie! So dead! Goodbye forever!"

I was in the hospital for six days. Dave and Jesse came to visit me every night, but I was otherwise on my own. I half-watched the television hovering over my bed and, once I started to regain my strength, ate a lot of Jell-O. Jesse reminded me every day how lucky I was that the doctors saved me. "Think of it," she said. "You could be a zombie right now—a real-life living dead person."

The whole experience meant I missed the first week of high school. Dave brushed it off like it was no big deal, but whatever anxiety I was already experiencing doubled with the realization that I'd be starting later than everyone else.

"Don't sweat it, Melanie—you'll make a grand entrance this way," Dave said. "Everybody will wonder what exciting things you've been up to. Maybe they'll think you were travelling around Europe!"

A paler version of me was discharged on a Saturday, meaning I could start school the following Monday. I went home to find a new purple pencil case on my dresser with a set of pens and a new green canvas knapsack. Inside the bag was a card: "Good luck, Melanie," Dave had written, followed by a note scrawled in kids' writing: "You should be dead right now."

There was also a gift bag with a sweatshirt inside. "Glad you're doing better, Melanie! Wishing you lots of luck in high school." The card was signed by Becky, who'd missed Dave's calls for help because she'd been visiting her mother up north.

My new school was a brown brick structure whose U-shape divided the building into three distinct sections—juniors on the left, gym and library in the centre and seniors on the right. The three flanks enveloped the courtyard, the outdoor area where most students assembled during recess and lunch, littering the pavement with cigarette butts and gum wrappers.

Dave dropped me off on my first day, waving goodbye as I approached the steps to the side entrance, intentionally chosen so that I could slink in as quietly as possible. I was early, so there were only a few other students around. In my hands was a sheet of paper with the number thirty-one scrawled on it.

I didn't have to look hard to find my locker; it was the only one whose door was still ajar. The front of it had been defaced with wads of chewed-up gum arranged in the shape of a heart. I grimaced as I poked my head inside. The interior had been spared the same injustice, though I did find a granola bar wrapper and an old shoelace.

The hallway filled up as students arrived for class. The buzz of chatter grew every minute as I fiddled with my combination lock, pretending to do something. I could only spin the dial so many times, so I took out my itinerary and decided to scope out where my classes were. I combed the halls and took in the smells, a strange mix of body odour, cleaning solution and cafeteria grease. There was a payphone in the hallway outside the office and a vending machine beside the gym. I did the same circuit twice, feeling the hallways swell with more commotion and laughter as students arrived. I still had another seven minutes to kill, so I circled back to my French class on the second floor and took a seat.

There were twenty-four desks in total; six rows of four lined up neatly. I settled on the third row, hoping I wasn't taking someone else's seat. I took out my binder and pens as other students started to pour in, bringing the easygoing banter of the hallway with them. The class was nearly full when a face I recognized walked through the door; it was Stacey, the girl who borrowed my bike when I first moved in with Dave. Her red hair and freckles had followed her into adolescence, but she was tall, at least as tall as Dave, and seemed much older than me and the other students. I watched her for a moment, then waved hello. She looked at me but didn't smile, talking instead to another girl seated beside her.

The teacher was the last to arrive. A dishevelled woman in her forties whose blouse was too tight, she opened the class by introducing me as Mallory and explaining I had been in the hospital. I felt the eyes of twenty-three other students look my way. The boy beside me leaned back in dramatic fashion and inched his desk away from me as if I had an infectious disease, interrupting the symmetry of the perfect rows. He stepped up his performance, pretending to cough as if he had contracted something, which made some of the other students laugh. The teacher ignored this and consulted the lesson plan on her desk before conjugating a series of verbs on the chalkboard. Nobody spoke to me for the rest of the class and, when we were dismissed, I watched Stacey get up and leave the room, still gabbing with the same girl. I gathered my things and headed to the cafeteria, where I bought a chocolate milk and took it to go.

I spent the rest of the day combing the halls and weaving in and out of already-established circles that were congregated in various corners of the school: the cafeteria, the bathroom, even the library. I tried to make eye contact, but the two students I recognized from elementary school didn't do much to welcome me. The most I got was a wave.

When Dave got home from work that night, I told him I wasn't going back.

"What do you mean?" he asked.

"It was terrible. Nobody talked to me. I don't want to go back."

"Give it time, kiddo," Dave said. "We're all new at some point in our lives."

I had no choice but to return the second day. I showed up wearing a baseball cap, keeping the visor low enough that I could avoid eye contact with others as I walked down the hall. But as I was returning to my locker from French class I noticed Emily, a girl from grade school, sitting by herself on the radiator by the window overlooking the courtyard. I didn't know her that well, but we'd worked on an art project together once before. I walked over to where she was sitting, hugging my binder in front of my chest.

"Hi."

She smiled at me. "I didn't know you went here," she said.

"Yeah, I kinda just got here. I had to miss last week so yesterday was my first day."

"Do you like it so far?" She stood up, much shorter than me, wearing a mustard T-shirt, light blue jeans and white running shoes. Her small frame was as unremarkable as her mousy brown hair, though her blue eyes were clear and bright.

"Yes," I said, lying. "I mean, it's okay. I'm still ... getting used to things, I guess."

"Yeah. Me too."

We still had another ten minutes before our next class, so we walked over to the cafeteria. We bypassed the other girl group gathered at the side of the hallway, greeting one another with exaggerated hugs. We talked about our teachers and classes. I told her about my hospital stay and showed her the scar on my stomach.

The radiator became our go-to place, where Emily and I would meet up between classes. One day after school, about three weeks after we forged our friendship, we were at our usual meeting spot when Emily asked me: "Did you want to come to my house?"

I looked around, watching the others leaving and gabbing in clusters. Everyone moved in groups, it seemed. "I can't," I said. "I have to pick up my little sister from school."

"Oh," she said. "It's okay—next time."

I thought of my options: bringing Jesse to Emily's, pretending I forgot to pick Jesse up, calling Dave to ask him to leave work to get her. Then I blurted out: "You come to my house! Can you?"

Emily called her mom from the payphone and made sure it was okay. We shuffled along together, gossiping about who was who. Emily passed down all the information her older brother had shared—who was dating, who had an eating disorder, who had a crush on the guidance counsellor. I took her on a short detour as I headed to Jess' school, explaining that I had to pick up my sister every day.

"I wish I had a sister," Emily said. "My brother's kind of annoying."

Jesse eyed my new friend when I got to her school but didn't say anything, preferring instead to drag her feet so that the rubber of her shoes made a grating noise against the concrete. As soon as we got home, Emily and I decided we were hungry. "Why don't we make a fancy dinner?" Emily suggested. "I can be the chef and you can be the sous-chef."

"What's a sous-chef?" I asked her.

"That's the next in command. It's a very important role."

"Okay," I said. "What should I do?"

She looked through the cupboards and then set the menu: Kraft Dinner with canned tuna on the side. I executed, following her instructions as she thought carefully about what to do next. "Sliced cucumbers can be our side of veggies this evening. With a hint of oregano maybe."

"On the cucumbers?" I asked.

"Yes, we need flavour."

I nodded and went to the spice rack. Dougie and Luke Skywalker encircled us in the kitchen, puddles of drool accumulating on the linoleum floor. Once the meal was ready, we set the table together. Each placemat had both a water and wine glass. We couldn't find any real linen to use as napkins, so I ran upstairs to get hand towels instead. "These should work," I said as I waved the stack in my hand.

Emily nodded in agreement. "Perfect," she said. "Except we're short a person."

"What do you mean?" I asked.

"There's four seats—we need five. For your sister and parents."

I lowered my eyes. "We only need four. My Mom's ... not around."

"Oh," Emily said. "Sorry."

Jesse poked her head in the kitchen to see what we were up to but didn't say anything. I pulled Emily by the arm and led her to the front room, where we watched *Saved by the Bell* as I kept my eye out for Dave. He pulled in fifteen minutes later, soon enough for the mac 'n cheese to still be relatively warm.

"Hi there," Dave said to Emily as he walked through the door. He tipped his baseball cap, his eyes smiling.

"Emily, this is my Dad," I said. "I call him Dave."

"Hi Dave," Emily said. "We made dinner."

"You did? Incredible—thank you." For the benefit of my friend, Dave acted surprised. He did not mention the many times I helped him do the groceries, prepare the meals or set the table.

"Should we eat before it gets cold?" I said. "I think you'll like it."

"You bet, ladies. Let me wash up and I'll be right there." We waited for Dave in the kitchen, the table looking its finest. "Wowzers, girls," Dave said as he surveyed the wine glasses and bathroom linen. "I'm wildly underdressed. You've outdone yourselves."

The three of us took our seats as Dave called out for Jesse to come join us. As we waited, I smelled something overwhelmingly foul but also familiar: dog poo. I turned to Dave and asked him if he smelled it. He stopped for a second to take a whiff. "Yes, I do," he said. We all stood up and, as soon as we did, both Emily and I realized it was all over the back of our pants. Dave turned around to take a look at his own backside, which had been spared. The poop had been placed on three of the four chairs—only Dave's regular seat was unscathed.

"Oh my God," Emily said. "It's so . . . gross."

"Dave," I said, staring at him, expecting him to know what to do. He looked toward the living room, where the dogs had been lounging on the carpeted floor.

"Dougie! Luke!" he called out. Both dogs responded immediately—as if they'd been summoned to dinner.

I looked at Dave. "Why are you calling the dogs?"

He looked down at Dougie and Luke, who lowered their ears at the sight of him.

"You can't be serious?" The hint of unintended teen-aged inflection had belied my anger. "You think the dogs pooped on the chairs?"

Dave stood there and didn't say anything. I turned toward Emily, too angry at Dave to be embarrassed about what had happened. She was more engrossed by the over-powering stench of poo, sniffing the back of her shirt to see if anything was on there. "Maybe I should go," she said as she walked toward the front door, slightly bow-legged as if she was afraid to move.

"Wait!" I shouted, meeting her at the front door. "I have a change of clothes—don't walk home in those."

"It's okay, I'm not far. I'm just going to go home and take a shower."

"I'm sorry, Emily," I said.

She hurried down the front steps of the porch and made a quick right, not bothering to say goodbye.

I turned around to find Jesse sitting on the couch. Dave was hovering over her. He looked pale and tired, a different guy from the one who walked through the door ten minutes earlier.

"Why'd you do that, huh, Jesse?" Dave asked. "You think it's funny?"

"What's funny?" she said, deadpan.

"Jess," Dave said, sighing deeply through his nose. "You need to apologize to your sister. You can't do things like that—it's not nice. You ruined Melanie's evening with her friend."

"Sorry," Jesse said.

Dave looked at me for a response. But I was too furi-ous. I hadn't had a smooth start to high school and Emily was my one friend.

"Well, Melanie?" Dave said. He nodded at me, trying to prompt me to say something.

Instead, I gave Jesse a dirty look, ran upstairs and changed out of my clothes.

* * *

The day after the dog poo incident, Emily acted like nothing happened. I met her at morning break by the radiator, where we walked down to get chocolate milk. When we met up again for lunchtime, she still said nothing. We were about to part ways for our afternoon classes when I brought it up.

"I'm sorry about yesterday," I said. "My sister got in big trouble. Sometimes, to get attention, she does stupid things."

"Oh my God, that was so gross, right?" she said, giggling.

I giggled back, feeling relieved. "Yeah, so gross."

We met up again after school so we could walk home together. Emily kicked the lid of a Tupperware container by the side of the road until she got bored and gave up, leaving it by the ditch.

"So," I said as we reached the juncture where she'd have to pick between my house or hers, "did you want to come over again? I can make sure my sister stays in her room. You can have free rein in the kitchen."

I watched her continue to kick her leg as if she hadn't already abandoned the plastic lid. "I can't," she said. "I promised my mom something."

"Oh."

"Yeah, she wants me to help her find a dress."

"Okay. Next time."

"See ya, Mel."

The next day, I noticed she started saying hi to people who usually ignored us in the hallway.

"I didn't know you were friends with Zeena," I said.

"We're in gym class, remember?" she said.

"Oh yeah," I said. "I forgot."

"You don't have to get all defensive, Mel."

"I'm not getting *defensive*."

"I mean, just because I have a mom and you don't, and just because I'm making new friends and you're not, doesn't make it the end of the world."

I told her I'd see her later and walked home myself.

That same night, Dave asked me if I wanted to go to the movies that weekend with him and Jesse.

"Which day?" I asked.

"I was thinking maybe Friday night."

"I'll think about it."

The next morning at school, I didn't see Emily at her usual place at the radiator, so I tracked her down at her locker. I didn't want to lose our friendship over what my sister did.

"Hi," I said. "How's it going?"

She was fixing her hair in her magnetic mirror and didn't look at me as she answered. "Okay, I guess. Having a frizzy hair day."

"Yeah," I said, combing my hands through my hair, which was not frizzy at all. "Me, too."

Emily ignored me.

"So," I said before the silence made things more awkward, "Dave and my sister are going out on Friday night so I was thinking you could come over if you wanted.

We can order a pizza and watch movies or something. Nobody will bother us. You can even sleep over if you like. We'll be home alone the entire night."

Emily paused for a few seconds. I was ready for rejection but then she said: "Let me ask my mom."

Later, she let me know she was in. "I'll bring my pyjamas and stuff to school so I can come over straight after."

I took this as a sign she had forgiven me for the dog poo incident. I needed to show her I was still a worthy friend, so I planned to make the night as fun as possible. We walked home together on Friday as agreed. I eyed Dave as soon as he got home so that he could leave with Jess. He nodded, getting the message, and hustled to get ready. "Bye girls!" he said as he led Jesse out the front door. "Pizza should be here soon."

We giggled as the door slammed shut, and I felt slightly guilty about not being with Dave. The doorbell rang twenty minutes later and Emily ran to answer it, flinging the door open in an exaggerated motion.

"Well, hi there," Emily said, lifting one of her knees so that she was standing on one leg, flirtatiously flamingo-style. "We are oh-so starving, so you're just in time."

At the door was a delivery guy, unsure how to react to Emily's performance. "Uh, one large pepperoni pizza. That'll be eleven dollars."

"Great," Emily said. "Let me call my guardian sex keeper. Melanie?"

I was standing around the corner in the living room, watching with my back up against the wall and my hand to my mouth to muffle the giggles. I took the twenty-dollar bill Dave left for us on the coffee table and gave it to the delivery guy in exchange for the pizza, managing not to make any eye contact out of embarrassment.

"Keep the change," I said as I closed the door, Emily and I bursting into giggles as soon as it slammed shut.

"You're so funny," Emily said. "Like, I can't believe you got embarrassed."

"I wasn't that embarrassed."

"It's okay," she said. "I was being sort of dumb."

"Yeah."

"Hey Mel?" she said, looking at me.

"Yeah," I said again.

"I'm sorry that I said that you didn't have a mom. I shouldn't have said that."

I didn't want to make a big deal about it. I was still trying to make it up to her. "It's nothing," I said, rolling my eyes to show I didn't care. "Honestly."

Over undercooked pizza and a made-for-TV movie about a kleptomaniac babysitter, it felt like our friendship had been restored. We were lying on the floor of the living room, talking and staring at the swirls in the plaster of the ceiling, when Dave and Jesse came home. Dave was carrying a sleeping Jess over his shoulder as he walked through the door, placing his keys on the console table in the hall.

"Fell asleep as soon as I started driving," Dave said quietly. "Going to bed now, girls. Don't stay up too late."

"Goodnight," Emily and I said in unison, the flickering light of the TV dancing off the walls. Dave headed upstairs as Emily changed the channel. "That movie was boring," she said. "What else do you want to watch?"

"I don't know. I'm sick of the TV."

"Me too."

"Want some ice cream? We've got a couple of flavours."

"Okay," Emily said, picking herself up off the floor and heading to the kitchen. She helped herself to the freezer, taking both containers of ice cream out, handing me the Neapolitan and keeping the maple walnut. "Grab the spoons," she said.

We sat at the kitchen table, picking away at our respective tubs with our teaspoons. I slowly worked my way through the rows of chocolate and vanilla ice cream, carefully avoiding the strawberry.

"So, I heard something about that girl in our grade, Stacey. Do you know her?" Emily asked.

"A bit. What did you hear?"

"That she's leaving school in November. Even though we just literally started the school year."

"How come?" I asked.

"Her family's moving somewhere far. Ohio, I think. Her dad's being transferred at work and they have to leave. Not for forever though—like a year or two and then they'll come back."

"Oh," I said. "I didn't know. Anyway, I don't really talk to her. She stole my bike when I was a kid."

"Maybe you can spend the next two years becoming the most popular girl in school so that when she returns you can make her life miserable."

"Yeah, we'll be old enough to drive by then, so maybe I can steal her car," I said.

"Yeah, steal it and smash it." We both laughed. "Switch?" Emily asked, holding out her ice cream container. I obliged, handing her mine.

An idea suddenly came to me. A crazy idea. I wasn't sure what Emily would think, or if I could even go through with it. But it felt like it was the ticket to making our night as fun as possible. I needed Emily to know I was sorry about the dog poo, and that I was a fun friend. I also didn't want her to think I was angry for saying I didn't have a mom. I just had to convince her to go through with it.

"Hey, you know what we should do? We should drive to Stacey's house right now and egg it. Make it really messy."

"That would be funny."

"No, I'm serious," I said. "Let's do it."

Emily put her spoon down and looked at me. "Egg her house?"

"Yeah. We can do a drive-by."

"In a car? We don't even know how to drive."

"Yes, I do. Dave has let me practise with his van. I got to drive around a parking lot like two, three times already."

"Oh my God," Emily said, half-giggling. "You're crazy."

"So, do you want to do it?"

"Do what?"

"Go to Stacey's house. I'll drive if you throw the eggs. It will be hilarious."

"You can't be serious, Mel. We'd get in so much trouble."

"It's just after ten. Let's wait until eleven when nearly the entire world will be asleep. There'll be no cars on the road. We'll take the van out and throw a few eggs, come back right away and be in bed by midnight. But we'd have to pinky swear that we wouldn't tell anybody about it. Not even your brother. Nobody could know."

Emily sat there for a few seconds. "I don't know, Mel."

"Come on, Emily."

She looked out the window then changed her answer. "Okay," she said. "Let's do it."

"Really? Do you mean it?"

"I guess," she said. "But we can only go on the side streets—no main roads. And eleven-thirty is better than eleven. The streets will be quieter."

"Deal," I said.

We sat and talked, going over all the details of our plan. I anxiously looked at the clock on the stove every five minutes. My hands felt sweaty and my breathing was quick. Eventually, eleven-thirty hit.

"Okay, let's go," I said. "But if we wake Dave we'll have to abort our mission."

"Roger that," Emily said.

We tiptoed to the front entrance, sliding our shoes on and grabbing our jackets from the coat rack. I slipped my hand into the pocket of Dave's leather jacket, where I found his wallet and two used movie tickets. "No keys," I said. Emily pointed to the console table beside me, where they'd been sitting since Dave got home. I clasped the set in my hand, keeping a firm enough grip so they didn't jangle. Feeling like I was moving in slow motion, I put them in the pocket of my jacket without a clink.

I gave Emily a thumbs-up and motioned for her to follow. "Wait," Emily whispered, grabbing the top of my left shoulder before I went any farther. She leaned closer so that I could hear how heavy her breathing was. I looked at her as if to say, 'What?' But Luke Skywalker distracted us as he circled our feet, wagging his tail in anticipation of a late-night pee. I shooed him away and grabbed the handle of the front door, managing to unlock it with one gentle click. With both hands clutching the knob, I pulled it toward me, making sure to give it some lift so that the bottom didn't scrape the sill. But it creaked anyway. Cringing, I paused for a few seconds to see if that caught Dave's attention. Nothing.

I tiptoed out first, with Emily following behind. Once we were out, I gently closed the front door, making sure to shut it all the way. I didn't bother locking it. We made our way to the van. Just as we'd planned, I unlocked the passenger door since it was farther away from Dave's bedroom. We climbed in, with me going first so that I could jump over to the driver's seat. Emily made sure to leave the door slightly ajar so that we limited the amount of noise we created. The next part, though, was the riskiest. With the key wedged between my thumb and index finger, I inserted it into the ignition and turned it quickly. The van roared to life and the engine whirred.

The next part of the plan required us to wait in the driveway for two minutes. If Dave's bedroom light turned on, or if he came out of the house, we'd tell him our preconceived story about needing to move the truck to the street so we could rollerblade on the driveway (although Emily had not brought her rollerblades). If the lights stayed off, then we knew he was still asleep. Emily counted methodically to one hundred and twenty and then said, "We are clear for takeoff."

Giddy, but trying hard to concentrate, I put the van in reverse and released the brake, easing my way out of the driveway and onto the street, which was dark and dead. I put my foot on the brake and switched the gear into drive, but stayed put for a few seconds as I gathered my nerve. Finally, I took my foot off the brake and let the van roll.

"See?" I said to Emily as the van inched forward. "I've driven dozens of times. This is a piece of cake."

"We're going really slowly," Emily said as she looked out the window. "It's, like, almost creepy or something. You need to go a bit faster so that you don't attract so much attention."

I tapped the pedal with my foot, and the van surged slightly. Feeling empowered, I pressed on it again, slowly applying enough pressure so that the van moved forward at a perfectly regular pace, one that did not suggest the vehicle was being driven by two fourteen-year-old girls who were out illegally on a late-night mission to egg someone's house.

"So, where does Stacey live exactly?" Emily asked.

"It's literally, like, around the corner," I said. "Get the eggs ready."

She put her finger on her mouth and said, "We never brought them."

"What do you mean? That's the whole reason we did this!"

"I know, I'm sorry. I remembered just as we were leaving the house, but then the dog came and I got nervous. Anyway, we'll just throw some sticks or a rock at her place or something."

"That's so lame."

"Okay, well, we'll figure something out when we get there."

"We're, like, basically here, it's right here where I'm turning."

I flipped the indicator and turned, hugging the corner a bit too tightly and nearly mounting the curb.

"Careful," Emily said. "You should slow down more when you turn."

"Okay, sorry. Her house is right there."

I hit the brake and came to an abrupt stop, where I pointed to the ranch-style home with the 'For Rent' sign on the front lawn.

"That's her house," I said. "All the lights are off."

"What should we do?" Emily asked.

"I don't know. We don't have any eggs."

"Did you want to throw anything else at it?"

"Like what?" I asked.

"I'm not sure."

We sat for another minute or so, staring at the brown brick bungalow with the brown garage.

"Anyway, let's go. We'll drive around the corner or something and then go back home before Dave kills me."

"Okay," Emily said.

I accelerated the van once again, giving Stacey's house the middle finger as I drove away. I didn't bother to show Emily the house where I used to live even though we drove right past it. Seeing it made me wonder where Mom was at that moment.

As I continued driving along the street, I felt like I was getting the hang of things. I had stopped at six stop signs so far and passed two vehicles without incident, successfully avoiding any unwanted attention. Emily agreed I knew what I was doing.

"You're, like, a pro," she said.

Once we reached Lucas Street, I had the option of turning left, which would have led us home, or going toward the main road with traffic lights. Everything seemed to be going well, so I chose to continue going straight. Once I reached Yonge, I indicated right and waited to merge. The headlights of a dozen cars flashed by as they zoomed past, leaving me little opportunity to turn. "I could have gone," I said. "But better safe than sorry."

Emily nodded in agreement. Finally, a break in traffic appeared, with no oncoming cars as far as I could see. I gently maneuvered the steering wheel, executing a perfect right-hand turn and landing centre in the lane.

"Woo hoo!" Emily shouted, my progress making her feel more comfortable. "You could almost teach driver's ed."

I accelerated a little, the glare of the streetlamps and storefront lights bouncing off the windshield. We passed the women's gym, the liquor store, the Persian rug shop.

"This is a piece of cake," I said, delighted at how easy it'd been so far. "Move over, everybody—Melanie's going places!"

An intersection loomed in the distance, its lights signalling green.

"Lights up ahead," Emily said. "Proceed with caution."

I kept a steady pace, but as soon as I approached the intersection, the light turned red. I slowly pressed on the brake, bringing the van to a halt.

"Good work, Melanie!" Emily said.

We waited patiently at the light, a car pulling up beside us in the left lane. Emily leaned toward my side of the van and waved at its occupants, but it was an older couple too engaged in conversation to notice us. The light turned green and I accelerated as Emily reached over to the dashboard to turn on the music. The dial was fixed on Dave's rock station, so Emily moved it around to find something better. Once she found a song she liked, she turned up the volume, raising both hands in the air as if she were on a roller coaster.

> *"The one good thing in my life*
> *Has gone away, I don't know why*
> *She's gone away, I don't know where*
> *Somewhere I can't follow her."*

We came to another intersection, again hitting a red light. I slowed down and brought the van to a steady and predictable stop, listening to the music as we waited for the light to turn.

> *"Good thing*
> *Where have you gone? (Doo, doo-be-doo)*
> *My good thing*
> *You've been gone too long (good thing)*
> *(Doo, doo doo-be-doo)"*

Once again, the green light signalled for us to continue on our journey, and I pressed on the gas and moved along Yonge Street as if it was the most normal thing in the world. Seeing another intersection up again, Emily asked if I could get in the left lane so that we could turn left at the lights.

"We should probably turn around and head back," she said. "I don't want to press our luck."

I nodded in agreement and switched on the indicator. After looking around for other vehicles, I eased my way into the left lane, slowly approaching the intersection to make my turn. As I did this, I noticed the bus shelter to my right, the last place I'd seen Mom.

I glanced at it for a second, but nobody was in it, so I looked back toward the upcoming intersection. I thought of Mom's profile, the way her face was illuminated by pink light, the sight of her head wrap blowing in the wind. Her face was all I could think about as I made my left-hand turn, the tires squealing as I did so.

Emily screeched at the same time, while the Fine Young Cannibals continued to sing in the background. I saw a flash of lights, heard two horns honk and then felt a thud as I hit a pole. We stopped moving so I opened my eyes.

I turned to Emily, who was clutching the sides of her seat, her eyes blinking repeatedly.

"Are you okay?" I asked her.

"We ... we crashed," she said.

I sat there for an undetermined amount of time and didn't say anything until I heard a tap at my window. I looked up and saw a man looking at me, knocking repeatedly and trying to get my attention. The radio was still playing.

"Hey ... are you okay? Open the window if you're okay." I leaned over and rolled it down halfway, looking at the guy briefly. He was an older man wearing a suit and tie; I could see his red sports car parked on the side of the road with its blinkers on. "I saw what happened— you took that turn way too fast. Don't worry, the police are right here. A cruiser was stopped at the red light when it happened ... I see an officer coming over now."

I nodded without saying anything. The man lingered at the window.

"Hey, listen, as long as you're okay that's the most important thing. Don't worry about your vehicle. I crashed my car two weeks after getting my driver's licence. Never been in an accident since."

"I'm fourteen," I said.

"What?"

"I said I'm fourteen. I don't have my licence yet."

The man's jaw dropped, rendering only silence as I sat and watched a car slow down as it passed by, the driver craning her neck to get a better look at the scene. Then I saw the blue uniform approaching. The man at my window turned and intercepted the officer before he could get to me, the two men speaking in hushed tones. The police officer nodded, looked my way, and nodded again. Thirty seconds later, he tapped on the window with his knuckles and motioned for me to roll it all the way down.

"Are you girls okay?"

"I think so," I said.

The police officer reached inside and turned off the van. He directed his next question toward Emily. "Are you hurt?"

"No?" Emily said. "I mean, no, I think I'm okay."

The police officer fixed his gaze on me.

"I heard you may not be old enough to operate a motor vehicle. Is that correct?"

"I guess so."

"Who does this vehicle belong to?" the officer asked.

"It's mine," I said. "I mean, my dad's."

"We'll need to call your parents and the van will have to be towed. Why don't you girls get out of the vehicle and I'll escort you to the cruiser. You can call your parents from the station."

Emily burst into tears. The officer ignored her and turned around to ask the man with the sports car a few more questions. Emily kept sobbing, her chest heaving up and down as she tried to catch her breath.

"Would you please stop crying?" I asked. "Please stop crying, Emily."

My begging only made her cry harder, so she hid her face in the sleeve of her jacket. I sat there until the police officer returned to open my door, lending me his hand to guide me out. We went over to Emily's side and he did the same thing, Emily sniffling as she stepped outside. The officer led us to his cruiser, the red and blue lights flashing without the siren. He placed us in the back of the car, a cage-like barrier separating us from him. I noticed another officer sitting in the passenger seat.

The officer pulled a U-turn and drove toward the station. Emily and I didn't say anything as we rode in the back, each of us staring out of our respective windows. I wondered what I was going to tell Dave. It was midnight; I knew he'd have to wake up Jesse and bring her to the station. And his van. I didn't even know how damaged it was. How long would it take to fix it? How would he get to work? For some reason I also thought of my mother, the last image I had of her, waiting for the bus in the wind.

Once we got to the station, the pair of police officers told us to call our parents. Emily went first, crying heavily as she told her mom what happened and asking her to pick her up. Then it was my turn. I didn't have the nerve to tell Dave, so I asked one of the officers if he could do it instead. He nodded.

Emily's mother was there in five minutes. She charged into the station, the heels of her boots clicking against the floor as her eyes searched for her daughter.

Emily threw her arms around her and continued sobbing as I sat on the bench, watching uncomfortably. Her mom spoke with the officers for a couple of minutes and then left. She hadn't even looked at me.

Dave got there ten minutes later. He held Jesse's hand as he walked into the station. They were both in their pyjamas. I knew I couldn't look him in the eye. I was so terrified that I felt like I had to vomit.

I knew there'd be hell to pay—and that I could also be arrested and charged. But what I was fixated on at that moment was Dave. For the first time in my life, I knew I had screwed up.

CHAPTER TEN

—◦◆◦—

DOTTED LINES

October 1990

THE NEXT MORNING was not good. I avoided Dave as long as possible, promptly putting my face back in the pillow as soon as I woke up so I could continue sleeping. I stirred again at noon, having to pee badly and knowing I'd stalled as long as possible. I got up and went to the bathroom before heading downstairs. Dave was at the kitchen table as if he'd been waiting for me.

"I hope you had a nice sleep."

"I'm sorry."

"The hell it matters."

I started crying.

"You screwed up big time. This is not a small thing. Number one, you could have killed yourself. Or your friend. Or someone else. Do you realize that, Melanie?"

I didn't say anything.

"Second of all, you messed up my van. I'll need to go this afternoon to see how badly, but what if I have to get something new? Do you know that I rely on it to get me to and from work? To and from the grocery store? To and from everywhere you and your sister need to be? I don't have the time or the money to deal with what you've done. I'm a single dad. Do you realize that?"

I knew better than to answer so I just stood there and stared at my feet.

"Finally, you know very well that you're a role model for your sister, who has her own issues to deal with. Don't you think of the example you are for her, Melanie? What about that?"

I looked around, aware of how quiet the house was.

"Where's Jess?" I asked.

"Not here," he said. "I think she's seen enough bullshit."

His voice was unsteady from anger, his face swollen from the lack of sleep. I'd never seen him like this.

The ball in my throat became tighter. "I said I was sorry, okay? It wasn't supposed to happen. I didn't mean for it to happen. It was an accident."

"It was no accident," Dave said. "And you know what I don't get? I thought you wanted to be the responsible one. The one who was going to grow up and show everybody how it's done. Instead ..." He paused. Maybe hesitating. But he said it anyway: "In some ways, you're just like your mother."

I couldn't believe he said that. I knew I'd screwed up, but I was nothing like my mom. And Dave knew it. Last night's events not included, I was the opposite of her: I was mature, I was responsible, I was good at school. I enjoyed artwork. I liked keeping the house clean. It felt as if Dave was just trying to get back at me, to hurt me for what I did. I turned around, ran up the stairs and slammed the door to my bedroom. I stayed there the rest of the afternoon, feeling around the back of my scalp and plucking my hair. By dinner time there was such a big pile at the end of my bed that I used the hair dryer to blow it all away.

I went to school Monday not sure what to expect. Emily was a no-show, so I walked over to the Grade Eleven lockers at morning break to see if I could find her brother. Though tall and attractive with nice brown eyes, Dan wore a studded black leather motorcycle jacket, kept his hair long and greasy, and hung out with a group of guys who all wore knee-high Dr. Martens. As I approached Dan's locker, I watched him speaking to his friends. I couldn't hear what he was saying, but by the way everyone was listening and laughing, I could tell he was telling them what happened. I turned around and went the other way before he had a chance to notice me.

Hoping that Dan wasn't popular enough to spread the story beyond his immediate group, I walked the halls in between classes that day without so much as a side eye from anyone. By the time the three-thirty bell rang, I was sure I was in the clear.

The next morning, though, everything changed. I got to school late, so the halls were empty as I made my way toward French class. I opened the door and, to the dismay of the teacher, the class erupted into giggles. Confused, she looked me up and down to see if she had missed anything before continuing with her lesson.

I took my usual seat, aware that nearly every set of eyes in the room was on me. As I put my bag on the floor, Shawn, my desk mate to the left, leaned in my direction. "I can't believe what happened," he whispered. "Did they put you in handcuffs?"

I shook my head as Steve, who was behind us, tilted forward, his butt off his chair: "You're so badass, Melanie! Sounds like you really wrecked your car."

The teacher stopped speaking again.

"Qu'est-ce qui se passe?"

Nobody said anything.

"Melanie?" she said, switching to English. "Is there something you'd like to share with the class?"

I looked at Steve, who'd been the one doing the talking.

"Me? No."

"Well, you seem to be doing a great job of distracting everyone. You also didn't get a late slip."

"Sorry."

"Last warning, please. No more disruptions."

A few giggles escaped from the back as Steve and Shawn returned to their seats. Marcus, who was sitting at the other end of the room, gave me a smile and a thumbs-up as the teacher resumed her lesson.

I sat there for the next hour, unable to pay attention, my mind wandering to Friday's events, to Emily, to Dave's angry outburst. I knew I had let him down. And that I'd jeopardized my friendship with Emily. I'd called her three times Sunday night. Twice there was no answer. The third time her mother picked up and said Emily couldn't come to the phone because she was grounded. "As you should be, too." Then she hung up.

Once first period ended, most of the class hovered over my desk, peppering me with questions and showering me with fake praise. The teacher kept a watchful eye, shuffling her papers so she could remain within earshot.

Guy with freckles: "Did you crash it on purpose?"

Me: "Of course not."

Marni: "Oh my God, I can't believe it."

Me: "Yeah, I know."

Naqeeb: "What did the cops say when they got there?"

Me: "That I had to call my dad."

Andre from the lacrosse team: "Are you going to jail?"

Me: "I don't think so."

Shawn: "Did they put you in handcuffs?"

Me: "You already asked me that."

When the crowd disbanded, I asked Marni how everyone heard about it. "Was it Dan?" I asked her.

"Who?"

"Emily's brother—in Grade Eleven."

"No idea. All I know is there's an article in the paper today and everybody says it's you."

I left class immediately and ran to the library, where the day's newspapers were displayed in a fresh pile beside the reference desk. I grabbed the city's tabloid paper first, scanning the news section. I flipped through the pages twice but didn't see anything, so I put it down. Next, I moved onto the *Richmond Hill Liberal*, the local paper that was more likely to cover less serious crimes. There, at the bottom of Page Eight, was the row of police blotter items.

> *Girl, 14, Takes Family Vehicle for a Spin, Crashes into Pole*
>
> *Police say a 14-year-old girl is lucky to be alive after crashing her family's van in a joyride gone wrong.*
>
> *The collision took place at Yonge Street and Major Mackenzie Drive shortly before midnight Friday, when the Chevy smashed into a traffic light.*

*According to officers, the girl and her friend—
neither of whom were licensed to drive—took the
vehicle for a spin without their parents' knowledge
and hit a pole while attempting to make a left-hand
turn. York Regional Police, who were at the same
intersection at the time, witnessed the incident and
attended the scene immediately.*

*The girls were not injured in the crash, and no
other vehicles were involved, but the van was badly
damaged.*

Police say charges are pending.

I read the article over and over again, taking a break in
between each time so it could sink in. I couldn't believe
it. On one hand, there was the shame and regret I'd
been dealing with since the accident. And, yet, seeing
the story in print—and knowing that everybody in
school knew it was me—was also strangely exciting.

Reality, though, tarnished my newfound notoriety,
particularly when I was charged with dangerous driving
and driving without a licence. Plus, I learned by eaves-
dropping on Dave's conversation with the insurance
company that he needed a new vehicle.

"I'll pay you back," I told him. "I'll get a job."

Dave didn't even consider my proposal. Instead, he
said, 'Shut up, Melanie.' He'd never spoken to me that
way before.

I was truly in the bad books—not just with Dave,
but also with Emily. She wouldn't talk to me; she said
she wasn't allowed. Every time I tried to get her attention in the hallway, she'd brush past me. "Come on Mel,"
she'd say. "You know we can't be friends anymore." She

kept ignoring me and started hanging out with a new group of girls—Laura, Zeena and Sarah. They were friends from gym glass, where they had bonded over the beep test.

A couple of days after the article appeared in the newspaper, I was in line in the cafeteria, waiting for my bagel to be toasted, when Kristine, a Grade Nine student who wore her long, blonde hair in a delicate headband, asked if she could borrow thirty cents. I found the change in my wallet and leaned over to give it to her.

"So ... do you have any injuries from your car wreck?" she asked me.

"Not really. I mean, I'm okay but my dad's van isn't."

"At least you're all right," she said. "You could have sort of died."

"Yeah, I know."

"Did you want to eat lunch with us? We're sitting over there." She pointed to a group of girls sitting in a perfect square, their cafeteria trays neatly lined up.

I had been planning on taking my bagel to the library. "Okay," I said.

Kristine and I joined the other girls at the table, each one welcoming me with a smile. I had expected more questions about the accident, but the conversation centred around a rumour that the Grade Eleven boys were hosting a party at the Polish Park on Friday.

I had never heard of the Polish Park and didn't know any Grade Elevens except for Emily's brother and his friends. I waited for a good time to speak, but never found anything valuable to say, so I ate and smiled as the others chatted and giggled. Finally, Kristine asked me what I was doing on the weekend. "Oh, I'm grounded," I answered.

"Oh yeah—of course you are!" she said. We both laughed, my anxiousness giving way to relief as the other girls joined in with their giggles.

The next day, Emily and I were chatting with our new clans in the hallway when we crossed paths. Emily flipped her hair as she looked the other way. I did the same, my hair flip exaggerated to prove I cared less.

Things at home were much more complicated. An uncomfortable silence swooped in for weeks; even Jesse managed to avoid any trouble. Without Dave's jokes at the dinner table or Jesse's usual antics, our daily routine became calm and predictable. Jesse and I went to school, helped with the chores and finished our homework. Dave hitched a ride to work for a couple of weeks until he settled on a used Honda. I didn't like the colour— green—but I knew better than to say anything. Dave didn't even tell me he bought it; he just came home with it one night with his usual rock station blaring as he pulled into the driveway.

I knew I needed to pay for my sin. How to do this was beyond me. Dave was barely speaking to me. Emily wasn't speaking to me at all. I decided to hunker down for a while and focus on my grades.

In November, my social studies teacher gave the class an end-of-term assignment. The instructions were both specific and vague. We were tasked with submitting a project on our upbringing. But we were left to decide how to tell this story, whether it was by creating a family yearbook, a short story or a comic strip. We all had to incorporate one aspect into our finished product: a family tree with pictures. Students were able to go as far back as they wished, depending on how much information they could get, or just focus on their immediate family unit.

The project, for me, should have been a breeze. I had enough designer construction paper and other art supplies to decorate a city street. But the problem was that I didn't have much of a story to tell. My family started with Mom and ended with Jesse. I also didn't want to bring attention to my fractured tree. What if the teacher or someone else asked about something? I didn't want people to know. Finally, there were the pictures—where would I get those? Mom wasn't exactly the type to snap photos of special moments. I knew there was one box of pictures that existed somewhere, but I didn't know where to find them.

I brought up the subject on a Saturday morning when Dave was sitting at the kitchen table, staring out the patio door while drinking his coffee.

"Morning," I said.

"Morning."

"I have to do a school assignment."

"Okay, get to it," he said, still staring outside.

"No. I mean I have a school assignment that I need help with. It's something I can't do without your help. It's ... it's sort of impossible for me to do on my own."

Dave swung around to look at me. I stared down toward my feet, embarrassed that my voice had wavered.

"What's up, kiddo?"

I blurted it all out in what felt like one breath. "I just, I have to do a project on my family history. It's worth twenty-five per cent of my final mark this year and I need to write a story and include photos and a family tree. How big would my tree be—one branch? I don't have any pictures of myself as a baby." I gasped at the end as I held back my tears. "I don't even know my real dad ... I don't have a family."

"Hey now, hey, it's okay," Dave said as he placed his coffee mug on the table. "You have a family, Mel Belle. You have me and your sister. And your mom—I know she's not around, but she's still your family. She'll always be your mom."

"You're Jesse's dad, not mine. How do I even include you in a family tree when we're not related by blood?"

Dave paused for a second. "Why don't you get a pencil and some paper and we'll sketch this out together."

I exhaled, dragging my feet as I went upstairs to my room. I gathered two freshly sharpened pencils, an eraser and a couple of pieces of plain white paper. I brought them back downstairs and sat down at the table with Dave. Beside him was Jesse, who had joined us to eat a bowl of cereal.

"So," he said. "I'm no artist, but if we're going to do a tree, then I say we pick a strong and sturdy one. Something that lasts during tough times. A survivor."

"A palm tree," Jesse said. Dave laughed. "A Christmas tree," she said.

"Stop it, Jesse," I said.

She made a face at me and took in a mouthful of Froot Loops.

"Let's pick something that's for all seasons, maybe," Dave said.

"What about a maple tree," I said.

"Great choice," Dave said. He sketched the base of the trunk in light grey, outlining the branches and shading them in with the pencil. "This is our background, our base. At the top, let's write your name." He wrote in large, block letters: Melanie Forsythe's Family. "Okay, we'll need to pencil in some boxes where we can add names. Let's start with the most important person in your life."

I looked at him and shrugged.

"That would be you, kiddo. We're starting with you." Dave wrote my name carefully, making sure all of the letters fit neatly inside the box. "Okay, now, above you we have two boxes for your mom and your dad. Dave sketched the two boxes that were connected with a line between them. He then connected mine to theirs. In the left box, he added my mom's name, Abigail Forsythe. He tapped his pencil on the desk and looked at me when he got to my dad's. "So ... what do you want to call him?" Dave asked.

"I don't know his name."

"Yes, so, should we call him what he is? First name Biological. Last name Father."

"Are you serious?"

"Why not? It's your family story—it's your history. We aren't making it up."

I thought about it for a few seconds. "Okay, fine."

"Great." He filled in the box, carefully crossing the "t" and dotting each "i."

"Okay, now, your grandparents."

"But we don't even know who my dad is."

"Your maternal grandparents," he said.

Dave drew two boxes above my mother's name and filled in Bill Forsythe followed by Irene Forsythe. Dave connected the boxes, drawing a line between my grandparents and then one linking them to my mother.

"Fantastic. Now we get to the fun part—me and Jess."

"Now it's going to get weird."

"You're weird, kiddo," Dave said, trying to get a laugh out of me. I didn't laugh; I sat there waiting to see what he was going to do next.

"Well, Melanie," Dave said, sketching a box beside Mom for him and one underneath them for Jess.

I studied the boxes, following the lines that connected them all.

"There's no link between us," I said.

"Huh?"

"You have a link with Jesse, who's your actual daughter, and I'm linked to Jesse and Mom. But you and I aren't connected in the tree even though you're actually my most connected family member."

Dave took a minute to think about it, grabbing his eraser. He sat for a second then put the eraser down, raising his eyebrows.

"Got it," he said.

Starting with his name, Dave made a dotted line, diagonally linking himself to me.

"You see?" he asked. "It shows that, while we're not biologically related, we're still family. You're still my little girl. And, here, I'm adding the same kind of line between me and your mom. We weren't even married, but we're still connected."

I looked at the tree and smiled. The dotted lines connected all of us, together. "So we're still family?"

"We are," he said. "Of course we are."

"It's perfect."

"Now, this is my rough draft. You need to do your own. But use this as a guide and do your thing with all your colours and your photos and I'm sure you'll get your A plus."

"And the pictures," I said.

"Oh yes. Those are in the basement."

"Are there any baby pictures?"

"You'll have to take a look. Your mother left everything behind."

I leaned over and gave him a hug, a real one meant for a real dad.

In the end, I decided against a piece of visual art to go with my family tree and, instead, wrote a poem.

He's Dave, not Dad
By Melanie Forsythe

He is to me a dad supreme,
A listener of rock.
He loves his daughters and his dogs,
He jogs but is no jock.
He taught me how to ride a bike,
And got lost on a boat.
He holds the bacon with his eggs,
As dad, he's got my vote.
I didn't know he'd be my dad,
He's really great—what luck!
I tried to follow all his rules
Until I crashed his truck.
He goes to work and bought our house,
He likes to barbecue.
He's not my blood but he's my Dave,
I really love him, too.

I put the pieces of the assignment together in a package: the family tree presented on a large Bristol board, the poem and a three-page report on how I put the tree together given the obstacles I encountered. I showed it to Dave when he got home from work later that week. He sat down at the kitchen table, his baseball cap still on, as I put the project in front of him, almost as if I was serving a meal. He started with the family tree, going through each branch, making comments about how nice it looked. Once he was done, he read the report line by line, nodding his way through it. Finally, he got to the poem. He held it with both hands as he read it, his head tilted toward the table, his face hidden by the rim of his baseball cap. I watched him for some time, unsure why he was sitting there and not saying anything even though I knew he had surely finished reading.

"Dave?" I asked.

He looked up at me. There were no tears in his eyes, but his face had changed, his eyes crinkled at the edges, his forehead more lined—almost as if he was fighting back against pain.

"Nobody has ever said such kind things about me before, kiddo."

"I'm glad you like it."

"I love it. If it's okay with you, I'd like to frame it."

And that's exactly what he did. Dave made me write out another copy for my teacher so that he could take the original to the local photo shop and have it professionally framed. He hung the poem on the wall of the hallway by the front entrance. Dave showed it to everyone who came by the house. "Here," he'd say, beaming. "Just look at what Mel did." I was embarrassed at first.

Jesse said the poem was stupid and the bright purple frame made it stick out. But it stayed there for as long as I could remember. Eventually, the purple frame managed to blend into the beige walls until I forgot it was there.

CHAPTER ELEVEN

MOM AGAIN

January 1991

I WAS BACK on good terms with Dave. I think the school project helped our relationship. He seemed to forgive me for what happened with the van and didn't give me a guilt trip when we were going through all the legal drama.

But things didn't stay calm for long.

I was nervous about going back to school after the Christmas break. Things, there, felt a bit strange. The crash had made me popular, but I learned quickly that it was only temporary. Emily still wouldn't talk to me. And by Christmas, everyone had forgotten about the accident. I was back to being plain old Melanie.

I didn't want to be plain anymore. I remembered the way Mom used to look. How everyone noticed her. Her long and dark hair, before it turned into a bird's nest, flowed so beautifully. She never cared what people thought and, yet, she captured everyone's attention.

I wanted to be beautiful, too. I was tired of being boring. While I had managed to escape having freckles, my skin was so pale I looked like the inside of a loaf of bread, a blob of barely baked dough. I tried explaining this to Dave on New Year's Day as he garnished the pot roast and peeled the potatoes.

"If I want to make a comeback, I need a serious make-over," I said. "You've gotta look your best to be a part of the in crowd."

Jesse rolled her eyes.

"There are definitely certain expectations," I said ignoring her. "I need to, like, put on my best face."

"You're a dummy, Melanie," Jesse said before getting up from the kitchen table and turning on the television.

"You got a bunch of new clothes for Christmas," Dave said. "That should give you a new look, right?"

"Yeah, but I need something more dramatic."

"Well, you've always been good at art. You're old enough to wear a bit of makeup now—as long as it's not too much."

I hadn't thought of that, but it sounded like a good idea. "Yeah, maybe," I said. "I'm also going to go on a diet. Like, immediately."

Dave took a sip of his can of ginger ale and then returned to peeling a misshapen russet. "Where'd you get the idea you need to lose weight?"

"I don't know," I said, stretching my hands above my head to lengthen my torso. "I mean, you don't have to be fat to want to lose weight. I just think it'd be in-credible to look like Cindy Crawford."

"Yeah right," Jesse snorted from the living room.

"Anyway, it means I can't eat your roast. Even though it looks good."

"Your loss, kiddo."

The next morning, I asked Dave for twenty dollars and went to the drugstore around the corner, where I bought a bright shade of purple lipstick, red blush and green eyeshadow. I rushed home and applied the colours in gentle strokes, the same technique I remembered Mom using.

When school resumed a couple of days later, I woke up earlier than usual. I slid into my new jeans and leather boots, carefully combing my hair and applying my new makeup. I looked at the clock—seven forty-five. It was time to get Jesse up. I went into her room and sat at the edge of her bed, gently nudging her to wake up, but she wouldn't budge.

"No," she said.

"It's the first day back at school. You gotta get up."

"I don't want to get up," she said, mumbling.

"You have to."

"I'm tired. I don't want to leave my bed."

I grabbed her comforter and sheets and, in one swipe, yanked them off her bed. "Get *up*, Jesse. School's starting."

"I said I'm tired."

"Well, too bad. Get up."

"Get lost, Melanie! I hate you!"

"You can't talk to me like that," I said. "I'm going to tell Dave and he's going to have a conniption."

"Tell him. I don't care."

Jesse got up only so that she could grab her sheets off the floor and put them back on her bed. I stormed out of her room and marched downstairs to the kitchen, grabbing the phone on the counter. I called Dave's work and had him paged, waiting impatiently for him to get on the line. By the time he got to the phone it was eight fifteen. I breathlessly told him what had happened and demanded that Jesse start to listen.

Dave sighed heavily. "Can you tell her I'd like to speak with her?"

I slammed the phone on the counter, walking back upstairs to call Jesse. I marched into her bedroom to find her out of her pyjamas and in front of her dresser.

"I'm dressed," she said. She made a face but didn't turn to look at me.

"Dave's on the phone," I said, trying to make my voice sound threatening. "You're in big trouble."

"Fine," she said. She turned around and headed downstairs. I followed her but stopped at the edge of the steps, sitting down as I listened in to her side of the conversation. She hung up the phone a few seconds later and stuck out her tongue at me. "Daddy says if we leave now we won't be late at all."

I walked down the stairs and flung open the door to the cupboard, finding a box of cereal. "I'm making myself breakfast and leaving this house in exactly eight minutes. If you're hungry I suggest you do the same."

"You're such a drama queen," she said, making another face as she passed the box of cereal and grabbed a banana on the counter. "I'll eat this on the way. So now I'm ready. And you're not."

"Get lost, Jesse."

"*You* get lost."

I approached her so that we were only two inches apart. "Why do you always have to ruin everything? You ruin *everything*." I spat my words at her as she winced in my face.

"Well you ruined everything by being *born*," she shot back. "You live in this house even though you don't belong here. You should go to an orphanage."

With that I grabbed Jesse by the shoulders and shoved her as hard as I could. She was flung backwards hard and fast, hitting the floor before her hands could break her fall. Jesse looked at me, her eyes wild with anger. My hands were trembling and my arms were still outstretched, locked frozen in the position I'd used to push her.

"I hate you, Melanie!" she screamed from the linoleum floor, the anger replaced by tears. "And you've always been mean."

I said nothing.

"You blame me for everything just because Mom left. I wish you weren't my sister."

I turned away from her and grabbed my schoolbag, leaving my bowl of cereal untouched on the table. We walked to the end of the street and then I turned toward Jess. "I'm going this way," I said, pointing right. "To my school. I'm not walking you today. You can get there all by yourself."

Jesse's green eyes flashed as she blinked; I couldn't tell if it was fear or anger. "You can't do that, Melanie. I'm not allowed."

"Well, I had to walk everywhere alone when I was your age. And, besides, you made me late for class. So you're walking yourself to school whether you like it or not. Bye." I marched away from her, knowing she was staring at me as I trudged along the sidewalk with my knapsack on my back.

I made it just in time for gym class, where I changed out of my new clothes and into shorts and running shoes.

As I was putting my jeans back on after class, I heard two voices around the corner in the main change room.

"Did you see Melanie?"

"Yeah, she finally got a new outfit." A pause, and then giggles. It was Melissa and Kristine.

"And did you see her makeup? She looks like a clown."

"I know. She's really not that pretty."

"You should tell her."

"Yeah right. You should."

My back was up against the wall and my jeans were halfway around my legs. I froze, wondering what to do next: stay put or storm out. Melissa changed the subject, asking which class Kristine was off to next, when the PA system crackled to life. "Attention, students. Could Melanie Forsythe please come down to the office? Melanie Forsythe to the front office immediately."

I had no idea why I was being paged. I considered waiting until the girls left, but then I wondered what was so urgent.

It was Jesse, I thought. It had to be.

With my jeans zipped up, I slid into my boots and stepped out of the shower stall. Melissa and Kristine watched in stunned horror as I passed them by. I ran to the front office, where the secretary pointed me to the phone on her desk.

"You have a call," she said.

I picked up the receiver to hear Dave's voice. "It's your sister. There's been some kind of incident at the school. I'm going to leave work as soon as I can, but I can't this very minute so you'll have to go and get her for me."

"What happened? Is everything okay?"

"I can't get into details right now. Can you please go get her?"

"What happened?" I said again.

"We'll talk about it later."

I signed myself out and walked back to Jesse's school, noticing there was already a scuff on my new boots. I walked into the hallway of Jesse's school and made my way to her classroom, where I knocked on the open door. The teacher, who was helping a student with an activity, glanced up at me but stayed crouched down by the desk. "She's in the principal's office," she said.

I turned around and made my way to the front of the school. The office door was shut, so I knocked on it and was greeted by a stern-looking woman with short grey hair wearing pink eye shadow and lipstick to match.

"I'm here for my sister," I said. She opened the door so that I could see Jesse sitting in a row of chairs. She was staring at her lap and didn't look up at me. "Is everything okay?" I asked the secretary. "What happened?"

"There was a fight involving this one and another student. Your sister pulled about half her head of hair out. There was quite a bit of blood. The other parents are threatening to call the police."

"Oh," I said. I turned toward Jesse, who was swinging her legs under her chair. "Can we go, please?"

"May want to wait for the principal to give his blessing … he's on the phone right now but should be out shortly."

We sat there for another twenty minutes as Jesse swung her legs and I stared at the secretary as if to say, 'How much longer?' Finally, an overweight man in a light grey suit came out and told us we could go. Jesse got up from her chair and shuffled past the secretary. "Bye," I said, leaving the office. Jesse said nothing and followed me out.

I got home expecting an empty house but found Dave on the couch in the living room, staring at the carpet. At first I thought he was there because of Jess, but then he told her to go to her room. From the way he was slumped over, I could tell he had something more to tell me.

"Melanie," he said once Jesse was out of earshot. His eyes were slits and his face was ashen.

"What's wrong?"

"Melanie, I ... just saw your mother."

I dropped my knapsack and my face went numb.

"What do you mean? You were just at work."

"I saw her driving. Shortly after I called you. I was on the road, not far from the shop actually, when she pulled up in the car next to me. We were at a red light so I had the chance to get a good look. It was her—I'm sure of it."

My heart thumped so hard and my breathing became so heavy I felt like I had to take a gulp of air to be able to speak. I couldn't believe it.

"What do you mean? That doesn't make sense. Mom doesn't drive."

"She was in the passenger seat."

"With who?"

Dave kept his gaze steady on me, despite his next sentence. "She was with someone else. Another man."

I bit my lip. Dave never made stuff up. "How did she look?"

"She seemed fine ... happy even. She was laughing about something."

I tried picturing her, her dark hair full and beautiful as she touched the arm of some stranger behind the wheel. But when I drew this image in my head, her face remained blank.

I peppered Dave with every question I could think of.

"What model of car was it?"

"I don't know," Dave said. He thought about it for a second. "It was blue."

"What was she wearing?"

"Something dark. I'm not sure."

"Where was she going? I mean, what direction was she headed in?"

"North—she was going north."

I needed more information. So I kept asking. "What about the licence plate? Did you get the number?"

"I didn't even think of it, Mel. It didn't occur to me."

"Why didn't you jump out of the car?"

Dave shook his head. "I didn't think of that either, Mel." He shook his head again. "It's not like she's been kidnapped."

I asked the only other questioned that mattered: "Did she see you?"

Dave stood up from the couch and went into the kitchen, where he got two cans of ginger ale. He returned to the living room, opened both cans and handed me one. He watched me take a sip as he pinched the space between his eyes. I waited for him to say something. Finally, he sat back down on the couch and took a deep breath.

"I guess I was staring at her for a while so it must have caught her attention. She turned her head and looked me right in the eye. She saw me at the stoplight and that's—that's when she stopped smiling. She stopped smiling and she turned away. She didn't want ... she didn't want to see me."

I knew it.

Something rose in my throat. I thought it was the bubbles of the ginger ale but it burned so fiercely that I had to swallow hard. We were silent for a few seconds and then I said, "So, what do we do now?"

"I don't know. I honestly have no idea. I guess we just move on, once and for all."

I thought about things for a moment and took another sip of ginger ale. She couldn't do this. She couldn't do this to me. "Are you going to tell Jesse? Do you think she should know?"

"No," Dave said, shaking his head. "It would confuse her. She doesn't remember your mother at all—and she's been through enough."

Jesse, I thought, hadn't really been through anything. It was me who lost my mother, it was me who didn't fit in. How could Dave even say such a thing? Everything was always about her. It was always about Jesse. The shock faded. And now I felt anger. I really hated my sister. I hated my mom. And at this moment, for the first time in my life, I even hated Dave.

"Well, it doesn't matter that Mom isn't coming back," I said, my voice rising up. "None of this matters. Because guess what? I don't need this family."

My hand was on my hip as I stared down at Dave. He was still sitting on the couch, holding his ginger ale and looking stupid and dumb.

"So I wouldn't get used to having me around for long," I said, feeling stronger, feeling brave. "Because I'm going to leave this house and I'm going to leave everyone behind. And you know what I'm going to do? I'm going to have another family—I'm going to have my own. And this family will be *real*, not like this pretend version that's full of shit and good for nothing."

Dave opened his mouth as if he was going to say something, but then he didn't. Instead, he got up from the couch and walked outside, not bothering to close the door behind him.

CHAPTER TWELVE

---⊷◇⊶---

LONDON

September 1995

THE RIDE TO London was long and frustrating, the highway jammed with weekend cottagers. The trunk of the car was stuffed with my suitcases, so Dave and I had to fit three boxes and two gym bags in the back seat, leaving Jesse squeezed up against the side door.

Dave drove west along the 401, slamming the top of the steering wheel every few minutes and shouting "Come on!" I watched Jesse in the side-view mirror as she listened to her Walkman, bobbing her head up and down while she looked out the window. Every vehicle was hauling something—boxes, bike racks, boats, trailers. I even saw a plaid couch tied to a roof. It was easy to spot the students. Unless their parents were driving, their cars were crappier, their back seats crammed with clothes and other things that weren't in boxes. I wondered if they were headed where I was headed, if any of them would one day be my classmate or my friend.

September had just started, but the weather was still hot and sticky. The air-conditioning in Dave's car wasn't working, so we had to drive with the windows rolled all the way down. If we were moving, we'd get a nice enough breeze to make it manageable. But with so much traffic on the highway, we were stuck sweltering.

"This is going to be a looooong day," Dave said. "We should have left earlier."

"You know what's even worse?" Jesse had taken off her headphones to share this piece of wisdom. "We're travelling to a city called London that's not even in England. How does that even make sense?"

I resisted the urge to run my fingers through my hair. "Would you guys stop complaining? We're not on a schedule. I can arrive at the dorm anytime."

The exit lane off the highway was bumper to bumper. The line was full of students and their parents inching their way to the university. "For Christ's sakes," Dave said. "This is worse than city driving."

By the time we pulled into the parking lot of the student residence, we were starving. "Let's get your boxes up to your room and then go grab lunch," Dave said. "We've got to make it quick so I can beat the traffic out of here."

"You're like a senior citizen, always hating traffic," Jesse said. "I can't wait to drive. One day I'm going to drive all the way to British Columbia."

"Before you do that, you need to help me with my boxes," I said, giving her one of my side eyes.

We pulled the suitcases and boxes out of the car and walked through the front doors. The massive, thirty-six-floor building was crawling with first-year students, music blasting from several windows.

"This place is awesome," Jesse said as she looked around.

The fact that I was finally starting university was thrilling. But school wasn't the only reason I was excited. After years of helping to take care of my sister, I wanted freedom. Freedom from home, freedom from responsibility and, maybe most of all, freedom from Jesse.

Dave, at first, was a bit nervous about my decision to go away. "What if you get sick?" he said. "Or need help with something?" I reminded him that I had spent a lot of my childhood on my own. Truthfully, I think he was more worried about Jesse not having me around. But I couldn't worry about her any longer.

Jesse, Dave and I took the elevator to the sixth floor of the residence where we found my room, a modest unit with two beds, two desks and a shared closet. I opened my suitcase and threw my clothes on one of the beds, staking my claim on the left side of the room. We made another trip to drop off the rest of my stuff and then went back to the car.

"Lunchtime," Dave said.

He drove south on Wharncliffe as he and Jesse argued about where to eat. Jesse was experimenting with vegetarianism and wanted to get Japanese. Dave ignored her and pulled into the parking lot of a plaza with a Subway shop and pizzeria.

"Separate restaurants," he said. "We can all get our own thing."

Dave and I grabbed a slice of pizza while Jesse wandered over to Subway to survey her options. She joined us at the pizza joint a few minutes later and ordered a cheese slice. "I don't feel like being healthy," she said.

Dave was less grumpy after lunch, but kept looking at his watch, wanting to get back on the road. "I've got an early shift at work tomorrow so we should really get going," he said. He dropped me off at the front entrance of the residence, got out of the car and gave me a hug.

"Be careful—no drinking," he said, squeezing me hard and patting my head.

"Yeah, don't get crazy drunk and wind up dead," Jesse said as she scooted around the car to take the front seat.

I had not expected it to happen, but I felt like I had to cry. Embarrassed, I waved goodbye and watched Dave get back into the car. Jesse raised her middle finger as Dave pulled out of the parking lot. I gave myself an extra minute for the tears to dry, then turned around and went back inside.

I returned to the dorm to find my roommate had arrived. The girl's long, straight hair was dyed an artificial black matched by her clothes and makeup. Her heavily pencilled lips and eyes contrasted sharply against her skin, a complexion so white it was startling. She wore a long see-through black chiffon top that draped over a black bra and jeans, punctuated by a set of leather boots with spiky silver studs.

"Hi," I said. "I'm Melanie."

"You should have knocked," she said. "It's called courtesy."

"Sorry," I said. "But I live here? I'm your roommate."

She kept her back to me as she arranged a row of plants on her bookshelf. "I still think there should be rules. We should knock."

"Okay," I said. "Good to meet you."

She paused for a moment as she admired the placement of her cactus. Without saying anything further she unzipped her luggage. It was stuffed with clothing, all of it black.

My new roommate never bothered telling me her name, so, a few days later, I leafed through some papers on her desk and learned it was Vanessa. She spent as little time in our shared space as possible. When she was in the room, she'd be at her desk, studying while her stereo blasted Marilyn Manson at full volume. While unsettling, her presence was at least predictable. She'd pack her weekend bag every Friday afternoon and disappear, not returning until Sunday. I assumed she went back home for the weekends, wherever home was, but she never said.

The hot, sticky weather clung to the first month of school, dotting the inside of the dormitory windows with condensation. The residence was often noisy and rowdy, with certain floors becoming congregation spots for students who wanted to hang out any time of day or night. Empty bottles and cigarette packs lined the halls as music blared. All were welcome to come and go as they pleased. The sixth floor was well below where most of the partying happened, so I caught only a glimpse of the action on occasion.

I tried to spend as much time out of the residence as possible, especially when Vanessa was there. By my second week, I felt like I'd hardly spoken a word to anyone. I called Dave on a Thursday night after dinner.

"I want to come home."

"What's wrong?" he asked.

"Nothing's ... wrong. It's just that it's like every other school I went to. I don't think I like it here."

"You only got there, kiddo. Give it time."

"I haven't made any friends yet," I said. "I feel like I don't belong."

"Melanie, you'll be fine. It's new still and things at the beginning always take some getting used to. Go out, join some clubs, check out the gym, the pool. Do all the things you wanted to do when you were busy helping me with Jesse."

"Fine," I said. "How is she, anyway?"

Dave sighed. "She's the same. You take care of yourself."

"I will," I said, annoyed he was brushing me off. "Talk to you later."

I decided to take Dave's advice. I got up early the next morning and walked over to the main campus to use the gym and pool. The student recreation centre was big and sprawling with multiple floors that were still unfamiliar. I was in the basement trying to find the girls' change room when I found myself in a dead-end hallway that led to three steel doors, all of them bolted.

"You must be lost."

I turned around to see who had called out. It was a guy in his twenties, presumably another student. There was something about his face. It was strangely familiar, yet I couldn't place it. Light brown hair, brown eyes, medium build, crooked mouth.

"I know you," I said. My mind raced and it clicked. It was Jason. The Jason from Saturday mornings when I was a kid. The Jason whose mom babysat me during Dave's running club days. "You're Jason, right?"

"Yes," he said. It wasn't clicking for him, though. I wondered if I looked that different from when I was younger. I hoped I did.

"It's Melanie from back home, remember?"

"Oh yeah," he said. He was looking at me, searching. "With the little sister?"

"Jesse."

"That's it," he said. "What are you doing here?"

"I'm looking for the change room."

"No, I mean, what are you doing *here*?" He motioned his hand to show he meant not the building but the campus.

"This is my first year. I'm doing my bachelor's degree. Art history."

"Nice."

"What about you?"

"I'm a teaching assistant. Engineering. Graduate work."

"Nice," I said, borrowing his word.

I studied Jason's familiar features: his face, his smile. He was an older version of the teenager I remembered, though his handsomeness was undercut by a boyishness that persisted into adulthood.

"So did you want me to show you where to go? You're pretty far off from the girls' change room."

"Sure."

I followed him through what felt like a labyrinth of long hallways and underground piping, aware of the loud squeaking my shoes were making.

"Go down this way and it's on your left," he said, pointing.

"Okay, well, thanks," I said. "Nice to see you. And say hi to your mom and dad."

"Oh, my mom's not around anymore. She died a couple of years ago."

Two vivid memories rushed back to me. The first was the time I met Marla, the image of her coral-coloured robe sweeping across the marbled floor. The second was the look on Jason's younger face when I'd told him the lie about my own mother—that she was dead.

"I'm so sorry," I said. I felt embarrassed for bringing it up. "I didn't know."

"Yeah, it was hard. My dad's still pretty messed up about it."

"What happened?"

Jason exhaled loudly as he looked down the hallway. "It was pretty sudden. Maybe I can tell you over a beer sometime."

He seemed annoyed at that moment. I realized he had probably not expected to be peppered with questions about his mother's death when he stopped to help what he thought was a stranger in the hallway.

"Sure," I said. "Anytime."

Feeling flustered, I thanked him again for helping me find my way, not sure when I'd see him again.

* * *

Two days later, I was in my dorm room when the phone rang.

"Hi, it's Jason—this Melanie?"

"Oh, hi," I said, tucking my hair behind my ears even though he couldn't see me. "Yes, it's me … How did you find me?"

"Wasn't hard. My dad had to remind me what your last name was, though. He remembers everything."

"Yeah, it's different from Dave's—my Dave."

"It's funny how our dads have the same name."

"Yeah," I said. "Funny."

"So, did you still want to go for that beer?"

"Sure," I said. "I mean, yes—yes I do."

We met up the next night at The Spoke, a pub in the recreation centre. Jason was waiting for me when I got there, playing pool by himself at a table wedged between the bar and lounge area. The sounds of clinking bottles blended with student banter, overpowering the drumbeat of an indiscernible song.

"Hey," he said as soon as he saw me.

I looked at him and waved, noticing the straight white teeth behind his slightly crooked smile.

"You play pool?" he asked.

'Not really," I said. "I can play cards, though. And checkers."

Jason let out a laugh; he must have thought I was joking. I laughed back, grateful he didn't detect the depth of my awkwardness. His age, his family, his wealth—so much about him was intimidating. I tried to push it out of my mind as he ordered two beers at the bar and I took a seat at the table.

"So," he said as he joined me, passing me a beer. "How do you like school so far? Campus is all right, no?"

"It's pretty nice," I said, nodding my head in agreement. "I'm still getting used to things ... and being away from home."

"I know what you mean. I've been here six years already and I'm still getting used to it." Jason smiled, crookedly, and I shifted my focus to his eyes. "So, why'd you decide to come here?"

I decided against saying anything about Jess—about needing a break from her, about wanting to be out on my own. "For the program, I guess. It's a good one."

"Art history?"

"Yes, but I'm doing a double major, actually—art and English. Don't get me wrong, I've always loved art and wanted to learn more about it, but I mean … I'm no Van Gogh."

"You mean, you're not?" He feigned surprise; it was his turn to be funny.

"I also don't really see myself working in a museum or anything. So I'm thinking about teachers college. Eventually."

"That's great," Jason said.

I didn't like so much of the attention on me. "And what about you?" I asked. "Why'd you decide to come here?"

"To be honest, I'd always planned to apply to the business program. Dad really wanted me to."

"But then?"

"But then … I was always more interested in machines. And the idea of actually building and creating things seemed more exciting to me. Mom was the one who encouraged me to do what I wanted, so I listened to her and enrolled in engineering. And here I am."

The mention of his mother led to a few seconds of silence. I wanted to ask, but I didn't know if it was too soon.

"Listen," I finally said. "I was really sorry to hear about your mom. I've been thinking about her ever since I ran into you the other day."

"Thanks." He leaned back and took a sip of beer. "It's been three years but it feels like three days. It's hard to talk about it, even now."

"I'm sure," I said. "Was she ill?"

"She had a brain aneurysm. Died instantly."

"What? Oh my God." I thought of poor Marla.

"It was one of those things. Completely without warning."

I leaned in, feeling terrible for Jason, but also needing to know more. "Where did it happen, Jason? How?"

He put down his beer bottle and massaged the inside of his left hand with his right thumb. "It happened at home. Dad was the one who found her. At first we didn't know what happened. But then the autopsy was done."

I wanted to ask so much more, but it felt like he was shutting down.

"How's your dad doing?"

"He fell apart after it happened. Obviously. There was a lot of guilt ... he wasn't at home at the time. My dad worked round-the-clock at his law firm and found her ... later."

"Oh my God," I said. "I'm so sorry. I mean, your mother—she was a nice woman. She was always really nice."

"Thanks," he said. "We were close, so it was difficult. I know you know how hard it is to lose your mom."

I nodded and didn't say anything. And then I changed the subject.

We stayed at the pub for another half-hour until Jason asked for the bill. "Don't even think about it," he said as he put one hand on the cheque. I smiled and thanked him.

"It was nice to see you."

I was about to get up from the table when Jason put his hand on top of mine so that he could say one last thing.

"I want to see you again," he said.

CHAPTER THIRTEEN

LIES

September 1995

THE NEXT WEEK, Jason invited me for dinner.

"You mean at your place?" I said, twisting the telephone cord around my finger. "Or a restaurant?"

"My place," he said. "If that's good for you."

"Sure. I didn't know you could cook."

"I didn't say I was cooking," he said, laughing. "I just thought we'd order pizza or something."

"Oh," I said, wishing I hadn't made the assumption. "Sounds good. You order pizza and I'll bring dessert."

I used my meal card to pick up two lemon tarts from the dorm cafetcria, which I placed in a Styrofoam container before heading over on foot. After passing the soaring tower of University College, I headed downhill, out the main gates of campus and then left on Richmond Street.

Jason lived on the upper level of a two-storey Victorian that had been carved into three separate units. The house was on a busy part of Richmond, a five-minute walk to campus, and was surrounded by the constant whir of cars. I approached the red brick house with the dark green trim and stopped in my tracks when I realized the front door had been boarded up. Unsure if I was at the wrong place, I walked around to the side to find a functioning door and three mailboxes. The door was ajar so I popped my head inside the entryway to find separate stairwells for the upper and lower apartments. I climbed the steep set of stairs and knocked on the door, suddenly regretful that I hadn't double-checked the address. I was about to head back downstairs when the door swung open. Jason was standing in front of me with dishevelled hair and a smile on his face.

"Hi there," he said.

"Hey. I thought I was in the wrong place for a second."

"Nope, you're in exactly the right place—come in."

I walked into the apartment holding the Styrofoam container in my hands as if I was presenting a special gift of some kind. "I brought dessert," I said. "For later."

"Thanks."

I looked around to survey his apartment. Despite the large exterior of the house, the upper unit was modest in size, a bachelor with a stand-in kitchen and washroom tucked away in the corner. The bed was placed beside the main window that overlooked the sidewalk. At the other end of the room was a loveseat sofa and a rectangular wooden coffee table that served as the eating area. I noticed the pizza was already waiting for us on top of the coffee table with a stack of paper napkins.

"Pizza just got here—it's still hot," Jason said.

I handed the tarts to him and took off my jacket, wondering if I should sit or stay standing.

"I've got beer," Jason said. "Or some wine maybe —somewhere."

"Beer's good," I said. "Beer and pizza are perfect."

He turned around and squatted in front of the mini-fridge. The kitchen was nothing more than a row of cabinets with a small sink and bar fridge, more befitting of a hotel room than an apartment.

"You don't have an oven," I said. "How do you eat here?"

"There's a cooktop under this thing," he said, lifting a white aluminum cover. "But now you know why I prefer to do takeout."

"Don't you get sick of it?"

"Eating out? Not really." He turned around to hand me a bottle of beer with a lime wedge stuffed in its neck. "We never cooked at home when I was growing up. We ordered in almost every night."

"That's insane," I said.

"Yeah, my mom didn't like to cook. It was just easier."

"Wasn't it expensive to do that every night?"

Jason shrugged his shoulders. "I guess." He popped the wedge of lime into his bottle and took a swig of beer. "Did Dave cook?"

"Oh yeah," I said, squeezing the lime juice into my bottle and feeling brave enough to sit down on the couch. "He did barbecue a lot, corn, salads, macaroni and cheese. Nothing too fancy."

I didn't mention the years of eating cereal for dinner.

"Sounds awesome. My dad doesn't cook at all."

Jason joined me on the couch and handed me the stack of paper napkins as an invitation for me to start eating. I took one and grabbed a slice of pepperoni out of the box. We each ate three slices as the conversation migrated to our favourite restaurants. But, after a couple of minutes, I ran out of things to say because I hadn't been to many interesting places.

"So," Jason said as he got up to get us more beer. "Are you and Dave still close?" I could tell he'd been studying my face, as if he was trying to figure me out.

"Oh yeah. He's pretty much my real dad. I'm probably closer to him than anybody else."

Jason nodded but didn't say anything as he handed me another beer.

"Is that terrible?" I asked.

"Why would that be terrible?"

"I mean, because I didn't say my sister."

"I'm not here to judge."

"It's just that Dave and I are really close. I don't know why it is, but he understands me best. I can be myself with him."

"I understand."

I wasn't sure that he did. "Is that the relationship you had with your mom?"

"Pretty much. It always felt like it was just me and her at home. Dad was always working."

"Was it lonely? I mean, you didn't have any brothers or sisters, right?"

He took a sip of beer before answering. "It was all right. Mom was always finding ways to keep me entertained. She was good like that."

"I get it."

"Now that she's gone, it's hard being back in the house. I go home a lot for my dad, but ... I don't like to be there anymore."

"I'm sorry," I said.

"Yeah, well, that's life. I just feel sorry for my mom. It wasn't her time to go."

I didn't say anything. Jason looked out the window as a group of people outside erupted into laughter.

"I'm just not really sure if I can ever get over it. I think about her every single day." He turned back to look at me. "Do you think that's a bad sign?"

I chewed the inside of my mouth for a few seconds, not wanting to continue the conversation for fear it would migrate to my own mother, to the lie I had told Jason when we were kids. "I don't think so."

"What was it like, when ... well, you know."

I knew I had to say something. The lie would get worse the longer it lasted. I closed my eyes for a second to gather my thoughts, but when I did, I saw Mom. She was standing at the bus shelter and her head wrap was blowing in the wind. "It was painful at the time, obviously. But you know..." I held my breath for a moment, scrambling, desperate for something meaningful to say. But nothing came to me.

"Yeah, I guess," Jason said. There were a few more seconds of silence before he spoke again. "God, this family stuff can get really hard. Can you even imagine having kids of your own?"

His question didn't demand an answer, but I needed him to know I wasn't going to be a screwup. I had a clear plan in life and I was going to follow it every step of the way.

"I definitely want my own family," I said, sitting up straighter. "I want to be a mom and I want to be good at it. Better than my mother was. Better than anyone."

Jason looked at me and didn't say anything. He either liked what I had to say or wanted me to stop talking because, before I had the chance to continue, he leaned forward, took my face in his hands and kissed me.

* * *

The first Thanksgiving home gave me a chance to catch my breath from the start of school. Dave put fifty dollars in my bank account so that I could take the Greyhound. I returned on the Friday before the long weekend to find the front porch decorated with the same tacky scarecrow that had been pinned to the mailbox every fall. I mounted the front steps but didn't even get the chance to knock. The door swung open and there was Dave with his arms wide open. "Welcome home, kiddo."

I threw my arms around him and took in the familiar smells. Jesse stood behind him holding a sign. "Welcome Home, Melanie!" it read in Dave's handwriting followed by "NOT" in Jesse's.

It was a relief to be back after all those weeks away. I dumped my bags on the floor of the hallway; in them was two weeks' worth of laundry and several books on history, conflict, betrayal and war.

The brown carpet had its musty yet comforting smell, its familiarity almost sedative after such a long time in such a strange place. The beige walls looked the same, still nicked with years of wear and tear. The blue plaid tablecloth Dave always used for company was out and the table was set.

"You went all fancy for me," I said.

"We've missed you here."

"The house is better quiet," Jesse said.

Dave ignored her. "Things are definitely different without you. But tonight will be like old times. Dinner is on the table!"

After so many weeks of cheese on toast and boxes of orange juice from the crappy cafeteria, the meal was exactly what I had hoped for—roasted chicken, mashed potatoes and gravy. Dave even poured me a glass of wine.

Jesse spent most of the meal complaining about her new teacher. "She sucks. She gives us too much home-work. And her hair's red like yours, Melanie." Dave interrupted as often as possible to ask me questions.

While Dave cleaned up, I captivated Jesse with a few tales from frosh week. "My second night there the student council rented a bunch of buses to take all the new students to a party, but one girl got so drunk she barfed all over the seats of the bus."

"No *way*."

"I'm serious. The bus had to turn around and go back. Nobody even made it to the party."

I actually hadn't been on the bus and had heard that story from my floormates, but she didn't need to know that. The stories made her interested in me. And, for the rest of the night, she peppered me with questions about what it was like to live with hundreds of other students my age.

"It's pandemonium," I said.

"What does that mean?"

"It means it's crazy, but in a good way."

After dessert, once Jesse had gone upstairs, I told Dave I was seeing someone.

"You are?" He paused for a second. "Who is it?"

"A guy. Another student. And he sometimes swims at the student pool, like me."

"Well, does he have a name, this swimmer? What is he studying?"

"He's a graduate student. Studying engineering."

"And his name?"

"Jason."

"So, can we meet him sometime? You've never had a boyfriend before."

I heard Jesse at the top of the stairs, so I changed the subject before I had the chance to tell him who it was. I didn't want her knowing. "Of course," I said. "Next time, for sure."

I tried to survive the weekend without getting into a fight with Jesse. I really did. But when I packed up my things on.Monday, I noticed a chunk of pages had been ripped out of my books. Hardcover. Brand new. More than fifty dollars apiece. I flipped through my textbook on modern Europe to find more than three quarters of it missing. I ran downstairs, where Jesse was drinking a glass of chocolate milk in front of the television.

"What the hell is this?"

I held the book by its spine and waved it in the air. It felt flimsy in my hands; the surviving pages flopped back and forth.

Jesse's eyes darted toward me before returning to the TV screen. "Looks like a book."

"Come on, Jess, it's not a joke—I'm going to tell Dave."

"Tell him. I don't care. I didn't do anything."

"The hell you didn't!" I shouted. "You wrecked three of my books—those cost a lot of money."

"Don't blame me for things I didn't do. We have dogs, you know."

She was lying and I knew it. But I didn't want to end the weekend on a bad note for Dave. He'd been happy to see me. Instead, I marched upstairs into Jesse's bedroom and yanked her blanket and sheets off her bed. Still unsatisfied, I opened her dresser drawers and pulled all of her clothes and pyjamas out, making a big pile on the floor. I did the same in her closet; anything on a hanger was pulled off and added to the heap. My breathing was heavy as I surveyed the room. Pink and purple T-shirts she hadn't worn in years were mixed in with her more recent clothes. I noticed a pair of jeans, several sweatshirts, her old ballet costume from her failed recital and then I saw it in the corner: a training bra. It was white cotton, with one of those three-loop clasps on the back. I thought of what I could do. The scissors—where were they? I rifled through her desk drawer, but all I could find was a broken ruler and some loose-leaf paper. I marched into the bathroom and opened the bottom drawer until I found what I was looking for. I took the scissors and, in each cup of the bra, cut out a large hole. I threw the disfigured remains in the pile in the centre of the room, noticing the purple stain on her ballerina costume, remembering how she'd missed her big recital. Instead of walking away I leaned over and put it back on the hanger. Just that one, I figured. Still feeling guilty, I folded the pink and purple shirts and put them away, too. From there I kept going, folding and hanging until everything was back in its proper place. Even though I'd found her bed unmade, I tucked the sheets under the mattress and smoothed the comforter on top so that there were no creases or bumps. By the time I was done, the room was in better shape than when I'd found it.

Later that afternoon Dave and Jess drove me to the Greyhound station, where I asked him for another twenty dollars so that I could get something to eat.

"Somehow," he said, handing me the money, "you're more expensive living out of the house than in it."

I smiled at him sheepishly and considered telling him what happened to my books. I needed two hundred dollars, not twenty. But Jess was sitting in the back seat and I didn't want to start anything. "Thanks, Dave," I said as I leaned over to give him a hug. "Later, loser," I said to Jess as I got out of the car.

I was still mad at her. The books were expensive and I couldn't afford to replace them. Although I'd taken out a student loan and paid my tuition in advance, I was learning I didn't have nearly enough money to keep me going until the spring.

I visited the job board in the student recreation centre the day after I got back from Thanksgiving weekend, but it was slim pickings. It was October, so most of the campus positions were already taken. I decided to venture into the city to see what I could find. Jason had his own car, so I called him up and asked him to chauffeur me around town for the afternoon. We drove up and down Wharncliffe, trying to scope out places I could work.

"So, what were you thinking?" Jason asked as we pulled out of the parking lot of the student dorm.

"Not sure," I said, remembering Mom's Mason jars. "Maybe waiting tables? You can pull in a lot of tips that way."

"Makes sense," he said. "There are a few places that should work. Do you have your résumé?"

"I do ... but there's not much to it."

"Doesn't matter. All you need to say is that you're a student—that's all they care about."

I put on my sunglasses as we started our tour, with Jason slowing down slightly every time we approached a plaza.

"Look at that one," he said, pointing. "A pizza restaurant."

"No way. I'd be eating nonstop."

"How about that?" he said. "A fast food joint."

"No tips." He nodded in agreement.

We kept driving, passing a drug store, supermarket, a dry cleaner. "Where else do you want to go?" he asked.

I shrugged.

"What about the pub further down?" Jason said. "There won't be as many students there ... but maybe that means higher tips?"

"Sure, let's go."

Jason drove a few more minutes before pulling up to a seedy parking lot with a dumpster in the corner and a light blue Chevrolet with a missing tire. A large emerald green sign spelled out "Ruthie's" in cursive, a four-leaf clover dotting the "i."

"I don't know this place," I said.

"Me neither. But you might as well check it out."

"Keep the car running just in case someone tries to murder me," I said.

The smell of stale beer hit me in the face as soon as I opened one of the large double doors. The place was dark and wooden, with a deep red carpet and matching velvet benches along the back wall that faced a series of dartboards. Behind the bar was a woman chatting with one of her customers, a guy in a blue baseball cap drinking a pint of something dark and frothy.

"Hi," I said. She stopped talking and looked at me, the guy in the blue cap turning around to see who I was. "I wanted to pass along my résumé. I'm looking for a job and wanted to know if you needed any help."

The woman, who was probably in her late forties, was small, thin and boy-like. Her tousled brown hair was tinseled at the sides and hung above a face whose moderate beauty had been faded by years of thick smoke and long hours.

"Are you from the university?" She looked at me closely as her customer returned to his drink.

"Yes. It's my first year."

"We don't get many students here. But we do need a bit of help on Saturdays. Care to stick around for tonight?"

"Tonight?"

"Training—*unpaid*," she said. "You can follow the girls around, learn from them."

"Sure, I can do that."

"Come back around four and we can get you started."

"Okay. I'm Melanie."

"I'm Ruthie."

"See you in a couple of hours."

"Thanks, doll."

I walked back into the parking lot, my résumé still in my hand. Jason looked at me confused.

"Well?" he said as I opened the door.

"I start tonight—*tonight*."

"Seriously? I mean, that's great. Do you want to work here?"

The fact that I was following in my mother's footsteps was not lost on me. But I needed the job. I needed the money. "I guess," I said. "I mean, why not? I can try it out."

I went back a couple of hours later in jeans and a black T-shirt since that was what Ruthie was wearing. I walked through the front doors to find a band setting up in the corner. Ruthie was behind the bar, putting glasses away.

"Take a seat," she said. "You're going to be working with Claire tonight. She'll be here soon."

I sat at the bar, two stools away from the guy in the blue baseball cap who was still there, taking a drag of his cigarette. He looked over at me and gave me a nod. "Hi," I said. He nodded again. I sat there for about fifteen minutes, watching the band perform their sound check, before someone tapped me on the shoulder. I turned around to see a petite blonde tying an apron to her waist.

"I'm Claire. You're going to be with me tonight," she said smiling.

"Hi, yes, I'm Melanie."

"Ruthie told me. So yeah, basically we do a bit of prep for the first half-hour to hour before things start to get busy," she said. "All you have to do tonight is watch and learn and do as I say. And, oh yeah, my tips tonight are just that—mine."

"Okay."

For the next nine and a half hours, I followed her around, watching her closely as she worked the room, darting from table to bar to kitchen to table. Claire was small, with a figure skater's physique and movements to match: quick and bird-like. Both hands were always occupied, handing over beers, writing down orders, waving hi to the regulars. She shouted over the music, remembered everyone's names and smiled the entire time.

I ended the shift dizzy, exhausted and even slightly drunk after Ruthie poured me an entire pint of beer to end the night. I wondered how Mom did it for so many years—the cleaning, the customers, the painfully long hours. Although Ruthie's was different from Sunny's, it was equally chaotic.

"Good work," Ruthie said. "You can come in every Saturday from here on out."

Jason shrugged his shoulders when I told him I'd be working every Saturday. "Guess I'll study," he said.

Ruthie gave me two tables to start for my first shift to try things out. I followed Claire around for the first hour until two men sat at one of my tables. I approached them with my arms crossed holding a tray up against my chest and asked them how they were doing. The men were in Saturday attire—jeans, T-shirts—and were clean-shaven, mid-forties. The guy on the left had a wedding ring and the one on the right, who was better looking but badly sunburned, didn't.

The sunburned one turned toward me as I asked him how he was, looking me up and down. "You new here?"

"I am. I'm Melanie."

"Well, how are you doin' Melanie?"

His tone was overly friendly, mocking.

"I'm ... okay."

"Aren't you a bit too young to be serving ale?" The band filled the dead air between us. "No, seriously. There's no way you're out of high school."

"Shit, Gavin, leave her alone," his friend said. "Just tell her what you want."

"What I want is to know how old you are," he said, grinning.

"I'm twenty-three," I said, adding four years to my age.

"You are not ... shit, I must be getting old."

The way he looked at me—intensely, invasively—made me think of the man with the horseshoe hairline. This time, I remembered Mom's advice about standing up for myself. "Yeah, you must be," I answered. "You kind of look it."

His friend laughed.

Sunburned Gavin laughed, too, but I could tell he didn't find it funny. "Why don't you get us a round of the usual, new Melanie?"

"What's the usual?"

"Ruthie knows."

I went back to the bar, still clinging my tray to my chest. Ruthie was watching. "Those two guys want the usual," I told her.

"Punch in two pints of Rickard's Red."

I did as she said, turning around when I was done to find her at the table. Her back was to me, but I could tell she was the one doing the talking, both men not saying anything. She turned around and gave me a wink as she left the table and went to pour their beers. They both had another round about an hour later and then left. On the table was a fifty-dollar tip, enough to replace one of my three books. I told Ruthie and she winked at me again.

I was at Ruthie's a few more weeks before picking up another shift, this time on Thursdays. Between both nights I was pulling in enough money to cover all my spending and even put away a little each week. But the job also meant I couldn't go home for long at Christmas —four days at most. Ruthie's was full-on during the holidays and I was expected to work. I broke the news to Dave, but he said he understood. "Gotta make a living," he said.

I worked Christmas Eve and came home the next morning, waking up early to take the Greyhound. Dave and Jesse met me at the station downtown. "Ho, ho, ho —Merry Christmas!" Dave said as I got into the car. Jesse had taken my normally reserved place up front, so I got into the back.

"Merry Christmas," I said as I slouched back in my seat. I was in my sweats, my face still unwashed. The pub hadn't closed down until well after two in the morning, and then Ruthie opened a bottle of Champagne, the fake kind I think, so that we could celebrate the holidays.

Dave ignored my bad mood as he pulled out into the street, making a U-turn so we could head home. The city streets were calm and quiet, with few cars on the road and all the shops shuttered. Becky had invited us to have lunch with Ron, Chris and Michael, but we had to be there for 1 p.m. sharp. Ron was on meds and had to take them with food at a certain time.

We went home so I could shower and change before we piled back into the car, arriving just on time. Dave handed me a bottle of wine and Jess a box of After Eights to give to our hosts.

"Hello lovelies, Merry Christmas." Becky answered the door wearing a black dress overlaid with a green and red apron that read "Santa's helper." Her hair was greyed and chopped off in a blunt style I'd never seen before, a sharp contrast from her usual long tresses. We handed her the wine and chocolates. "Oh my, how fancy," she said. "Thank you. Come on in."

We stepped inside to the smell of roasted turkey and the sound of Chris and Michael arguing about something they were watching on television. "Hang up your coats and get a drink," Becky said. "You know what to do."

The house was just as tidy and organized as ever. We walked into the kitchen to find Ron sitting at the table, looking pale and thin. He nodded our way in a friendly manner, the windows slightly fogged from the cooking.

"Merry Christmas," Dave said.

"Merry Christmas," Ron said.

Becky placed the turkey, potatoes and bowls of greens on the table so that we could start eating.

"Looks great, Beck," Dave said. "There's food for miles."

"Actually, Chris and Mikey stuffed the turkey," she said. "And mashed the potatoes, too."

"No kidding. Nice work boys," Dave said over his shoulder so they could hear him.

Becky handed Dave a beer as we took our seats. Chris and Michael walked into the kitchen, taller and more mature looking than when I'd seen them last. Everyone started to dig in with the exception of Jesse, who played with a spoonful of mushrooms on her plate.

"Eat up," Becky said, motioning toward the turkey with her fork.

"No, thanks," Jesse said. "I only eat vegetables."

Dave's plate was piled in his usual way: slice of turkey, topped with mashed potatoes, followed by a sprinkling of peas. He repeated these layers so that it looked like he was eating a piece of cake. I chewed my food and spoke when spoken to, but the only thing I could think about was Jason. I replayed moments from our first weeks together over and over again, wanting him to be here but also feeling guilty I hadn't told Dave it was the Jason from my childhood.

Everyone seemed a bit sleepy after lunch, so Becky got up from the table and put on a pot of coffee. Chris, Michael, Jesse and I watched *Married with Children* while the adults sat at the kitchen table, chatting over blueberry pie, shortbread and goblets of brandy.

Chris and Michael both planned on doing their apprenticeships to become electricians like their dad. I heard Becky telling Dave how proud she was of them, but then her voice became lower. "Truth is I can't wait for them to get on their feet so that we can move on. We want to downsize and move half-time to Florida. We're sick of the cold ... and we're sort of sick of the kids, too."

The three of them chuckled because it was supposed to be a joke. I kept my eyes on the television screen, pretending that I was still watching.

"What about you?" Becky asked. "How are things with Jess?" I leaned in closer, but Dave's voice lowered to such a whisper that I couldn't hear anything. He spoke for such a long time that, by the time he'd finished, we had moved on to another episode with Al and Peggy Bundy.

Eventually, it was time to go. We said our goodbyes, and Becky gave each of us a hug. As we made our way down the driveway, Dave threw me the keys and asked me to drive. This prompted Jesse to call shotgun and run to the front passenger door, relegating Dave to the back seat alone. "That'll teach me for drinking so much," he said.

As soon as we got home, I ran to the phone and called Jason at his Dad's house, but no one answered. I still hadn't wished him a Merry Christmas, so I decided to leave him a voice message on his family's house line.

I plopped in front of the television and resigned myself to sleeping on the couch. Though I had only been away at school for a few months, things had changed at home. For starters, Jesse had taken over my bedroom and moved all of her belongings into my drawers. The clothes I had left behind were stuffed into garbage bags and shoved onto the floor of her former bedroom closet, where most of her clothes were still on hangers.

When I accused Jesse of taking ownership of both rooms, she brushed me off. "I haven't finished moving everything over yet."

A few other things were also out of sorts. The house, while usually well-maintained, had started to show some cracks. The trusty Kleenex box on the console table by the front door, for example, was absent. Outside, garbage bags spilled out of the cans, which were missing their lids. Finally, the day after Christmas, when I went to wash all the dirty laundry I'd brought home, I noticed Dave had been using fabric softener instead of detergent.

When I had a minute alone with Dave, I asked him what was going on. "Well, you know your sister keeps me busy. And I don't have you to give me a hand any longer, kiddo."

"Whatever," I said. "The house looks like crap."

Dave threw his hands up. "Melanie, I'm tired. I can't do everything all the time. I really can't."

Jason didn't call me back. I tried reaching him a second time, but once again nobody picked up. At the end of my four-day stay, even though he was only a few minutes away from Dave's, I hadn't spoken a word to him. I briefly considered dropping by his place but decided against it. Instead, I took the bus back to London and replayed everything I had ever said to him. I wondered and worried about what I did wrong.

The day after I got back, I wrote him an email: "I hope you had a good Christmas with your family. I tried reaching you a couple of times. See you at school."

I clicked 'send,' wondering if things between us were over. I thought they were—I didn't get an email back. But, a few days later, I heard his voice when the phone rang in the middle of the night.

"Melanie? Are you awake?"

The sky was black, so I turned over to look at the alarm clock: 4:59 a.m.

"Is everything okay?"

"I'm okay. But there was a fire. My place burned down—it's completely gutted."

"Oh my God. Is your dad okay?"

"My dad? He's fine. Not my family home—my place in London. The house burned down."

I rubbed my eyes and sat up in bed, confused.

"What?"

"It was terrifying, Mel—the whole thing, it burned up in a blink of an eye."

"What happened?"

"The guys who live on the main floor—when they got home around two-thirty they saw all this smoke and light coming from the basement. At first they weren't sure what it was, but then realized there was a fire. One of the guys threw a rock up at my window and broke it —the sound of shattered glass is what woke me up. Thank God it did. I ran out in my pyjamas without even a winter coat on."

"Holy cow."

"I know. It was crazy. There was so much screaming and commotion. Apparently we're not allowed to go back inside to get our things ... basically I'm up a creek."

"Actually, it sounds like you're lucky to be alive."

"I guess. I just—I'm not thinking clearly. I'm wearing someone else's coat now, and I'm not even sure whose it is. I need to sleep."

Jason came to my dorm to get some rest and figure out what to do. His adrenaline made it difficult to fall asleep but he finally crashed around 8 a.m. When he woke up three hours later, groggy and confused, I handed him a glass of water and asked if he wanted to get something to eat.

"Sure," he said. "But first I want to see the house."

As soon as we turned left on Richmond, we saw a fire truck on the street with its ladder extended and a huddle of men on the sidewalk. "Looks like some of the crew is still there," Jason said. "And, shit, that's my landlord." We got out of the car at the side of the road. The stench of burnt wood and rubber hit me immediately.

"I can't believe it," Jason said, his eyes widening. "I think it's still smouldering."

The exterior of the house was standing, but the red brick façade was charred. The roof was non-existent— either it had been incinerated or it had collapsed. The inside appeared entirely gutted; everything looked black, twisted, unrecognizable.

"Look," Jason said, pointing through the burnt-out window to his unit. "My apartment is gone—it's all caved in."

We tried to get closer but one of the investigators asked us to step back. Jason spoke to the huddle of men on the sidewalk for a few minutes, exchanged some information and took my hand to leave. We drove to a restaurant close to campus, a place that had a plastic egg as its welcome sign. Jason and I took a seat at the back so that we didn't have to look into the kitchen, where a giant, greasy man was frying bacon over a hot stove.

"So what are you going to do?" I asked.

"I don't know. Maybe live in my car for a while? I need to talk to my dad."

"Did you want to stay in my residence? I could see if they have an extra room maybe."

"Nah, I'm too old for that place. I wouldn't fit in anymore."

"Yeah, all the girls would probably think you're old and creepy."

Jason gave me a tired smile. And then he tapped the fingers of his right hand on the table, as if he was playing the piano.

"You know, I have another idea. I think it's a good one."

"You do?"

"What if you and I were to ... you know. Move in together."

I studied his face to make sure he wasn't joking. His eyes were swollen but they looked serious. Instead of waiting for an answer, he kept talking. "When you look at our situations—I need a place, you dislike your roommate. Plus you now have a job. Doesn't it all make sense?"

I actually didn't think it was a bad idea. I loved the idea of leaving residence, of being with him, of finally feeling like an adult. Something, though, nagged at me, something I didn't have the courage to bring up: he abandoned me over the holidays.

Jason waited a few more seconds, then offered one of his crooked grins. "Well, Mel? What do you say?"

I was afraid of wanting it, I was afraid of everything. But, more than anything, I wanted to say yes. And so I took a deep breath and used all my energy to stifle a squeal. "Let's do it," I said. "Let's move in."

Chapter Fourteen

GARLIC BREATH

January 1996

The pages of *The Gazette* peered out at me from the table of the coffee shop, its wilted pages looking forlorn. I'd spent an entire week searching for an apartment, and all I could find was a handful of vacancies, none of it promising. I circled a couple of options in the student newspaper, then crossed them out when I read the details. Double the price? Nope. Shared space? Never.

I managed to line up three appointments, one of which got cancelled the night before. That left us with only two options within walking distance to campus. The first apartment seemed promising enough—the upstairs unit of a brown brick bungalow on a side street. But the landlord never showed up to the appointment, leaving me and Jason to wait in the car for forty-five minutes before we gave up.

The final place was a small and dreary basement unit with low ceilings and limited light. The bedroom was tiny and the bathroom was so small that Jason didn't fit under the shower head without squatting. But the place was affordable and a short walk to our classes. We took it and moved in the next day.

All of Jason's items were burned in the fire, so we borrowed a futon from one of his friends to sleep on. With no table or chairs, our sole piece of furniture did double duty when we wanted to sit while eating. As cozy as I found it, Jason wasn't impressed.

"This is shit," he said. He was seated on the futon, hunched over a box of takeout noodles and sporting a spot of soy sauce on his chin. "We've got to fix this place up a bit."

I leaned over and dabbed his chin with a napkin. "It's only temporary," I said. "We'll get some furniture soon."

"We better," he said. "I mean, who the hell can live like this?"

I shrugged my shoulders and took in another mouthful of noodles. He was being such a baby. My mother and I had lived in semi-furnished rentals for years. Nothing about it was ideal, but we seemed to do just fine.

The next afternoon, Jason came home dragging several boxes through the door. "Table and chairs," he said. "I need a place to eat—and to study." We assembled the pieces together, taking our time to follow the instructions given by stick people on paper.

As soon as I got the phone line installed, I called Dave and told him I had a new number, explaining that I'd switched rooms in residence because I didn't like my roommate.

"What was wrong with her?" he asked. "Besides all of that strange black clothing."

"She was a bit odd," I said, hating myself for lying. I knew I needed to tell him, but not yet.

That wasn't the only thing eating at me. I still hadn't talked to Jason about why he hadn't called me over the holidays. Why had he dropped me only to reconnect when his place burned down? More importantly, there was the big lie. The one about my mother dying. The longer it continued, the worse it got.

It took us a few weeks, but we finally got everything sorted at the apartment. By February we had new dishes, a bed and a television. Jason even got new clothes to replace what had been destroyed in the fire. To celebrate our accomplishment, we decided to go out for dinner. Jason chose a restaurant where everything was made with garlic, even the ice cream. It wasn't until we were seated that I realized it was the first time we were out at a proper restaurant.

"Cheers," Jason said as we clinked our glasses of wine together and waited for our meals to arrive. "And thanks for making such a big move in the middle of the school year."

"Yes, it was a big move," I said. "Feels surreal."

"I bet. You're living in sin away from your nutty family."

I gave him a confused look. It was true I was happy to be on my own. But how could he say such a thing? He hadn't even seen Dave or Jesse since we were kids. It bothered me. Wondering how to respond, I took another gulp of wine with one hand as I twisted the corner of the tablecloth with the other. Finally, our meals arrived. Instead of grabbing my fork, I rested my elbows on the table, leaned forward and finally asked him what had been on my mind.

"Can I talk to you about something?"

"Shoot," he said, twisting his fork into his pasta.

"You never called me over the holidays. Even when I got back to school, you ignored my email and didn't contact me until your house burned down. What happened?"

Jason looked up from his plate. "If I did, it wasn't intentional." He dabbed his mouth with a white linen napkin, the faint outline of an old wine stain apparent from across the table. "I was busy at home with things."

"I thought we were through."

"That obviously wasn't the case," he said, smiling weakly at me.

I examined Jason's features: the boyish hair tousled in front of his eyes, his heart-shaped face. Even though he was the older boyfriend, he looked more like a teenager to me. "Well, *obviously* something happened," I said. "Maybe if you had called me, you would have seen that my family is—*obviously*—not so bad after all. Don't you think you—*obviously*—owe me an explanation?"

"Owe you?"

"Yes. Don't I deserve to know why you just disappeared and then randomly popped back up again?"

"Uh, it wasn't random. My house burned down."

"Yeah, I know—you needed something. So you called me ... after ignoring me through the holidays."

"Listen," Jason said, leaning in and touching my hand. I could smell the garlic on his breath. I didn't feel like eating anymore. "I'm really sorry. I thought we'd just connect again in January, which we did. Can't we just forget about it?"

"Fine," I said, shrugging my shoulders. I wasn't satisfied with his explanation, but I felt like I'd made my point. I picked at my plate, deciding to let it go, promising myself to never eat garlic again.

We skipped dessert and walked down the street toward our basement hovel. The slushy streets of London buzzed with overworked students trying to blow off steam. Alanis Morissette blared from a basement bar, its purple lights hitting the sidewalk from the slit of its sole window.

Jason slipped his hand into mine so casually I didn't even realize it until he tugged at me to cross the street.

"Where are you going?" I asked. "Home's that way."

"I know, but it's still early. Want to head somewhere else?"

"It's cold out. Where do you want to go?"

"I don't know, let's just walk for a bit."

We took a U-turn and headed back south, our fingers linked as we passed by a group of other twenty-some-things encircling a girl vomiting at the side of the street. We kept walking until Jason squeezed my hand and motioned his chin forward, where a large emerald green sign beckoned. "Look what's up ahead," he said. The four-leaf clover dotting the "i" flickered maniacally as if its light bulb was on its last hours. "Want to pop in?"

"On my day off?"

"Why not? For once you can be the guest. We'll stay for one drink."

I shrugged my shoulders. "Sure," I said.

We approached the door to Ruthie's and walked in as the band was signing off for a break. The hum of chatter swelled as glasses clinked and smoke swirled. I spotted Ruthie in her usual spot behind the bar and gave her a wave as Jason and I took off our coats and sat down in front of her.

"You miss me that much?" Ruthie said.

"I guess so. Ruthie, this is Jason."

They both exchanged smiles and nods. "Good to meet you," Ruthie said. "You here for drinks or grub?"

"Drinks," I said. "Beer, I guess."

Ruthie poured two pints and put them in front of us. I sipped the froth threatening to spill over the rim, watching Jason as he did the same.

"So, is this how it happens?" Ruthie said, leaning back up against the cash register.

I gave her a funny look. "How what happens?"

"Is this how you tell me you're quitting? You know," she said, leaning toward Jason. "She's actually not that good of a waitress."

"Hey!" I said. "No fair! It's hard work, okay? Besides, I'm still learning."

Ruthie laughed and moved on to another customer as Jason swivelled his chair around to face me. He must not have liked how our previous conversation had ended because he took both of my hands in his. "Mel, I really am sorry about not calling you over the holidays," he said. "I didn't forget about you, believe me. The truth is I have my hands full when I'm home."

I could still smell the garlic on his breath. "What do you mean?"

"There's something I haven't shared with you, but my dad—he's not at his best right now. Ever since my mom ..."

"Oh," I said.

"It's been hard."

I didn't know what to say.

"If I'm going to be honest." He looked at me, seriously. "My dad's not the person you remember."

I could tell it was difficult for him to say that.
Suddenly, a wave of embarrassment came over me. Here
I was giving him a guilt trip about something incon-
sequential when he'd been dealing with real problems. I
looked like someone who couldn't keep her schoolgirl
emotions in check. Exuding neediness, immaturity. I
needed to stop what I'd started.

"I get it," I said. And I did. "Let's just forget about it,
okay?"

"Okay," he said, squeezing my hands. "I really am
sorry. He does need me and things get pretty intense
when—"

"It's okay. We don't have to talk about it again."

Our conversation was over, so both of us sipped our
drinks. The smell of garlic hung in the air, its unpleas-
antness matched by the uncomfortable silence.

* * *

I called Dave the next morning and told him I'd be
coming home for a few days.

"Well, that'd be nice, kiddo," he said. "I feel like I've
hardly heard from you lately."

"Sorry, I've just been busy. I'll take the bus the week
after next if you're able to pick me up. Sunday morning?"
I hesitated before making the next suggestion. "And
maybe don't bring Jess this time. We can catch up."

Dave agreed and met me in the usual place on the
street beside the bus station. I climbed into the car, relieved to see we were alone, and gave him a big hug. It
had been nearly two months since I last saw him, but
something seemed different. He felt thicker. Softer. I

leaned back to get a better look at him. His shoulders were larger; his face was rounder.

"You've changed a bit," I said.

"More handsome, you mean?"

"Sort of like, um, more fat."

Dave laughed and patted his belly. "I know, Mel Belle. Too many late-night visits to the pantry."

"You should take up running again."

"With this crickety old body? I'd have a heart attack right on the street."

"You're not that old. Oldness is a state of mind."

"Well," he said, pulling out onto the main road. "My mind is focused on frying up some nice burgers for lunch."

I wasn't sure how to bring up the subject of Jason. I played the opening line in my head ("So here's the thing, Dave ...") and then I lost my nerve. But as we drove along the usual stretch of highway, we hit a traffic jam. Hundreds of pulsing brake lights loomed in the horizon. It looked like we'd be in the car for a while. Staring at the sea of red, I blurted it out.

"I've moved in with someone."

Dave tightened his grip on the steering wheel and turned to look at me. "What." He didn't tilt his voice up to intonate a question.

I cleared my throat. "I've been living with someone. You know him, actually."

The row of traffic inched ahead of us after a brief pause, but Dave didn't touch the gas pedal, sitting still instead. "I know him? Who? What do you mean?" The car behind us gave a quick tap of the horn to encourage Dave to move forward.

"It's Jason. His dad is from the running club you were in a long time ago. Remember?"

Dave's eyes widened. "Dave and Marla's son? That's the Jason you've been seeing? How did this happen? And what about residence?" The car rolled farther ahead, catching up to the one ahead of us.

"I bumped into him at the beginning of the school year. We recognized each other. And then we started dating." I waited for Dave to say something, but there was a long stretch of silence. "Listen, Dave, I know you might think I'm not ready, but I really hated my dorm. My roommate was mean and I didn't fit in. Jason is nice and we're both really happy. I'm also thinking of staying in London for the summer. I really like working at Ruthie's."

I blurted it out, a stream of consciousness, none of it rehearsed.

After more waiting, Dave finally said, "This is a big surprise, Melanie."

"I know. I figured it would be. But he's a nice guy. We're not getting married or anything. I'm barely twenty."

"Just don't make the same mistakes as your mother," he said.

"What does that mean?"

"You know exactly what I mean." Dave merged lanes as traffic started moving.

"It's sad about Marla," I finally said. "Jason told me that she died."

"You're telling me."

"You knew?"

"Well, I heard. Such a tragic way to leave your family."

I looked at him, defensive. "I mean, how was she to know?" Dave furrowed his brows. "It wasn't exactly her fault."

"You think?"

"How can anyone have control over a brain aneurysm?"

Dave shook his head. "Marla didn't die of an aneurysm."

"What do you mean? Jason told me the story."

"What story? From what some of the guys said, Marla was found dead in the pool at home. I don't like to repeat rumours, Melanie, but it was no secret that she liked to drink." Dave took a second before he continued. "It sounded like she passed out and drowned."

I didn't understand what I was hearing.

"No," I said. "Jason told me what happened. His dad found her. She died of an aneurysm and an autopsy confirmed it."

Dave shook his head again. "No, I didn't hear that. I don't know anything about that."

"It's what Jason told me," I said. "Jason told me the story. Do you ever see his father anymore?"

"Listen, kiddo, I don't know what's true and what isn't. Jason's dad, from what I understand, went a bit off the deep end after Marla died. I haven't talked to him. I haven't even seen him. And from what I understand, nobody was invited to the funeral."

I sat there, feeling numb and confused. I thought of everything Jason had told me. Why would he lie about it? I also thought of my own lie, the one about Mom dying. Why had I let it continue for so long? I didn't know what I could say now, or what to believe about Jason.

With traffic picking up, it took another twenty minutes to get home. I climbed out of the car and mounted the steps. Dave held the door for me as I carried my duffel bag. The house hadn't changed much from the last time I'd seen it. It was quiet inside, as if no one was home.

"Where's Jess?" I asked.

"She's around."

I went to the bathroom to wash up. When I came down, I found her in the kitchen pouring a glass of milk. Dave wasn't the only one who'd changed. Jesse's blonde hair had bright pink streaks in it, a highly artificial colour that made her pale skin appear sickly. Her blue jeans were exceptionally baggy and hung perilously off her thin hips. A crop top, black cotton, exposed her belly button, the pale white of her midsection visible.

I looked at Dave. "You let her dye her hair? She's only eleven."

"Course not," he said. "She did it with a friend after school."

I turned toward Jesse. "Since when do you dress like that?"

"Since when did you get so ugly?"

"You look ridiculous," I said, afraid her jeans would fall to the floor any moment.

"Stuff it, Melanie," Jesse said as she walked upstairs. "You haven't even been home in forever."

Dave ignored our exchange and pulled out a package of burgers and French fries from the freezer. "You hungry, Mel Belle?"

"Yes," I said, lying. "Is Jess going to eat with us?"

"I doubt it. She's still not eating meat, but we can leave her some fries and salad."

I set the table as Dave manned the frying pan, flipping the burgers with his oversized barbeque spatula.

"I thought it was just the two of us," I said to him.

"This won't go to waste, Melanie."

He joined me at the table a few minutes later with a large platter of food. He grabbed two cans of ginger ale out of the fridge and sat down at his seat. "So," he said, taking a bite out of his burger. "You really like that bar you're working at?"

"It's hard work, but it's not bad," I said, salting my fries. "Decent tips."

"I bet," Dave said. "And cash money, too. They giving you enough hours?"

I nodded as I ate. "Ruthie's good to me."

"Happy to hear that, kiddo."

"So," I said, licking the salt off my fingers. "Are you guys going to be okay without me? If I don't come home this summer, I mean."

Dave took another bite of his burger. "It would be nice to have you home," he said with his mouth full. "I do worry about you. But, I get it—you've got to live your life."

"What about Jess?" I asked.

"What about her?"

"Is she, you know, giving you a hard time? She's dressed all weird and everything."

Dave finished his burger in two more bites and chewed for a long time.

"Jesse," he said as he reached for the platter, helping himself to another burger, "has and always will be her own person. But I'll manage just like I always do."

* * *

I stayed for three days, taking the Greyhound back to London on a weekday afternoon. All I could think about on the bus ride home was Jason's mom. Marla, glamorous Marla. I couldn't get her out of my mind. The image of her body floating in the ice-cold water of her basement pool permeated every thought. I needed to talk to Jason about what had happened to her, but when I got home I found a note on the refrigerator: "Gone to see my dad," it said.

I was sitting down at one of our new kitchen chairs when some kind of movement caught the corner of my eye. On the kitchen counter, right beside the dingy stainless steel sink, was a rat. Its body was white and spotted. Its eyes looked dark and red. I was so surprised to see it I couldn't even scream. I sat frozen, unsure about what to do.

The rat peered inside the sink and scoped out whatever was in there. Then it scurried along the counter, jumped down to the kitchen floor and ran inside the bathroom.

I leaped out of the chair, closed the door to the bathroom and ran to the bedroom, where I grabbed the phone and called Jason at his dad's.

"There's a fucking rat in the apartment!" I shrieked.

"Melanie, I can't talk right now."

"Did you hear what I said?" I was panting, breathless. "There's a rat in the apartment! I trapped it in the bathroom."

"Okay, Mel, I'm with my dad right now, so I can't really help you from out here."

"What am I supposed to do?" I thought of all the things my mother had to deal with when we lived in our series of rundown rentals: silverfish, spiders, centipedes, a mouse. But never something as big and ugly as a rat.

"Can you call someone? Call an extermination company. You're going to have to deal with this yourself."

"Oh my God, Jason, I really wish I wasn't alone right now."

"Sorry, Mel." His voice grew quieter. "We actually just got back from the hospital."

"What?"

"My dad was having some chest pains. They ran some tests and kept him last night for observation. We just got back home now."

"Oh," I said. "Is he going to be okay?"

"I think so. He just needs some rest ... and so do I."

"Wow, Jason, sorry. All I saw was the note on the fridge and so I didn't realize. I hope everything's okay."

"Yeah, me too. It's just that I might ... I might need to stay here for awhile."

"What? For how long?"

"I don't know, Mel. I just need—I just need a bit of time."

I didn't hear from Jason for three days. I was alone. In the dingy basement apartment I'd dubbed the rat-hole. The exterminator had managed to remove my un-wanted visitor, but it didn't matter. Every time I heard even the slightest noise, I panicked.

Finally, I got a phone call. The good news was that Jason's father was doing fine. The bad news was more surprising.

"I need to stay here a while longer. Maybe until the end of the school year ... which isn't that long when you think about it. It's just another month or so."

"You're not coming back?" He had to be kidding.

"I *am* coming back. Just not now. Dad needs me for a few more weeks, so I'm going to take a leave from school and teaching. I'll be back by April."

"But I just moved out of residence … to be with you. We just got settled." I felt like I was going to cry.

"I know. I'm sorry."

It felt like Jason was waiting for me to say something. "Is your dad doing better?" I finally asked. "Did he have a heart attack?"

"We're not sure."

"Do you know what it is?"

"Not yet …. Listen, Mel, it's only a few weeks. I'm really sorry to do this to you, but I'll be back as soon as I can. Promise."

It wasn't his fault. I couldn't be mad at him. But I was deflated.

I finished the school year alone in the rathole. The winter was long. The time went by slowly. Despite being a part of a busy campus, I felt isolated.

To help me cope with everything, I decided to take up running. On a cold and grey morning, I headed toward the Thames River, a less impressive version of its namesake in Britain. Though quite narrow, it meandered through the city with purpose and enveloped parts of the campus I'd never seen before. I found a path that shouldered the river and jogged sluggishly at first, picking up speed as I went along. The water moved slowly for the most part but sped at certain points—as if it was racing toward something finite.

To complement my new running routine, I studied hard and focused on my final exams. By the end of the year, my marks were so high that I received a congratulatory letter from the dean's office.

I called Dave and told him right away.

"Well that's great, kiddo—I'm so proud of you."

"Thanks Dave. I'm hoping it'll help me get into graduate school."

"You mean there's another school after this one? When does it ever end?"

I gave him a chuckle. "You know, I was thinking about being a teacher."

"Well, I think that's great, Mel Belle. I'm so proud of you."

"Thanks, Dave. But don't be proud yet. I still have to graduate."

Jason got back to London, finally, in May. Although it was a longer stay than he'd expected, he returned just in time for us to sign a new lease. After weeks of searching, I found a great new place I thought we should move into: a bright downtown walk-up on top of a clothing store with large windows and reasonable rent. Though further from campus, it had two bedrooms, high ceilings and was a short walk from Ruthie's. I brought Jason to see it the same afternoon he got home.

"Looks nice, Mel," he said afterward, standing on the sidewalk outside. "Really modern. Really bright."

"Thank goodness," I said. "I'm done with the rathole."

"Hey," Jason said. "I hope this is a better place for us. I'm really sorry about leaving you before." I nodded as he put his arms around me. "And thanks for being so understanding about everything. My dad really needed me."

I was still feeling bruised. I'd abandoned student residence and then spent the rest of the semester alone.

"I get it," I said. "And I hope he's better now? What are the doctors saying?"

"Not much—just that he should take it easy and stay on top of his meds."

"Does he have a pacemaker?"

"Pacemaker? No. It didn't end up being a heart attack. It's really more like ... what I guess you'd call ... psychological attacks."

"Psychological?"

"Anxiety."

"Oh."

"It may not sound that serious, but he gets these bad attacks. It's pretty intense."

I remembered what I could of Jason's dad: the taut running shorts, the knee-high socks, the sunny disposition. It was hard to connect that person to the man Jason was describing. But I didn't disbelieve him.

"So what happens now?" I asked.

"I cross my fingers that he's all right and then we move into this apartment," Jason said, leaning toward me to kiss my forehead. "A fresh start is what we need."

I wasn't sure where I'd heard it, but I knew I'd heard that before.

———◦◦◦———

Chapter Fifteen

JUST THE BEGINNING

January 2000

Three weeks into Y2K, Jason said he wanted to take me somewhere.

"It's a surprise," he said. "But we have to go back home for the weekend."

"Where are we going? I need to know what to wear."

"Daytime event. Something nice but not too formal."

I didn't have any other details, but I wondered if the surprise involved being reintroduced to his father. Despite our childhood connection, despite dating for several years, despite living together, I'd not seen his dad since I was a child. I wondered if it had to do with the death of his mother. Even though we'd been together all this time, Jason still didn't know I knew the truth. Or maybe he was embarrassed of his father. Or of me. I didn't have any answers, so I waited patiently and respected his privacy. Secretly, though, I wondered how much privacy he needed. All throughout high school and now in university, I had felt like an outsider. That outsider status continued even in this relationship. But, if Jason and I were ever going to have a future together, the wall that existed between us needed to come down.

We went home in early February, pulling into the underground parking lot of a downtown hotel. I looked at Jason curiously, wondering if we were going to meet his dad for lunch. To look respectable for the occasion, I'd put on a long black skirt and a tweed blazer.

I tapped on Jason's shoulder as he led me into the elevator. "Is there a restaurant we're going to?" I asked.

"Restaurant? No. This is something else. You'll see."

As soon as the elevator doors opened, I had a stronger sense of what was going on. Jason led me by the elbow as he followed the signs that promised "Items of Prestige." We walked into a large ballroom where rows of jewellery, vases and other items were on display. Jason stood beside me as I stared at a glass case that housed dozens of rings, necklaces and bracelets in a bedding of royal blue velvet.

"Am I supposed to be doing something?" I asked him.

"I thought you could pick out a ring," he said, grinning.

"A ring."

"Yes, an engagement ring. My mom used to go to auctions all the time. You can find some nice things."

Jason smiled and my stomach flipped. But the excitement was tinged with a sense of bewilderment. I really hadn't expected an engagement to come before meeting his father again.

"Is something wrong, Mel? I thought you'd want this. We've talked about it for ages. Please say yes."

"Yes," I said. "Of course."

He grabbed me in his arms, lifted me up off my feet and twirled me around the hotel ballroom. A small group of spectators clapped and cheered, and Jason placed me back on my feet. He saluted the group with his boyish smile and then turned back toward me.

"Would you prefer a proper jewellery store?" he said quietly, aware we still had a small audience. "We can do that instead if you want … I thought this place might have things with more history. More character."

"No, no, this is perfect," I said. "Let's take a look."

We shuffled through the aisles of the ballroom and scanned the items on display. I saw chunky gold bracelets, ruby earrings and an emerald ring, most of them gaudy relics from the eighties. "This is really fancy," I said. "Are you sure this is a good idea?"

"Keep looking," he said. I obliged and walked around the row of glass enclosures until something caught my eye. Lot item #121 was a simple but beautiful solitaire, a rounded diamond on an elegant band of white gold.

"That one," I said, nudging Jason in the side. He leaned over to get a better look as I grabbed a catalogue. I flipped through the list until I found it. "Minimum bid is two thousand," I said.

I finished eyeing the items but didn't see anything better. Jason took me by both my hands. "So," he said, looking at me. "What do you think?"

"It's nice," I said. "I like it."

"Me too. It's perfect."

"So what happens next? Do we put a bid on it now?"

"Not yet," he said. "We come back tomorrow. This is just the viewing. Tomorrow's the auction."

We headed back to the car in the underground lot. Jason did three donuts, circling up the levels to the exit. His turn signal was on as he waited for a break in traffic. I wondered if there was a second part to the surprise, if being engaged meant I could finally meet his father again. Too many aspects of his life still felt shrouded in secrecy. I needed to throw it all out in the open.

"So," I said, turning to face him as he looked through the side window. "Does getting engaged mean I'm finally going to meet your dad again? Or will you continue to keep me away?"

The traffic had cleared, but Jason kept his foot on the brake.

"What are you talking about?" he said, turning toward me. "You're not separate from my life—whatever that means."

"I really don't know about that, Jason. Why haven't I seen your dad since we started dating? We've been together for *years.*"

Jason drove out of the lot, but immediately pulled over to the side of the street. He kept his gaze fixed straight ahead as the indicator clicked rhythmically.

"Melanie, maybe this is hard for you to understand, but this isn't about you. Things are very complicated. My dad hasn't been great since my mom died."

"I know that."

"Yeah, I know."

"And so? Now we're supposed to be getting married. Why haven't I been back to meet him?"

"When I say Dad's not well, I mean it. He went mad after Mom died. He hasn't worked since. The house is in a state of disrepair."

"So you keep me away? As if we're not in a relationship? And you tell me lies?"

"These aren't lies," he said.

"The story about your mother." I'd held back on bringing it up for so long that the words came out by themselves. "My dad told me what really happened. As if I wouldn't find out? Why didn't you just tell me the truth?"

"Like I said, Mel, things are complicated."

"Stop lying to me, Jason. Every family is complicated."

Jason turned to look at me. "What, like yours? Tell me then, Mel, why haven't you told me the truth about your own mother? I know she left you as a kid. I know she's probably still alive. And you've never talked to me about it—never."

I was shocked that he knew. How did he keep this to himself all this time? It felt like there'd been so much secrecy between us.

"It's different, Jason, it's not the same."

"Really? How so?"

"I told you that lie as a kid—I was eleven and I didn't know what I was saying. It was something I needed to tell you about, something I planned to tell you about. But when I found out about your own mom and how she really died, it became awkward for me. I didn't know how to bring it up."

"You needed me to tell the truth before you could?" He looked incredulous.

"I guess you could say that."

"Mel, you can't even compare the two situations. You don't understand. Dad lied to me about all of it. He tried to keep the truth from everyone. He didn't want anybody knowing what really happened."

"Which was what? Tell me what happened."

Jason adjusted the rear-view mirror and relaxed his shoulders. He cleared his throat as if exercising his vocal chords. As if there was a lot to say.

"I went home on a Thanksgiving weekend and Mom wasn't there. Dad was home alone and pretty much freaking out, pacing around the house in his underwear. His eyes were bloodshot and his hair was a mess. You should have seen the look on his face when he saw me walk through the front door. He clearly wasn't expecting me. I asked him what was going on, where Mom was, and he told me the story of finding her dead, calling the ambulance, trying to revive her and having the coroner arrive.

"There were empty bottles of wine and gin all throughout the basement and I suspected—I *knew*—what had happened. But Dad denied Mom had been drinking and even suggested the possibility that somebody had drugged her. It was all bullshit, I knew it was, but he was in absolute denial and said an autopsy would determine the truth. When he finally got the results, he wouldn't let me see it, but he said it showed she died of a brain aneurysm. I didn't believe him, but when he caught me looking for the report in his office, he wrestled me to the ground. He told me that, if I loved Mom, and if I wanted to remember her fondly, that I needed to stop challenging the truth and let things be. And so that's the story he's stuck to and that's the story he tells."

I felt so many things at that moment—surprise, guilt, doubt, relief—but I didn't know which one to trust. "I'm sorry," I said.

"Me too. I should have told you, but it was just one of those things that was easier to ignore, especially because my dad's still pretty messed up about everything."

"I get it." I paused. "I'm also sorry for not telling you the truth about my mom. She left right after Jesse was born. Poor Dave was left all alone to raise us and I'm not even his daughter."

Jason let a few seconds of silence pass. "That's rough," he said.

The right-hand turn signal was still clicking. "It's been a source of anger and, I guess, shame my whole life. It's created so much …" I didn't even know if I could say it.

"What?" Jason asked.

"Insecurity."

"I guess that's to be expected."

"How did you even know about my mom? Did your dad tell you when he learned we were dating?"

"Yeah, it was my dad," Jason said. "Your Dave never told him, I don't think, but it was one of those open secret things with the running club. I guess those guys gossip like everyone else."

"I guess," I said.

"Listen, you can meet my dad. In time—it needs to be at the right moment. He's asked to see you, honestly."

"Okay, I understand. I really do. And I'm sorry about your mom. It's such a terrible story. But we're getting married now. We're going to be family. We need to stop keeping secrets from each other."

"I didn't want to keep anything from you."

I felt like I needed some time alone, to process everything. "Okay," I said. "Maybe just take me back."

With his left hand, Jason reached out and tucked a strand of hair behind my ear. Then he flipped his turn signal, merged back onto the street and headed north to Dave's.

* * *

The next morning, I was washing dishes at the sink when the phone rang. "The auction starts at one," Jason said. "I'll be by to get you at noon."

He arrived right on time, tapping the horn lightly to signal he'd arrived. I walked out of the house wearing heels, a dress and a parka. It was an icy winter day, the kind where the wind slices through everything like a meat cleaver. I smiled weakly as soon as I saw him, still feeling overwhelmed by our conversation the day before.

"Hi," I said as I sat in the passenger seat. "Wasn't sure I'd ever hear from you again."

"Yeah right," he said.

We got to the hotel with twenty minutes to spare. The ballroom we'd visited the day before had been outfitted with a podium and chairs, so we took an aisle seat. People filed into the room steadily; almost everyone arrived in pairs.

The auctioneer started with the first lot item, a loose canary yellow diamond. There were two bidders—an overweight lady with bright red hair and a long green dress, and a balding middle-aged man with dark circles under his eyes. I turned to my side and watched both of them as they raised their paddles until, finally, the tired-looking man relented and the fat lady won. Jason elbowed me in my side as my neck remained twisted. "Could you try to play it cool?" he said. "Stop turning your head every time someone makes a bid."

"Sorry," I said. "This is exciting."

"Just let me do the bidding when our time comes."

"I want to hold the paddle," I whispered.

"No," Jason said, keeping his head straight. "Sit there and don't move."

The auctioneer went down the list. A gold geometric necklace whose replica was worn on the set of *Dynasty* resulted in a bidding war between two men. Three sets of gaudy earrings went unsold without a single bid. About halfway through the auction we got to my item, the simple solitaire. The auctioneer introduced the ring to the audience and opened the bidding at two thousand. I tried to turn around to scan the room, but Jason took my hand and squeezed it hard. He raised the paddle slowly and waited.

The auctioneer spent a minute inviting others in the room to put in an offer but nobody was interested. I held my breath as I waited for something to happen. The man pointed to Jason and said "Sold!"

I clapped my hands and bounced up and down in my seat, a display of excitement that caused Jason to look away in embarrassment. We sat through the rest of the auction and paid at the end, collecting our ring from an office adjacent to the showroom.

The ring was in a tiny plastic bag with the lot number affixed to it. I took it out immediately, slipping the diamond onto my finger.

"Looks nice," Jason said. "Fits, too."

I wriggled my finger around to see if that was the case. It was loose, but I tried not to notice. "It's perfect," I said.

With my newly minted finger, Jason and I headed to the lobby and found the hotel bar. Jason ordered us each a glass of Champagne, which I toasted with my left hand so that I could admire my gem. "It's so sparkly," I said. "Does it suit me?"

"Pretty nice," he said. "It was a good score."

I waved my fingers as if I was playing a piano, admiring how the diamond caught the overhead light. The ring's history intrigued me: who owned it before me and why didn't they want it any longer? Sipping my Champagne, I pictured someone else's dead skin cells trapped in the grooves of the white gold. "I should really clean it as soon as I get home," I said.

Jason looked at his watch after we finished our drinks. "Let's go," he said, tapping its face. "There's somewhere we need to be."

"There is?" I asked, looping my arm in his. "Should I not have dressed up?"

"You look perfect."

The suspense of our destination did not last long. "So," I said as soon as Jason had merged onto the highway. "Where are we going?"

"You know where we're going," he said. "Just do me a favour—let's not talk about the engagement yet, okay? I need to pace things out with my dad. He's pretty fragile."

I nodded, feeling my heart flutter at the thought of being back in his family home. I took the ring off my finger and tucked it into the side pocket of my purse. Forty minutes later, we pulled into the long and narrow driveway. The red brick Georgian with double doors looked like a faded and decrepit version of the house from childhood.

"This place isn't what it used to be," Jason said. He turned off the vehicle and put his keys in his pocket.

As we got out of the car, the dilapidated house came into focus. The shingles of the roof were weathered and torn while the overgrown evergreens cast a pall over the facade. The brass pineapple doorknocker was badly tarnished and the black lacquer of the front double doors had dulled with age and neglect.

Jason grabbed the blackened handle on the pineapple and tapped it six times with a brief pause between the fourth and fifth beats. "I guess it's kind of a secret knock. He doesn't want me having my own keys."

We waited for at least a minute until we heard a series of locks being unfastened. Jason fidgeted. I smoothed my hair. Finally, the door swung open.

"Hello!"

A man was standing before us with long grey hair and an overgrown beard. His dark green sweatpants were too short for his legs and his sweatshirt was dirty, torn and ragged around the neck.

"Hi Dad," Jason said, walking through the front door as he held my hand.

"Entrez-vous! Don't mind the mess." I looked around and took in the walls I hadn't seen in more than a decade.

It was as if the house had been stopped in time. The grand entryway, with its elegant staircase and crystal chandelier, was coated in dust. The lights were off and the house was draped in darkness. It was ice cold, the hum of the furnace absent.

Jason's dad leaned toward me, taking both of my hands in his. The skin of his fingers was cracked and dry, like rough leather.

"How's your father?" he asked.

"He's well. Busy with my sister and still making airplane parts. Not running anymore, though—he gave that up ages ago."

"Oh well. At our age, that's to be expected." He turned to Jason. "So ... you had a good day?"

"We did."

"That's great."

"Spent the afternoon downtown."

"That's terrific. Really terrific. Well, I don't want to keep you. It was good of you to stop by."

We stood there, the three of us in the foyer of the home. We still had our coats on. I squeezed Jason's hand, unsure what to do.

"Thanks, Dad," Jason said as he leaned over and gave his father a hug.

"Great seeing both of you. Say hello to your father, Melanie."

"I will," I said, following Jason's lead as he opened the door to go back to the car. We could hear the series of locks being fastened as we walked away.

I didn't say anything until we were back inside the car. "Does he have running water?" I asked.

"Of course he does ... but he doesn't take good care of himself. I hope you're not too spooked."

"Not spooked. Just a bit sad, I guess."

"When Mom died, he fell apart. He didn't even try to hold it together. A couple of months after it happened, I tried to organize a trip skiing—just the two of us. But when we got there, Dad didn't want to ski. So we just sat around, most of the time in the hotel lobby. Dad drank gin and tonics all day, talking to anybody and everybody who crossed our paths. He'd speak about

Mom nonstop, telling them all the same story about how she died of an aneurysm. By the end of the week, nobody would go near us. It was just awful."

"I'm sorry."

"After we got home, he left his law firm. It was supposed to be a temporary break at first, but he never went back. He became more and more of a hermit. Now he hardly leaves the living room—it's where he eats and sleeps. The other parts of the house have been abandoned."

"And what about the rest of your family? Your mom had a brother, right? You have cousins?"

"They were strung along with Dad's story the same as me. We were never really that close, but my uncle got pissed at Dad and now we barely talk. Usually it's just a phone call over the holidays. I'm not sure they fully understand how severe Dad's descent has been."

"Wow," I said. I put my hand in the side pocket of my purse, making sure my ring was still there. "So, what do we do about the wedding? Would you want your dad to come?"

Jason put the keys in the ignition and looked in the rear-view mirror as he reversed out of the long driveway. "I don't know if it's a good idea, Mel. I don't really see him coming."

"But he's your dad—"

"I know, but I don't want to complicate things," he said. "We need to move forward with no expectations. Let's please just try to move forward."

With that, he put the car in drive, pressed his foot on the gas and sped away.

* * *

We got married a few weeks later at London City Hall on a Friday. Dave walked me down the aisle as Jesse, Becky, Ron, Ruthie, Claire and a couple of Jason's engineering friends looked on. I wore a pale yellow dress and Jason wore a blue suit. Jesse arrived wearing head-to-toe black with a shoulder-length veil for effect. Unsurprisingly, Jason's dad didn't come. We'd invited him, but he said he didn't feel up to making the trip out.

We went out to dinner afterward at an Italian place downtown. The party was elegant and simple—no obligatory dancing, extravagant cake or silly speeches. But at the end of the night, Dave pulled me aside to speak to me privately.

"I couldn't be happier for you, Mel Belle," he said, squeezing me with both his arms.

"Thanks, Dave." My face pressed up against his chest.

"It's just that ... you've already been away longer than I expected. Are you sure you two want to stay here in London? I was kind of hoping you'd return home one day."

Dave was right: I took an extra year to finish my degree so I could spend more time working. But now six weeks away from graduation, I'd been accepted at the local teachers college. Jason had a full-time position at a food processing plant and I had another side job at a daycare centre around the corner. It may not have been what Dave wanted to hear, but it looked like we'd be there for some time. The pieces of my life that I'd planned for so long were finally falling into place. "I think so," I said. "It just feels right."

"Well, you do what you've got to do. And you know you can always count on me, just like always."

"I know."

"I really am proud of you, kiddo. I know you always felt like you didn't have a family of your own, but after your mom left, I want you to know I did the best that I could."

I could taste my lipstick as I bit my lip. I may have been marrying Jason, but Dave was still the most wonderful person in my life.

"I know you did," I said, trying not to cry.

Releasing me from his arms, Dave took both my shoulders in his hands so we were eye to eye. "But now it's your turn to build your home and the life you've always wanted. And this," he said, motioning to the party with one of his hands, "is just the beginning of—"

The sound of shattered dishes and a woman's gasp cut Dave off. We turned toward the commotion and noticed someone sprawled on the floor. Whoever it was, they had managed to take half the tablecloth and most of its contents down with them.

"Oh my God," Becky shrieked. "Are you okay?"

A small crowd gathered around as two waiters rushed to clean up the mess. I peered through the circle of bystanders, noticing a hand clutch the table, and then a black veil.

It was Jesse. Of course it was.

"It's fine, I'm fine," she said as she stood up, holding onto the edge of the now-barren table. Miraculously, her other hand maintained its grip on a wine glass that had managed to survive the tumble.

I turned back toward Dave. "She's drinking alcohol, you know." I didn't mention the fact that she'd also interrupted a special moment for me.

But Dave just smiled and shrugged his shoulders. On a day like today, not even Jesse could break his spirit.

Chapter Sixteen

HOME

May 2000

I DISCOVERED A new running route, this one away from the Thames. I traded the serenity of the river for city sidewalks and its adjacent residential pockets. The buzz of downtown traffic and random encounters with Ruthie's regulars may have been chaotic, but it felt comforting.

Along this route I discovered a peculiar-looking home west of downtown. It was tiny, a storey and a half, and unusually close to the sidewalk. The powder blue siding was accented with white shutters and a painted white door that was slightly off-centre. The porch was a simple slab of concrete (no handrails); the landscaping was a flat mane of grass (no flower beds). It was so cute and small, I half-expected a gingerbread family to emerge from the front door.

I continued to casually admire it until the Sunday morning I jogged by and noticed a For Sale sign posted on the front lawn. I stopped and stared at the house, its charming blue hue, the steeply sloped roof and the lack of driveway. Skipping the next leg of my run, I went back home, tapping Jason on the shoulder while he was still asleep.

"Wake up," I said. "There's something I want you to see."

He rubbed his eyes and looked at his watch. "What is it?"

"It's a surprise. But you have to get up."

I drew the curtains open and then jumped back on the bed, rubbing the small of his back. As soon as he slid on his jogging pants and sweatshirt, I grabbed his hand and led him down the stairs. "But I haven't brushed my teeth," he said.

"No need. Let's go."

I held his hand as I led the way, walking the nine minutes it took to get there. "You see?" I said, standing at the foot of the concrete path that led us to the white door. "It's adorable. And perfect for us." It was also the perfect place to start a family, something I didn't have the courage to say.

Jason stood with his hands in his pockets, his face being pelted with a rain that had picked up unexpectedly. "It's small," he said. "And it probably needs a lot of work."

I ignored his comment and set up an appointment so we could see it later that day. I knew it was ideal and didn't want to lose it—the price and location made it the perfect place for us.

Jason was silent as we made our way there again, this time in the car. Once we'd parked, we walked up the concrete pathway and climbed the steps to the front door. The realtor greeted us cheerfully, showing us the main floor and two bedrooms upstairs. While the outside siding was blue, everything inside was white: white paint, white floors, white cabinets. But instead of feeling sterile, the home felt warm. The wood countertop in the kitchen and fireplace in the living room made everything cozy.

Jason dragged his feet behind us. When we were done, we thanked the realtor for his time and walked back to the car.

"So, what do you think?" I asked. "Adorable, right?"

"It's not bad," he said. "But we can't afford it."

"What do you mean?" I asked. The house, while charming, was not out of reach. And we were both working. I had two jobs, in fact (though my waitressing gig at the seedy downtown pub paid more than my respectable daycare position). We did, however, need a down payment. "We could easily make the mortgage on that," I said. "We're both bringing in decent enough money."

"You still have a year of teachers college ahead of you," Jason said. "Besides, we don't have a down payment. We don't have the money."

"We have some," I said. "Plus," I added, hesitating as I held my breath.

"Plus what?"

"Plus ..." I shouldn't have even had to say it. "You have your father to help."

"You want *my* family to pay for it?" He looked at me, eyes wide, as if I'd asked for the moon.

"I'm not asking anyone to pay for all of it. What I'm saying is, I have money to contribute, money that I've saved. And you have options, too."

"Listen, Mel, I don't know what you're thinking, but I'm not made of money."

"If I thought you were made of money, I would have taken you to another house."

"It's not fair to even ask. There are certain family … reserves, but I'm not sure I have access to those. I'd have to talk to Dad. I don't think I can do that right now."

"Fine," I said. "I don't want you to have to ask your father. I thought you'd have something of your own. And just so we're clear, I'm not asking you to buy me a house. I'm asking for us to buy a house together. I thought this would be a nice place to start our life."

The rain pattered against the windshield as we sat in silence. Jason started the car and the wipers jolted to life. It was early afternoon, but the sky was a dark grey. A car drove by with its lights on. Jason put his on, too. He pulled away from the curb, letting me have the last word.

The house sold three weeks later. Two months after that, an older woman moved in. The new owner liked to garden at the front of the house and planted a small bed with red and pink snapdragons. I wondered why she'd moved there and why she lived alone, if her husband had died, or if she'd recently retired. I wanted to ask her why she chose that house. Instead, I took notice from the sidewalk, careful to maintain my jogging pace so that she didn't suspect I was watching.

With the house sold to someone else, I resigned myself to painting the apartment. The ceilings were high and beautiful, but the walls were scuffed up. I wanted something fresh. Jason and I went to the paint store and scanned the colour board displayed on the wall, the sample chips spread like a mesmerizing fan. It was easy to make our choice: pale yellow. We bought the paint and brought it home.

Jason and I moved the furniture, taped the sideboards and started painting. Once we got the first coat on the walls of the living room, the place started to feel more familiar. We moved on to the kitchen and then the main foyer. "It's almost like we're bathing the skin of a turkey in warm butter," I said. "It's nice, isn't it?"

Jason looked up and then teeter-tottered his head, as if to say "so-so."

I was about to open our second can of paint when I heard the phone ring. Pulling off my gloves, I ran to the kitchen and picked up the receiver.

It was Dave, breathing heavily.

"It's Dougie," he said. "I'm at the vet right now. He's been swollen for days and so I took him in. But I knew, Mel. I knew it was bad."

"Oh no," I said.

Just shy of seventeen, Dougie had been blind and limping for the past year and a half. Identical in age, Luke still had his eyesight, but he would not move from his favourite spot on the floor of the living room unless he had to pee. Both were well beyond the life expectancy of their breed.

"The vet says we really have no choice but to put him down. She'll wait for you if you can come home today."

Sensing the pain in Dave's voice, I cancelled my shift at Ruthie's the following night and took the next Greyhound back to Toronto. At the station, I jumped into a taxi and went directly to the vet, where I met with

Dave in the waiting room. He brought me to Dougie, who was lying on a table. His eyes were closed and his breathing was shallow. I put my hand on his side and waited for his tail to wag, but it didn't move.

"Thanks for coming, kiddo," Dave said as he patted Dougie's head. "The last couple of years have been really tough for this guy."

The vet came in a bit later and the lump swelled in my throat as I watched her prepare her tray. "I can't watch," I said. "I need to wait in the hall."

Dave nodded and moved out of the way. "Don't be too sad. The vet says we have the oldest collies she's ever seen. He's been a good dog and he's had a good life. Say your goodbyes."

I leaned over and put my face to Dougie's, rubbing the space behind his right ear. "Goodbye, Dougie," I said. "Don't worry about Luke—we'll take good care of him."

I gave his face a kiss and left the room, waiting in the hallway until it was over. Dave emerged less than half-an-hour later with the blood drained from his face. "Let's go," he said as he put his arm around me. It wasn't until we were in the parking lot that I thought to ask about Jess.

"She stayed with a friend this weekend," he said, taking his keys out of his pocket.

"But didn't you call her?" I asked. "Didn't she want to be here for this? I came all the way from London."

"She said she was busy and that it'd be too sad."

"I don't know how this is okay," I said. "She's known Dougie since she was born."

"Melanie, I'm tired of arguing with her about things. Your sister's a very different person than you are. If I told her what to do all the time, all I'd do is push her away even further."

"She's sixteen, okay? Not twenty-one."

Dave sat in the driver's seat of the car and put the keys in the ignition. "Yes, I know, but she needs a lot of freedom. In a lot of ways, she's like ..." He started the car without finishing what he'd set out to say. "You know what, kiddo, I honestly think it's sometimes best to let people be. And that's what we need to do with your sister—just let her be."

I wanted to let it slide, but I couldn't. Dougie had died only minutes ago and here Dave was bending over backwards to defend Jesse. But the truth was she should have been there for Dave. She should have been there for Dougie. Instead, like usual, she was allowed to do what she wanted.

"You know what?" I said, turning toward him. "You're wrong." Dave slumped his shoulders and gently sighed. "Jesse gets away with everything. She gets a free pass all the time. But she should have been here today— she should have been here for her family."

Dave kept his focus forward, not bothering to turn toward me in the passenger seat. "Parenthood, Melanie, is not what you think. You can't always control your children."

The more he spoke, the more he reminded me of Mom. Telling me how hard it is. Telling me that life follows its own, stupid path. But I wouldn't hear it. I was done with it. I was done with it all.

"You can say whatever you like—you can defend Jesse until you're blue in the face." I was angry now, angry for Dougie. Angry for all of us. "But if Jesse had been my daughter, things would have been different. I would have straightened her out a long time ago and turned her around for good."

I studied Dave's face, searching for a reaction, wondering how he'd respond to the dagger I'd flung. But Dave didn't give me the satisfaction. Instead, he simply put the car in reverse, pulled out of the parking spot and drove home.

CHAPTER SEVENTEEN

BACK TO SCHOOL

September 2002

LEGS CROSSED AT the knee, high-heeled foot jiggling, I sat and admired the view from my desk. It was the end of my first day teaching Grade Two and the classroom looked pristine. My students had been dismissed twenty minutes earlier, and I'd just finished tidying things up. On my desk were several plastic containers, each one filled two-thirds of the way through with paperclips, pipe cleaners, cotton balls and popsicle sticks. Behind me, my black background gleamed. I had soaped and wiped every square of my lesson board, leaving not even a hint of chalk dust.

I was feeling pretty good about myself when I heard my cellphone buzzing at the bottom of my purse. I reached under my desk and answered the call on the fourth ring, right before it would have been sent to voicemail.

"Melanie, you there?"

It was Dave.

"Hi," I said. "Are you at work?"

"I'm home today. I called because I wanted to check in on you ... and talk to you about a few things."

"What is it?" I said, sitting up in my chair. By the sound of his voice, I could tell it was important.

"It's your sister. She's moved out."

"What? What do you mean?"

"She's moved out of the house—with her boyfriend."

"She's eighteen!" I said.

"No kidding. And not only that, she's dropped out of school. Imagine that, her final year and she's just not bothering."

Dave couldn't see me, but I shrugged my shoulders. "Well, no surprise there," I said.

"I'm at my wit's end with her. It's constant worrying and wondering where she is. Not coming home at night, never giving a damn about her studies. And this boyfriend that she's got—his name's Gruff, for Christ's sakes. What kind of name is that? I don't like him one bit."

"Ugh," I said. "I don't want to meet him."

"Believe me, you *don't*."

"So what happens now? What do we do?"

"What can I do?" Dave asked. At this point, his voice wavered. He sounded like he was about to crack. "She's an adult now. I can't control her."

"I don't know what to tell you," I said. "I'm sorry you have to deal with this."

There was a long pause at the other end of the line, and I wondered if the connection was lost.

"Thing is, I'm not sure what I did differently."

"What do you mean?"

"What I mean is, I don't know what I did differently with her than you. Of course, you were a bit older when I took over as your dad. But somehow I thought, and forgive me for saying this Melanie, but I thought that

Jesse would have had a better shot at things. She was never dragged around from house to house the way you were as a child. And she never knew the pain of having her mother leave her. In many ways, I like to think, she had a better upbringing."

I knew what he meant.

"You know," he said. "At this point, I don't even give a rat's ass about her schooling. I just want her home and away from this deadbeat. She just met him this summer—she hardly knows the guy."

I felt bad for Dave and knew I was partly to blame. Jesse was one of the main reasons why I'd left home. Instead of staying to help my family, I had run away from it. "I'm sorry, Dave. I wish she'd listen to me. I wish I could call her up or even go to see her and talk some sense into her, but you know she won't listen, you know she won't—"

"I know, Mel."

"Why's she so difficult?"

"I just don't know," he said. "On the bright side, at least I know where she's at. I can check up on her when I need."

"That's good."

"Yeah," Dave said, sighing. "Anyway, kiddo, how are you doing out there? How was your first day in the classroom?"

"Pretty good," I said. "I have a great group of students."

"That's good, Mel Belle. Take care of yourself."

We said our goodbyes and he promised to keep me posted.

I drove home in my new car, which was not really new but a used sedan I bought as soon as I got the job offer. It had low mileage and good fuel efficiency, perfect for someone like me who didn't know cars and didn't like to drive. I parked in one of our rented spots behind our apartment and walked inside to find Jason on the couch, watching TV.

"Hey," I said. "You're home early."

He got up from the couch and gave me a kiss on my forehead. "How was your first day?"

I didn't feel like talking about Jess. I didn't want her drama tainting the energy of my special day. "Super," I said. "They seem like sweet kids." Jason smiled. "I'm thinking I need to get some of those stickers, you know the ones you put on assignments that say 'Terrific!' and 'Well done!' You ever seen those?"

Jason shook his head.

"I guess they don't give those out in private school. Anyway," I said as I dropped my purse on the floor and headed to the kitchen, "I'll figure it out." I poured myself a glass of water and turned back around to find Jason looking at me. He was grinning ear to ear.

"What is it?" I asked. "And why are you home so early?"

"A happy reason," he said. "I've got an appointment—and you're coming with me."

"An appointment? For what?"

"Don't get too excited, but I've been talking to a woman just outside of Windsor who breeds Corgis. Sweetest little things. She's got a litter on the way and so I thought I'd head out there, see the mom and maybe … put down a deposit."

"A dog?"

"What do you think?"

I wanted a baby, not a dog. And Jason knew that. "I'm not sure, Jason ... I just don't think ... I don't think it's the right time."

"Think about it, Mel—you love dogs."

"I know I do." I took in a deep breath. "But you also know I want to have a baby soon, and—"

"Here we go again," he said. He crossed his arms across his chest and stared at me as if it was a showdown.

I'd had the courage to bring it up, so I wasn't going to let it go so easily. "You know, I don't get you," I said. "I really don't. This was always in my plan. Our plan. And I thought you always wanted what your parents had."

"I wanted their marriage, Mel, but kids? I do, Mel—I mean, I will. Just not right now."

"I want a family," I said. "I've always wanted one. And you know that. You just want a dog because you're trying to stall me. This is your way of trying to shut me up."

"What? How can you even say that?" He moved his hands to his hips, as if he'd been offended.

"I want to start a family. End of story."

"I know, Mel. And we will. But it isn't easy—you of all people should know that."

"Don't pull that with me, Jason. That's not fair."

"The point is, I think it would be great to get a dog for the time being. You just started teaching. Let's focus on that and the pup. We've got lots of time to have a kid."

He wasn't wrong, but I didn't care. "A dog feels like a stand-in," I said.

Jason walked over and put his arms around me. "A dog is not a stand-in. A dog is a dog."

I thought of Dougie and Luke Skywalker—both gone. Luke died just weeks after his brother had to be put down.

"A dog is ... fine," I said. "But it's not a permanent replacement. And I'm not driving to Windsor either. I want to turn in early and get a good night's sleep."

Jason kissed me on my forehead. "You're going to be so happy."

* * *

We brought Roxanne home a few weeks after she was born. She was a sweet girl, a playful corgi with caramel-swirled fur. Her tiny body trembled in my arms the entire car ride back to London. It was supposed to be Jason's dog; he was the one who brought her into our home. But it was me Roxanne was closest to. She followed me from room to room, constantly licked my face and curled up by my feet whenever I was on the couch.

Our daily walking routine gave us time to bond and explore the city. I took her by the river, where she liked to jump in the water, and sometimes we'd walk past the blue and white house. Jason had been right; getting a dog was the right decision. Any talk of a baby was put on hold.

I'd just returned from walking her one morning when Dave called to give me an update about Jess. There seemed to be a lot of them, and most weren't good.

"She's back home," he said. "Thank goodness."

I felt a surge of relief but wondered how long the reunion would last. "What happened with What's-His-Name?"

STEPHANIE CESCA

"Don't know. But Jesse has agreed to go back to school—and she says she'll enroll in a college program."

"Huh," I said. "You think it's for real?"

"Well, I hope. I'm just glad to have her back. And, so far, everything seems to be fairly calm."

"Huh," I said again. "I hope it is."

But Dave knew just as well as I did. Even when things were calm, they never stayed that way.

CHAPTER EIGHTEEN

THE ACCIDENT

April 2005

IT WAS EARLY spring and London was still trying to climb out of a dumping when another storm struck, this one more fierce. Shops were shuttered, schools were closed and transit buses were cancelled. Many offices told their employees to stay home. Those who had no choice ventured out in trepidation, cursing their bosses or whatever responsibility forced them to confront the unusual April weather.

Jason was one of the unlucky ones who not only had to work but had to work late. His boss needed help with a production issue, so he stayed through dinner at the office. I planned for a quiet evening at home.

I was in my pyjamas getting ready for bed when Roxanne scratched the foot of the bed. I put on my winter coat, took her down the stairwell, slipped on my boots and stepped outside. With the snow piled up, we weren't able to navigate the sidewalk, so we walked along the side of the street, which had been plowed. Even though there was a lot of it, the snow was not the wet, slushy kind streaked with grey and brown, but was fresh, white and powdery, blanketing the city as if it were a snow globe.

Roxanne and I were alone on the street. I saw a car drive by and heard a snowplough off in the distance, but, otherwise, downtown felt abandoned. We were about to turn around and go home when I noticed the headlights of a car in the distance, driving at a regular clip despite the blurry conditions. It was the only car on the road, its windshield wipers in full swing as they struggled to keep up with the snow that barreled down. As it approached the intersection, the traffic lights turned yellow. I stopped and waited at the lights, despite the absence of other cars. The oncoming vehicle also tried to stop but skidded instead, the tail of the car twisting. I tightened the dog leash, taking three steps back as Roxanne started to yelp. The barking took my attention away just long enough to delay my reaction as the car turned 90 degrees and veered in my direction. The sight of the passenger door was the last thing I saw before I was knocked down. When I opened my eyes, I was sprawled out on my back on the sidewalk, the leash no longer in my grip. I had not actually been run over; instead, the car flung me to the side like a bowling pin.

Sensing I wasn't badly hurt, I sat up and wondered where Roxanne was. I heard the door of the car open, and saw a man get out and run in my direction.

"Are you okay?" he asked as he crouched beside me. It was a guy in his thirties wearing a sweatshirt and a winter hat, but no jacket.

I ignored him for a second as I turned around. "Have you seen my dog?"

He followed my gaze, looking for a sign of life around us. "I don't see one ..."

"Roxanne!"

"Are you sure you're okay?"

"I think so," I said. I looked down and felt the right side of my ribs. "My side hurts, though."

I tried to stand up, but the man put his hand on my shoulder as a way to coax me to stay put. "Sit down," he said. "I'm calling an ambulance."

The police were the first to arrive. I told them what happened and asked if they could help me find Roxanne. One of the officers did a quick scan of the intersection and even checked under the man's car; there was no sign of her. I begged him to do more so he promised to drive around the neighbourhood looking for her. It was only when the ambulance whisked me away that I thought I should have looked for her paw prints before they were covered by snow.

The driver put on the siren, which I found unnecessary since I wasn't seriously injured. "We don't need to make a scene," I told the paramedics. "There aren't even any cars on the roads."

Two men pulled me out of the back of the ambulance at a hospital I had never seen before. "Where are we?" I asked. "We're not near campus."

"We're on Commissioners," one of the paramedics said. "Try not to move so much."

They wheeled me into a cordoned-off area on the main floor of the hospital, where I was examined, asked a series of questions and then finally moved somewhere else for testing.

"So, things don't appear to be too bad," the doctor said, looking over my chart. "You've got a slight fracture in your rib, but nothing punctured or anything of that sort."

"That's good," I said. "I knew my side was hurting."

"You never mentioned you were pregnant, though."

"Mentioned what?"

"On the report here … you're pregnant?"

"I'm … no. I'm pregnant? No."

The physician's eyes narrowed. "Right here," he said, tapping the chart. "You don't know?"

"I'm not sure," I said, clutching my side. "I mean, I don't know. My period's been a bit all over the place recently. Are you sure?"

"It appears so," he said. "Everything looks fine. It's still very early."

It was all so overwhelming—the accident, the dog, the pregnancy. I had to call Jason, I had to tell him. But I worried about how he'd react. If he was ready. I looked at the doctor. "Can I make a phone call?"

I broke the news to Jason, recounting in detail how the car slid and hit me, that Roxanne was lost, that the doctor said I was pregnant. Jason seemed confused by the tsunami of news. Mostly, though, I think he was in denial about the baby. "I don't understand," he said. "Are you sure? How come you didn't notice?"

"I guess it's because it's still pretty early."

Before I was discharged, the doctor encouraged me to follow up with an obstetrician as soon as possible. "Could have been a lot worse. Consider yourself lucky."

Our luck, though, ran out when it came to Roxanne. She was nowhere to be found. Once we were home, I called Dave to share the news while Jason visited the site of the accident. He did the same thing every day for the next two weeks, walking around the area and visiting the nearby parks that flanked the Thames. He put up "Lost Dog" signs all over the city in the hope that someone would help us reunite. We even visited the local pound. But each time, we returned home feeling like we were no closer to finding her. There was no sign of her anywhere, no leads to follow. It was as if she simply vanished.

But Jason wouldn't give up. He spoke about Roxanne endlessly. He even called Ruthie, asking if her regulars could keep their eyes open. To me, his determination bordered on obsession. Part of me wondered if fixating on the dog allowed him to avoid the reality of what was happening. If only he could find Roxanne, the whole series of events would undo themselves and I would no longer be pregnant.

I tried to mourn Roxanne but was distracted by everything going on in my body. Every day without Rox was another where the baby flourished. It hadn't sunk in and I had to keep reminding myself: I was going to be a mother.

CHAPTER NINETEEN

IT WASN'T
SUPPOSED TO BE

October 2005

TO NO ONE'S surprise, Jesse dropped out of college. Dave called me one afternoon to let me know she hadn't bothered going to class in weeks and wasn't going back.

"So, what now?" I asked. "How will she support herself?"

"I don't know. She's thinking of applying to be a cashier or something else close to home. She may want to try hairdressing school eventually."

"Do you think she'll bother?"

Dave sighed at the other end. "I don't know Mel. It's her life and her decision to make. She was obviously never going to be a doctor. She's just different."

"Like Mom, you mean."

"What I mean is that school was never the right place for her. She never wanted to be there."

"How's a job going to be any easier?" I asked. "She'll still have to show up on time and get along with people."

Dave sighed again. "Like I said, I don't know. Now that you're going to be a mom, you'll realize that you can't control everything about your kids."

I put one of my hands on my belly and felt around for the baby, who was wriggling about. "Let's hope this baby doesn't have those same genes—wherever they come from."

Dave sighed a third time. "Bye, Mel."

"Talk soon."

I placed my other hand on my belly, rubbing it in circular motions. The pregnancy had been terrible. Nausea and vomiting had started at the two-month mark and stalked me into my second trimester. By eight months, I'd gained only seventeen pounds. I talked about it with my doctor, but he didn't seem too worried. "Try to eat small, frequent meals," he said. "Lots of fruits and vegetables."

And then suddenly, with only three weeks to go, I felt better. Stronger, less tired. By then Jason had warmed up to the idea of being a father, especially once he felt the baby move. "I can't believe my mother did this for me," he said. "It's so crazy."

I shrugged my shoulders and turned on the television. "Better get used to crazy," I said.

I climbed into bed that night and Jason put his hand on my belly. "Must be sleeping," he said.

The next afternoon I was at the grocery store when a thought tugged at me. I hadn't felt the baby move all day. I bought a carton of orange juice and drank half of it at the cash register, hoping it would spur the baby into action. I paid my grocery bill with my hand still on my mid-section, desperate to feel even the slightest of movements. I ran home, where I drank the rest of the carton. I lay down, closed my eyes and waited for the rest of the sugar to kick in. I didn't feel anything.

I picked up the phone to call Jason, but when I looked at the keypad I called 911 instead. Keeping my voice as steady as possible, I lied and said I had an excruciating pain on my side and couldn't feel the baby. The paramedics arrived a few minutes later and took me to the same hospital I was treated at when I got hit by the car.

"My side doesn't hurt but something's wrong," I said to one of the paramedics as he helped me into the ambulance. "I'm not crazy."

"I believe you," he said as he squeezed my hand.

Once we got to the hospital, I was wheeled into a room and told to wait. A doctor came in a few minutes later and asked me a bunch of questions, felt around my belly and then did an ultrasound. I watched his eyes narrow in the blue light of the machine. I could feel him concentrating, searching.

"What's wrong?" I asked.

"I'm looking."

The doctor put down the transducer and left the room without a word. A few minutes later, another physician came in and did the ultrasound all over again.

"Why are you doing another ultrasound?" I asked her. "What's wrong?"

"I'm very sorry," she said. "There doesn't appear to be a heartbeat."

It felt as if my own heart had stopped. I tried to say something, but couldn't catch my breath. I'm not really sure what happened after that. I remember someone holding my hand. I remember the doctor telling me the baby was likely strangled by its umbilical cord. I remember feeling confused when someone said we could do an autopsy.

"How can you have an autopsy when you've never even been born?"

I kept telling the doctor about the car accident, about my fractured rib. But she didn't think they were related. She kept shrugging her shoulders. "I'm very sorry," she said again.

At some point, Jason showed up. I was freezing and couldn't stop shaking. "How come you're here?" I said, rocking back and forth in the hospital bed. "Who called you?"

"You did," he said, staring at me.

Jason did not come near me or say anything further. He sat in a chair in the corner of the room with his shoulders slumped and watched me as I tore my hair out, pulling out a section strand by strand. Eventually, a nurse came in and told us what needed to happen next.

We returned to the hospital the next morning. Following the instructions we'd been given, we took the elevator to a floor that led to a small room with nothing but a phone. Jason looked around and picked up the receiver. An unsmiling nurse came to get us a minute later.

She led us to a room with a bed, a chair and a door to the washroom. Everything but the bed sheets were grey. I tucked my overnight bag out of sight and under the chair. There seemed nothing left to do. Within a half-hour, another nurse knocked on the door and introduced herself. She was young and stout with dark hair and eyes. The badge clipped to her chest identified her as "NURSE AMY," but the picture looked like a much slimmer version of the woman standing before me. Amy had three clipboards, but before she went through them, she sat on the edge of the bed and grabbed my hand. I flinched at the unexpected gesture but didn't pull away. Jason sat in the chair with his face in his hands as she provided details on the drug that would be administered, the contractions that would follow and the end result.

Amy handed over a pile of paperwork to fill out and a gown to change in to. "I'll be back," she said.

The drugs kicked in as she had explained and I braced for what happened next. I vomited eight times. But after hours of struggle, there was still no delivery. By the end of the day I was sitting up in the bed without the slightest sign of any movement. "It's not happening," I said to Jason.

Finally, another nurse came in. "Let's take a look and then call the doctor."

She came back with two doctors and another nurse. It was time.

Jason stood in the corner as I followed orders. It was only when they stopped telling me what to do that I knew it was over. The doctors and nurses moved furiously with their tools, their blankets, their containers. I looked at the ceiling and waited.

One of the doctors placed the baby in a blanket and passed it to the nurse.

"She's here," the nurse said. "Did you want to hold her?"

I was too scared, so I shook my head. No. But she leaned over the bed and placed her in my arms anyway.

The baby in the blanket was a small but perfect version of the newborn I'd always imagined: pink face, pixie nose, pea-sized mouth.

Jason emerged from the corner of the room to sit on the edge of the bed. "She's so small," he said. "Look at her foot."

He pressed the pad of his index finger on her nose and then her eyelids. He took her tiny hand in his.

We sat there for some time, cradling the baby, caressing her face. And then someone knocked on the door and took her away.

* * *

Jason and I stood on the stoop of the red brick building with the set of double black doors and waited. He hit the bell three more times, growing impatient as the wind whipped our backs and the rain pelted our faces.

"It's fucking freezing," he said.

It was early October, but the misery of the season had already settled in. The smell of dead leaves clung to the air and the grey sky flirted with shades of green and black.

"Would you ring it again?" I said. "Instead of just complaining."

Before he had a chance to act, one of the doors swung open to a middle-aged man wearing a black suit and yellow rain boots.

"Please come in," he said, ushering us into the warmth of the entryway. "I'm Jonathan. You must be Jason." He shook Jason's hand before turning to me.

"I'm Melanie." A pause. "The mother."

The man led us through the long, carpeted hallway and into the back office. The room was lined with granite slabs; its furnishings were dark, heavy, wooden. At the centre of the room was a large table with a pile of papers and a box of tissues.

"Please sit down," he said. "I'll be back in a minute."

I took a seat at the table, but Jason didn't budge. He stood at the back of the room, his hands in his pockets.

"Are you going to join me?" I asked.

"I'm good."

I stared at the table. I thought of turning around but didn't have the energy. We waited for several minutes in silence until there was a gentle knock at the door. Jonathan poked his head into the room, making sure it was safe to return.

"Thanks for waiting," he said.

He walked back in wearing shoes instead of boots. "Please, first let me say how very sorry I am that you're here. It's never easy making these kinds of arrangements." I heard the floorboards squeaking as Jason shifted his weight. "I want you to know that there is support for you, there are programs and—"

"Listen," I said. "That's all very nice, but I'm not interested. We need to do what we need to do and then get home. I'm not feeling well."

He nodded.

"I'm going to leave you with a catalogue with some options," he said, putting a booklet in front of me. "Take a few moments together to look through it. I'll come back in about ten minutes to answer your questions." He got up from the table and left the room, closing the door behind him.

I put my hand on top of the catalogue but didn't open it. "I don't want to look at this alone," I said to Jason. "Can you please sit here with me?"

The floorboards creaked again but Jason didn't approach the table. "This didn't have to happen," he said. "It didn't have to happen this way."

I turned around to face him. "I know. It wasn't—"

"No," he said. "This wasn't supposed to be. I didn't even want this baby. This was your idea. And look what happened. Look at where I'm standing right now. I'm in a *funeral home*."

"Are you seriously blaming me? Do you not realize what I've just had to go through? How could you?"

Jason was about to say something else, but he sobbed instead.

"Fine," I said as I flipped through the pages of the ornamental urns. "I'll look alone."

I wanted to cry too, but the tears wouldn't come.

CHAPTER TWENTY

TRUTH OR DARE

October 2005

JESSE CAME TO stay with me right after the baby died. It was her idea, not mine. She called me up saying she needed to get away from Dave and that she thought I could use the company. I was home at the time, taking a leave of absence from teaching, so I agreed to have her stay for a week or two.

She arrived on a Greyhound in the early afternoon, carrying a black duffel bag and her army green backpack that was adorned with dozens of pins she'd been collecting over the years. One had an image of Che Guevara and another said, "I did not have sexual relations with that woman." I waved to her from the back seat of the taxi as soon as I saw her. At that point, I hadn't seen her in years. She was thin and pale, her hair long and dark brown, much different than her natural blonde. Maybe it was the hair, or because I hadn't seen her in so long, but she really reminded me of Mom.

"You look exactly like her," I said as she scooted toward the centre of the seat so that she had space for her bags.

"Who?"

"Mom."

"Really? I wouldn't know."

"You've seen pictures," I said.

"Well, you still look pregnant."

I flinched and put my hand to my belly, as if the baby was still there. But there was nothing to feel other than a swollen and hollow mass. "Don't be a jerk," I said. I knew I shouldn't have let her get away with it, but I couldn't let things boil over in the first thirty seconds.

Jesse ignored me and looked out the window, surveying the gritty sidewalks of London. It was lunchtime, but the streets were quiet. I surveyed the back of her head and noticed how her hair was knotted in several places. "Your hair's long now. Longer than I remember," I said, feeling the small bald patch at the back of my own head. She kept looking out the window, not reacting to what I was saying. "Hey," I asked. "Are you hungry? I've got soup at home. Or we can drop off your bags and go out to eat somewhere?"

"Home's fine," she said. "I need to pee." She wiped her nose on her sleeve, a hint of glazed eyes.

We pulled up to the storefront below my apartment a few minutes later. "Forgot what this place looked like," she said. "It's so weird that you live on top of a store."

"You get used to it. It's not so bad."

We climbed the narrow staircase to the front door, which I'd decorated with a hanging rubber spider for Halloween. Jason had asked me why I even bothered when there were no passers-by to admire it. "Just feels like a wasted effort," he'd said.

Jesse dropped her bags on the floor and I reminded her where the bathroom was. Once she was out, I showed her to her bedroom, which had been wiped clean of most of the baby items, except for the crib, which I didn't know what to do with.

"Make yourself at home," I said. "Towels are in the dresser."

She started unpacking. I noticed the clothes in her bag hadn't been folded.

"Here," she said, throwing me a jumbo box of Ritz crackers that had been mixed amid her things. "A gift."

"For what?" I said.

"For your hospitality. It was on the counter at home so I swiped it. Now it won't go to waste."

I went into the kitchen to heat up vegetable soup and slice some cheese while Jesse took a shower. She was in there for so long I was sure there'd be no hot water left. I was about to knock on the bathroom door to see if she was okay when the taps turned off. She came out a few minutes later, her hair wet and combed straight.

"So," she said, meeting me at the kitchen table, "what's new?"

I looked up at her from my bowl of soup, the awkwardness of the question hanging between us. At that moment my breasts tingled as a wave of milk rushed in; I winced in discomfort and waited for the pressure to relent.

Oblivious, Jesse sat down, took a spoonful, then looked out the window. "You like living here?"

"It's not bad," I said, following her gaze to the row of shops across the street. "We're sort of in a routine, you know?"

"I guess," she said, taking a slice of cheese.

"What's new with you? What are you going to do now? Do you think you'll find a job?"

Jesse squinted her eyes as she leaned back in her chair. "God, you sound just like Dad."

"What do you mean?"

"Whatever. Forget it," she said. "You mind if I take a nap after I finish eating?"

"Of course not. You know where your room is."

Jesse let out a yawn as she got up from the table, her long jogging pants dragging on the floor by her feet. She shut the door behind her and didn't emerge from her bedroom until four hours later, when I was starting to think about what to put on for dinner.

By the end of the week, Jason asked me how much longer she'd be staying. "We have a lot going on right now," he whispered in bed. "It's a big distraction."

"I have nothing going on," I said. "I've been sitting around the house feeling sorry for myself. She's here to help me."

"How is she helping? She's spent so much time lounging around on that couch one of the cushions has a permanent imprint."

"She won't be here much longer," I said. "She'll want to go home soon—she gets bored of things easily."

But Jesse only seemed to get more comfortable. She slept at crazy hours and her bedtime was always irregular. Sometimes she'd be up all night; other times, she'd pass out before nine. She napped during the days, but not always. A couple of times I was up early to use the bathroom and found her in the living room playing video games. I shrugged my shoulders and went to pee.

The effect on my own sleeping habits was destabilizing. I'd go to sleep wondering where she was and wake up doing the same. I went to bed later, woke up more frequently and spent the day feeling lethargic. Jason insisted he was sleeping fine, but I noticed he, too, looked more tired than usual, as if the skin under his eyes had been shaded with the shavings of a black pencil crayon.

By December, Jesse was still there, her contributions to the household chores nonexistent. I was standing at the sink doing dishes one morning when I tried to bring up the subject of her going home. "Doesn't Dave miss you?" I asked. "I don't like the idea of him being alone all the time."

"Oh, whatever, he's fine," she said from her place on the couch, the television converter in her hand. "We just fight all the time. Besides, you need my help recovering from the baby."

I kept waiting for Jason to bring up the subject of her leaving again, but he didn't. Instead, he and Jesse forged a strange bond drinking at the kitchen table.

There were several things I learned about Jess while she stayed with us. Besides the fact that she drank a lot, she had friends in London she visited frequently. She also smoked pot daily. For all her flaws, she could sometimes be fun. She was always good company when the alcohol was flowing.

A week before Christmas, we were drinking a bottle of wine and watching a Chevy Chase movie when Jesse turned to me. "Did you want to get a tree?"

Jason and I had never had a Christmas tree in our tiny apartment before. I looked at her, the wine glass in my hand, and shrugged my shoulders. "Sure, why not?" It would give us something to do. The next day we drove to Canadian Tire and chose the second smallest tree in the pack: a five-footer narrow enough to get through our stairwell and sit in the corner of the apartment without disturbing our window view. We decorated it with candy canes and strings of popcorn. Jesse coined it the edible tree.

I decided Dave would come to us for Christmas Day. Jesse said it was a bad idea and that she came to London to escape him, but she didn't have a choice. To make it official, I created an online invitation and emailed it to him. I waited for him to mention it, but he didn't, so I called to ask why he hadn't responded. He said he hadn't checked his email in weeks, so I invited him over the phone.

"Please come," I said. "It would be nice to see you."

"Oh, I don't know," Dave said. "Are you sure there's enough room for your old man?"

"Don't be silly. There's more than enough room for everyone."

Dave arrived on Christmas Eve, taking the Greyhound because of the weather. Snow squalls made the two-hour drive on the highway too dangerous, and Dave said he didn't want us to have to plan his funeral on Christmas.

I took the car to pick him up at the station, leaving Jason and Jesse waiting at the apartment. I got there early and parked at the side of the street until I heard a tap at the window. I smiled and motioned for him to come around the other side. Dave slid into the passenger seat smelling like aftershave and chewing gum. "Hey kiddo, it's good to see you."

I leaned over and gave him a hug, noticing how much thicker he felt around the middle.

"How you feeling?" he said.

"Not bad. Not good. You know."

"I know," he said. "You need to take care of yourself."

I nodded and managed not to cry.

We got to the apartment a few minutes later, with Dave carrying his overnight bag in one hand and a large plastic bag with gift-wrapped boxes in the other. We made our way up the narrow steps as Dave breathed heavily through his nose. "Wow, I'm out of shape," he said during a short break halfway up the stairwell. "Quite a way's away from my running days, aren't I?"

I opened the front door to let him in the apartment, where we found Jesse and Jason watching television. Jason got up to greet us as Jesse let out a terse, "Hey, Dad." Dave's arrival relegated her to the sofa, so her duffel bag was sitting on the floor in the centre of the room.

Dave shook Jason's hand, then said "Hiya, Jess, how've you been?" She got up from the couch and gave Dave a hug, carefully avoiding his gaze before sitting back down. Dave didn't seem to notice and smiled ear to ear. "So good to have both my girls here. Been far too long."

We stayed up late his first night there, chatting at the kitchen table while sharing the better part of a bottle of Bourbon, something Jason had put out even though he was the only one who liked it. Despite the late night, we were all up early on Christmas, exchanging gifts at eight in the morning while standing in the kitchen in our pyjamas. Dave gave me and Jason a proper set of cutlery, something I'd been meaning to get since we got married. We gave Dave a new scarf. Jason and I got Jesse a bottle of vodka while she gave us a bottle of wine. Jesse got Dave a gift card to a coffee shop (although I had to loan her the money for it) and Dave gave her a sweater.

Jason and I didn't exchange gifts. He'd asked me what I wanted and I'd said nothing.

We had a special Christmas dinner planned, but we were up so early we decided to make it lunch instead. I made Jess peel the potatoes while I chopped up the rest of the vegetables. Dave set the table as Jason orchestrated the main event: the roasted chicken. The potatoes and rest of the vegetables were cooked by noon, but the chicken needed more time. Jason uncorked the first bottle of wine to keep us busy while we waited. Jesse drank it out of a white ceramic mug emblazoned with 'Rich Girl' in red cursive.

"This is much better than coffee," she said, lifting it in the air to signal cheers. By the time the chicken was roasted, the vegetables were cold, so we put those back in the oven and opened up more wine.

After most of the second bottle was finished, we finally sat down at the table, Dave giggling as he carved the chicken.

"Great looking turkey," he said. Jason, Jesse and I started laughing. Nobody corrected him.

Our plates were piled high with chicken and gravy, shrinking gradually over the next hour. Dave organized his meal in the usual way he did at the holidays: slice of poultry topped with a layer of mashed potatoes followed by a sprinkling of greens and repeat.

His chair screeching, Dave got up from the table as soon as he was finished eating but before I had a chance to serve dessert. Without saying a word, he stumbled to his bed with his hand on his belly and passed out for the next hour and forty-five minutes.

STEPHANIE CESCA

With our second bottle complete, Jason got up to open another but this time bypassed the wine. "Should we move on to the vodka?"

"God, no. Please," I said.

"Okay, not much else unless we want to drink our Christmas gifts," he said, closing the freezer door and moving on to the fridge. "We've got some bubbly."

"That sounds nice," I said. But Jesse pouted her lips in exaggerated fashion.

Jason closed the fridge and opened the door to the pantry. "Okay, ladies, it'll have to be brandy."

"Deal," Jesse said.

Jason grabbed three clean coffee mugs from the cupboard and put them in the centre of the table, our dirty plates still in front of us. He flexed his wrist to pour three generous servings, the fumes of the alcohol stinging my nasal passages. We each took a gulp, with Jesse holding the mug on her lap as if she was nursing her morning coffee.

"So," she said. "Want to play truth or dare?"

"What are we, thirteen?" I said. "No way."

"Come on, Mel, why do you have to be such a stick in the mud?"

"I'm not being a stick in the mud. I'm just drunk and feeling pretty lazy right now."

"We won't make it difficult. Dares will not involve us leaving this apartment. It will be low-key. Who's starting?"

"Not me," I said.

"What are you afraid of? That Jason's going to ask you a bunch of questions about Mom or something?"

"Jason knows everything about my upbringing," I said, smiling at him. "No secrets here."

"So there's nothing to be afraid of," she said.

Jason shrugged his shoulders and grimaced like an idiot. I just sighed and took another swig of brandy.

"Here, I'll start," Jesse said.

"Don't we have to spin the bottle or something to see whose turn it is?" Jason asked.

"We're not playing spin the bottle, we're playing truth or dare," she said, the edges of her voice starting to curl from the liquor. "And I'm going first. I choose truth."

Jesse sat up straighter in her chair to show she was ready, her hands clutching her coffee mug.

"Okay," I said, hoping the game would end after a minute or two. "Tell us about your last relationship."

"Ooohh, okay," Jesse said. "His name was Brian. Lasted three weeks. Found out he was still seeing his ex-girlfriend. Next!"

She giggled and turned toward me.

"Dare!" I blurted out, looking at Jess.

"I dare you to put makeup on Dad's face while he's sleeping."

"No, I won't do that."

"Come on, Mel. Live a little."

"I'm not doing that, Jess . . ."

"Don't pretend to be such a goody two-shoes," she said. "You're the only one in the family who's gotten arrested."

Jason turned to me, his eyebrows raised. "What?"

"You mean, you don't know?"

"Jess," I said.

"How could you not know this?" she said, perking up in her seat.

"Jason went to private school, remember? He wouldn't have heard about it."

"Oh yeah," she said, turning to him. "Pretty boy. Anyway, Mel made quite the impression in her first year of high school. She stole Dad's van and crashed it into a pole. Got in trouble with the police and everything. And she always pretended like I was the troublemaker."

She smiled as she took another sip of brandy, exuding pride in the fact she'd revealed this piece of my history.

"I can't believe you did that," Jason said. "You never told me."

"It's not exactly a bright shining moment. Moving on," I said, looking to Jason.

"Okay," he said, his eyes flickering with excitement. "Truth."

Jesse didn't hesitate. "How many women have you slept with?"

"Jesse!" I yelled. "You can't know that. Don't answer that, Jason."

"Why can't I know that? You know that, I'm sure."

"This is going to end badly," I said. "Game over."

Jesse cupped her hands around her mouth to project her displeasure. "Down with the host!" she shouted. "Host is a lame-o!"

Jason laughed as he poured her some more brandy. "You're going to wake up your dad," he said.

"Okay, fine," she said, trying to contain her giggles. "No more games. But next time we have a party," she said, whispering in his ear, "let's be sure not to invite Debbie Downer."

Chapter Twenty-One

———◆———

DEPARTURE

February 2006

JESSE STAYED UNTIL mid-February. She said that was a better time to return home to look for a job. "Everyone's still hungover in January," she said. "Everyone's broke and no one's hiring."

I was back at work by then so couldn't drive her to the bus station. Jason was able to take the morning off, so he agreed to do it for me.

"Here," I said, handing her a peanut butter sandwich I'd made earlier that morning. "For the road."

"Thanks," she said as she tucked it into her pocket. "I might need to swipe your jug of O.J., too. Peanut butter sticks to the roof of my mouth."

I was relieved to see her go. She'd been with us four months and, over that time, she'd become more of a parasite than a support system. Not once did she buy any groceries or clean up after herself. Never did she ask me any questions about the baby. Dave, I knew, was also getting antsy. "She needs to come home and get her life sorted out," he said. "She can't run away from her responsibilities forever."

Jason ended up having the most patience with her. Plus, I could tell he liked having a drinking partner. They sat around the kitchen table most nights, the aroma of pine tree emanating from their gin and tonics. Sometimes they even went to the bar together without me.

After giving Jess a hug goodbye, I left the apartment and went to work. I met my Grade Two students in the hallway, where I helped them take off their snowsuits and switch their boots for indoor shoes. It felt good to be back in the classroom again. The students were bright-eyed and eager to learn. They drew me pictures of parks, picnic tables and fields of flowers on reams of brightly coloured construction paper. "Ms. Foresight," they called me.

I went home after work to find Jason on the couch, still wearing his jogging pants from that morning.

"I thought you were going back to work in the afternoon," I said.

"Not today," he said, yawning. "Back tomorrow."

"Did you want me to put on some dinner? Or maybe we can go out? Celebrate our newfound freedom." I laughed at my attempted joke, but Jason kept a straight face.

"Don't know," he said as he changed the television channel. "I don't feel like going out. Dinner would be great, though."

The next day, Jason worked late. I texted him repeatedly. But he got home well after eight and said he wasn't hungry.

"Sorry," he said. "Crazy day at the plant."

Things between us became even more unpleasant after that. If he wasn't working late, he was watching television—only if I wasn't beside him. Everything I said seemed to irritate him.

"What's wrong?" I tried asking him.

"Nothing," he said. He didn't even bother to look at me.

I also noticed what I thought were changes in his relationship with his dad. While Jason had always been the one to call his father—every Sunday, without fail—Jason's phone was ringing incessantly, sometimes in the middle of the night. The conversations were always brief. Always tense. Jason seemed annoyed.

It went on like this for weeks until late March. Jason came home from work one night and told me he was taking a leave to go back home. "It's my dad again," he said. "I need to spend some time with him."

"Is he seeing a doctor?"

"He's seeing his doctor. But I don't feel comfortable with him being alone right now."

"I understand," I said. Although I didn't. "How long do you think you'll be gone for? A few days? A couple of weeks?"

"For as long as it takes, really. I'm hoping it won't be too long."

With his suitcase on the floor of the bedroom, Jason packed his clothes as he whistled the tune to "Little Drummer Boy." I sat at the edge of the bed and watched as he zipped up his luggage. I asked if he wanted me to make him breakfast before he went, but he shook his head. "No thanks," he said. He checked his cell phone and gave me a peck on the forehead before heading downstairs.

Jason checked in the next day—his dad was the same, still the same—but there didn't seem to be any solution in sight. I asked him everything I could think of: did we need to consider another arrangement for his father? Should we think about moving back home? What about hiring full-time help? Jason told me to stop pressuring him and asked me to have patience.

March turned to April. And then we approached May.

While Jason was away, I learned the gingerbread house was available again. For weeks, I had not seen the lady during my runs. Or any visitors. Even though it was spring, the garden was bare, the windows veiled by curtains. Finally, on a weekday afternoon, I noticed a black car out front. As I jogged by, I saw a woman carrying an empty box into the house.

"Hi," I said from the sidewalk, the woman's back to me as she headed toward the front door.

She turned around.

"Is this your family's house?" I asked.

"It's my mother's."

"I jog by several days a week," I said, to which I was greeted with a blank stare. "I live nearby."

"Sorry ... do you know my mother?"

"Not really, though I did see her quite a bit in the neighbourhood. Is she okay?"

The woman's eyes lowered. "Actually, my mother died last month. She had a stroke."

"Oh, I'm sorry."

"Thank you," the woman said, the box suddenly looking heavier.

"I've always admired this house. I think that's why I noticed your mom, planting flowers in the garden and coming and going."

"My mom really liked it here," she said, turning toward the façade. "Well, I should be going."

"Bye," I said.

I jogged to the end of the street and pulled out my phone. I had to tell Jason. I called his cell phone three times. No answer. I sent him a text message asking him to call me back. But nothing. Two days later, on Sunday, the text remained unanswered, a peculiarity even for Jason. I called his cell phone again, but still couldn't reach him. Frustrated, I called his dad's house line. There was no answer there, either.

By Sunday night, I knew something was wrong. I called Dave to see if he knew anything. He said he hadn't seen or heard from Jason at all. I asked to speak to Jess, but he said she'd been away for the weekend.

I texted Jason again. A simple 911 so he knew it was urgent. I waited and heard nothing. Eventually, I went to bed. The apartment that night felt quieter than usual. It was as if I could hear it breathing in and out, waiting for something and then sighing when it didn't come.

By five-thirty in the morning, my head ached from a lack of sleep. My neck was knotted from tossing and turning. I rose from my bed, moving swiftly and quietly through the apartment. After calling in sick at work, I made three quick pit stops: bathroom, closet, kitchen, done. I was out the door within twenty minutes, on my way to catch the 6:15 bus. I was in no state to drive.

The ride back to Toronto was long and bumpy, the bus approaching a consistent layer of thick fog that remained on the horizon but we never seemed to reach. During those two hours I thought of Jason, mostly, but also the father-in-law I barely knew, the house we didn't buy, the baby we lost. I couldn't deny it: disappointment beleaguered every aspect of our life together, a life that increasingly felt like I no longer shared with him.

In many ways, his disappearing act was not a surprise. I wanted to think he needed time after the baby. Or needed time with his dad. But I needed things, too. I needed a real home. I needed a family. I needed an explanation. As disappointed as I was with the way things had turned out, I didn't want our marriage to unravel. I thought of couples that stayed together for fifty years or longer, the kind of people you read about in the paper. They're with each other for so long that when one dies the other follows. At that moment, the thought of staying married for fifty years seemed unfathomable. And, yet, I also did not want to let him go. So, on the bus, I was on a mission to fix our relationship before the gulf became too wide.

I arrived in Toronto at a half past eight, a time when traffic had surged downtown. I hopped in a taxi and gave Jason's father's address to the driver. We pulled up to the dilapidated mansion an hour later. "Keep the meter running," I said as I got out of the taxi. The driver stayed in the driveway as I marched toward the house.

I knocked on the door—three times loud and clear —the brass pineapple knocker staring me down as I waited for someone to open. A minute went by and nothing happened. The hum of the taxi emanated from the driveway. The driver watched me as I waited.

I knocked again, this time using the doorknocker, which felt cold and slimy in my grip. I waited for another minute, my arms crossed in front of my body. I tapped my foot. Nobody was answering.

I thought of his dad and wondered if he was hiding behind the curtains, trying to catch a glimpse of who was at his door. And then I remembered. The secret knock. What was it, five or six taps? With a break in between. I lifted my knuckles to the door again. Knock, knock, knock, knock. Rest. Knock.

I waited another minute. Still no answer. I raised my fist and banged on the door as hard as I could at least a dozen times. "Open the door!" I shouted. "Open the God damn fucking door!" I kicked the bricks in front of the house knowing the taxi driver was probably watching. "You fucking hermit!" I screamed. "You can't hide in there forever!"

I turned around and stomped toward the taxi, flinging the back door open and slamming it shut.

"Take me home," I said.

"The address please, ma'am," the driver said in a small voice.

I spat Dave's address out and then whipped out my cell phone to check to see if I had any texts. I wondered if Dave knew something by that point.

I got to the house. It was a dark and grey day, but the lights were off inside. I paid the driver, jumped out of the cab, mounted the front steps, put my key in the lock and was greeted by the familiar smells of a home I no longer inhabited. Nobody was there, at least from what I could tell, so I got a glass of juice from the fridge and sat down on the living room couch, trying to calm down. I checked my phone to see if I had any messages

—still none. I texted Dave—"Call me"—knowing that he was at work and unlikely to reply anytime soon. I turned on the television and flipped through the channels, though I paid no attention to what was on the screen. I was at this for about twenty minutes, remote in my hand, when I heard footsteps shuffling down the stairs. I looked up to find Jesse, wide-eyed and pale in the face.

"Melanie, what are you doing here?"

"I'm looking for Jason. Have you or Dave heard anything?"

She looked out the window. "Did Dad know you were coming?"

"No, I didn't let him know … Don't you want to know why I'm looking for Jason?" My tone was sharp; I was speaking quickly.

Whatever blood was left in her face seemed to drain in the next few seconds. She opened her mouth to say something and then didn't.

"What's going on, Jess?"

"Nothing," she said, her eyes darkening, her arms crossed in front of her body.

"Jess, please. I haven't been able to reach him for days. He's not answering my texts. I don't know where he is."

At those words, Jesse's face crumpled. Her eyes tightened shut, her lips pursed together, her nose crinkled.

"Jess?"

"Melanie, I have something to tell you. I'm so sorry, Melanie."

My heart raced; my breathing picked up.

"I didn't know you'd be here, but it's something I've needed to tell you, so I should just do it now ... It's not easy, Melanie, oh my God."

My heart was pounding so loudly in my ears it was as if I was listening from underwater. Suddenly Jesse fell to her knees, landing on her hands so that she was on all fours. She was gasping, crying, trying to speak through her tears.

"Melanie, I don't know how to tell you this. I don't know what I'm going to do."

Fear gripped my throat as my mind raced. I could barely choke out the next words. "What, Jesse? What *is it*?"

"I'm pregnant, Melanie."

"Oh my God, Jess." I suddenly felt a surge of relief. "Does Dave know?"

She was sitting with her legs tucked behind her now, but her crying intensified, a string of drool linking her mouth to the top of her thigh.

"No, Melanie, you don't understand." Her crying became so intense that her chest heaved as she gasped for more air. "You don't *understand*."

"What is it, Jess? What's *wrong*?"

"Melanie, the baby ..."

"What's wrong?!"

"The baby is Jason's."

No.

"You need to understand what happened."

No.

"Melanie, please say something."

No.

I stood there, stunned, my gaze focused on the saliva that had formed a small puddle on her jeans.

A few things raced through my mind. The first thing was the baby. My baby. Remembering her in my arms, holding her tiny foot. I could still see Jason's face as he looked at her. I could recall every line in his expression.

My next thought was Jesse in my apartment all those months. What had happened? What had I missed? My stomach flipped as I replayed scenes of Jason. Packing in March while humming a Christmas carol.

Finally, I thought of Dave. Did he know about the affair? Did he keep it from me, too? How could he not say something? I needed to talk to him.

I wanted answers. I needed to know. I would have asked Jesse all of these things, but I felt like I did the time I dreamed a strange man was in my room; when I opened my mouth to scream, nothing came out. Instead, I picked up my bag, walked out of the house and took the next Greyhound back to London.

Chapter Twenty-Two

FOUR HUNDRED AND THIRTY-SEVEN STRANDS

May 2006

DAVE CALLED ME a dozen times later that night. I didn't pick up the first time, not because I was ignoring him, but because I was on the floor of my bathroom hoping I could throw up. The pain had started in the centre of my gut on the bus ride home and grew into an orange-sized stress ball that stung so fiercely I could feel it pulsing with every breath. I tried hovering over the toilet for half an hour as soon as I got home, but nothing would come out, so I went back in the living room and stared at the items that belonged to Jason: a photo of his parents, a wood carving he bought during a trip to Jamaica, an ugly fruit basket that came from who-knows-where. There were so many things about him I still didn't know, things I would never learn.

Dave could hardly speak when I finally picked up the phone. His breathing was shallow, his voice was shaky. He asked me if I was okay. I said I wasn't. He stayed on the line for the next several minutes and listened to me cry.

I asked him if he had known about Jason and Jess and he said he didn't until Jess told him after work. I believed him but my relief was mixed with a strange frustration at not being able to be angry at him. I needed to lash out at someone.

Jason did not text or call. I sat on the couch and checked my cell phone, obsessively, every five minutes but found only a blank screen. I was consumed with anger. I felt disgust. I imagined them together; the thought of their intertwined bodies made me shake. I didn't know what to do, so I grabbed a tuft of hair at the back of my head. I pulled as hard as I could and felt a strange mix of pain and relief. I pulled out some more. And then some more. By the time I was done there was a gaping hole at the back of my head, much larger than the small bald spot that had already existed. I sat on the floor of my living room and counted each strand, one by one. By the time I was done, I had counted to four hundred and thirty-seven.

Time went by slowly. I should have returned to work, but I didn't. I couldn't. Instead, I stayed home and waited. For what, I wasn't sure. But this terrible thing had happened to me and so, I felt, that it was only fair for something else to happen. Something else had to happen if I was going to emerge from this anguish and confusion.

Three days later I was at the kitchen table when I heard keys scratching the lock of the front door. I watched as the door swung open. Jason looked at me, his eyes hooded and tired.

I waited for him to say something but he just stared at me as his lip quivered. I continued to wait because I didn't know what to say. The silence was the worst thing because I had nothing to distract me from the look in his eyes.

"Melanie, I fucked up so badly I don't even know what to say."

I started crying.

"I know you hate me. And you don't have to ever forgive me. I'll understand if you don't. But I also need to tell you that I haven't been happy. I don't know how else to say it, but after the baby died, I just—I don't want to be married anymore."

I hadn't expected him to say that. I'd expected him to beg for forgiveness.

"What?" I said. I couldn't believe what I was hearing.

"I know what I did was wrong. It was such a huge mistake. But, when I think about it, I think I did it because I'm a mess emotionally."

"What are you saying, Jason?"

"What I'm saying is, I need to be on my own."

I was stunned. I didn't think there was a way he could hurt me even further. "How could you do this to me? After everything we went through—after the baby —how could you do this?"

"I'm sorry. I really am. And I don't know what else to say."

* * *

I remained in a catatonic state over the next couple of months. I woke up each morning, went to work, came home and slept. This predictable routine was all that kept me going—that and the support I got from Dave.

I think he was in as much shock as I was. He didn't make excuses for Jesse, he didn't bring up Jason's name and he didn't suggest I try to save my marriage. Instead, he called me every day and asked me how I was.

In July, about two months after learning about the pregnancy, Dave called to provide me with an update about what was happening.

"She's keeping the baby," Dave said.

"Huh."

"She considered an adoption and, um, the other thing but ... well, I guess she's not." I knew he could hear me crying. He gave me a minute and continued. "She and Jason are not together. Obviously. But Jason knows she's keeping it and he's agreed to support the baby once it's born."

Then, Dave said something I did not expect.

"I kicked her out of the house, Mel."

My eyes widened slightly as I stayed slumped in my chair. "You did?"

"She's living in a basement apartment with a friend. I couldn't have her here after everything. I felt like I needed to draw a line in the sand."

I wanted to feel bad for Jesse, but I didn't. "I'm just ... surprised," I said. "Are you okay with your decision?"

"I think it's the right thing for now. The only problem is, I don't know what will happen."

The baby was born in November. Dave called to tell me that Jesse was still in the hospital and that she'd decided shortly before the delivery that she was going to give it up for adoption. After learning this, Jason said he would step in. He agreed to take the baby back to London and raise it by himself.

I wanted to ask Dave a bunch of questions—who was at the hospital? What did the baby look like? But I asked only one thing.

"Boy or girl?"

"Girl," Dave said, and paused. "Her name's Emma."

"Nice name," I said, tears streaming down my face. It felt so strange to be curious about a baby I should have hated. "I'm surprised Jess would pick out such a pretty name."

"Actually, Melanie, Jesse asked me which name I preferred. She said she didn't want to do it, and so I thought it was nice."

Dave broke down and started crying.

"I'm so sorry about all this, Melanie. I'm still mad as hell at Jesse."

"I know."

"But it's not the baby's fault," he said, struggling to get through his tears. "She's just an innocent child—just as you once were."

CHAPTER TWENTY-THREE

ALONE

January 2007

THE INTERIOR OF the house had changed over the years. The outside was still white and blue, a pastel that whispered your name as you admired it from the sidewalk. But the inside had undergone several recent changes, some of which slightly eroded the character.

While everything before had been whitewashed, the bedrooms and bathroom walls were now painted a dark blue that flirted with grey. The butcher block countertop in the kitchen had been replaced with a white stone. And the white ceramic floors had been updated with slate.

Thankfully, a few of the original features, including the wood-burning fireplace, remained untouched. That fireplace, and the house, became mine after I approached the previous owner's daughter. We executed a private sale. Dave helped me with the down payment, transferring fifteen thousand dollars in my bank account while I got the paperwork completed. And, then, I moved in. Alone.

After Jason left, I had no choice but to move on—at least in the physical sense. I had never wanted to remain in that apartment anyway and, knowing the gingerbread house was vacant, I decided to make an offer.

Though cute, the home and its charms were undercut by the fact I was moving in all by myself, a broken woman with no family. Despite what I was dealing with, I did try to make the best of it. I hung photos of me and Dave in the hallway. I bought a plant for the living room. I painted my bedroom yellow.

I stayed home a lot. And, for some reason, I thought of Mom. Everything she'd warned me about, everything she'd said. She was right, of course. Life couldn't be planned. Things weren't always fair. Sometimes things get thrown at you, sometimes you cannot choose. I wished I'd listened to her, I wished I knew better.

A few days after moving in, I was lugging some grocery bags inside when a man from next door stepped out onto the tiny concrete slab that protruded from his front door. The house was one and a half storeys tall like mine but in a beige and weathered siding. Although I'd jogged by it for years, I never noticed it until I moved in next door.

"Hiya," the man said while settling down on an aluminum chair with brown and yellow vinyl webbing. The chair was parked in the centre of his lawn, slightly lopsided due to a pile of January snow. "I'm Charlie."

"I'm Melanie."

"Good to meet ya."

"Good to meet you, too." I looked at him and noticed he was wearing only a sweater. "Isn't it a little bit cold to be sitting outside?"

He held up both hands, revealing an unlit cigarette in one hand and a lighter in the other. "Won't be here for very long. So, where ya moving from?" he asked as he leaned in to light his cigarette.

"Around the corner. I'm from the neighbourhood."

"Don't ya have a gentleman friend to help you with all your bags?"

"No gentleman, I'm afraid."

"Sorry, it's so hard to know these days," he said, blowing out smoke. "Your lady friend, then."

"No lady friend, either. No friend at all. I'm divorced. Or divorcing. It's just me."

"That's a shame. I'm alone here as well. Wife died ten years ago."

"I'm sorry."

"Thank ya. It's been a bit lonely without her. It's hard being alone. So it's good to have ya here, Melanie."

"Thanks. Nice to meet you."

I went inside and shut the door behind me. As I put the groceries away, I noticed a black spot in the grout of the kitchen backsplash. The furnace seemed to rattle instead of hum. Maybe buying this house was a mistake, I thought. Maybe everything in my life had been a terrible mistake.

I paced around the house before calling Dave, struggling to keep my voice steady. "I'm getting everything sorted," I said as I dragged my finger below the fireplace mantel, tracing the outline of a single brick. "It's looking really good."

Dave said he was glad and then promised to visit soon. "Looking forward to seeing you, kiddo. Maybe I'll drive out when the weather's a bit nicer."

"No rush," I said.

In the end, though, Dave never drove out. He never even saw the house he helped me buy. I invited him once or twice, but maybe he couldn't muster the energy. Or maybe it would have been too painful for him to see me that way.

I really wish that I'd been more persistent. Or that I'd taken the time to visit him more myself. Because despite being consumed by an unbelievable amount of grief, the biggest blow was still to come.

CHAPTER TWENTY-FOUR

DAVE'S DAUGHTER

April 2009

ALL I KNOW is what I was told when I got to the hospital.

Dave was at the Coffee Time at seven in the morning when he abruptly left the line. He didn't say anything, but he must not have been feeling well. Just as he was trying to leave, he collapsed in front of the exit. Someone called 911. The ambulance came within minutes.

While he was sprawled out on the tiled floor of the coffee shop, Dave asked for someone to call his daughter. Dave had asked one of the bystanders the same thing twice: "Call my daughter."

The hospital assumed that daughter was me; I was listed as his emergency contact. When I first got the call, I was told there was a "medical incident" and that Dave had been rushed to urgent care. I dropped everything and jumped in my car. The two-hour drive back to Richmond Hill was a strange blur. Everything in my body was racing but the car seemed to move so slowly. During the drive I wondered if Dave could have possibly been asking for Jesse instead of me. I may have been the responsible one, but I was not his daughter. Even still, I told myself, it wouldn't have made sense for him to want Jesse. She was never reliable and, besides, she had moved to B.C. Living with a friend. Somewhere temporary.

As soon as I got to the emergency room, I raced through the doors and told the front desk why I was there. Someone led me to a tiny room, where I waited a total of thirty-nine minutes until a doctor arrived. He was accompanied by a woman who stood there and watched as the doctor told me Dave was dead.

"I'm very sorry," the doctor said. "Both the paramedics and the emergency room physicians did everything they could to resuscitate him. We believe it was a heart attack."

My entire body went numb. "Dave," I said. I repeated his name: "Dave." I felt like I couldn't stand up any longer, so I crouched down on the floor, my head spinning. The doctor helped me to my feet, led me back to the chair and recounted the details passed along from witnesses.

I sat there, alone, for the next while. I don't know for how long. When someone finally came back into the room, I was asked if I wanted to see the body. I asked for a few more minutes alone.

I called Jesse's cellphone but there was no answer. I waited a few minutes and called again. This time, she said hello in what sounded like a daze.

"It's Dave," I said. "I mean Dad. Dad's died, Jesse."

"Melanie?"

"He's dead, Jesse! The doctors think he had a heart attack."

A long pause. It was the first contact we'd had since she told me about the baby.

"Oh."

Even through that single syllable I could tell her speech was slurred.

"You should come home," I said. "You need to come home, Jess."

Another pause and heavy breathing. "Okay," she said in what sounded like a drug-induced drawl. "I need to come home."

She breathed heavier now. Everything sounded muffled but I could tell she was on something.

"Melanie?"

"Yeah?"

"Is this a joke? I mean ... are you trying to get back at me?"

"No, Jess," I said. "He's gone."

As soon as I said this, she let out a howl, a sound that cut through my skin, a sound that will haunt me forever.

Chapter Twenty-Five

❦

FUNERAL DIRGE

April 2009

DAVE'S EYES WERE half-moons.

Smiling with his mouth closed, squinting from the sun, he was sitting on the back deck with his head gently cocked to one side. From the way the light hit him, and the direction of the long shadows, I could tell it was late afternoon, probably July. He was wearing a red cotton T-shirt, sitting on a lawn chair. A bottle of beer was in his right hand. The other hand was rested on his knee, which was crossed over the other leg. His skin was ruddy in certain spots, especially around the neck. That was how he had aged—not many lines or wrinkles, but the type of skin that became goose-pimply, like the flesh of poultry. His smile was easy and calm. He looked happy. It wasn't clear who took the picture. Maybe Becky. There was no way of ever knowing that this was going to be the photo used in Dave's death notice, the face that would signify the end of his life.

Everyone stopped to admire the image, which was mounted on an easel standing beside me in the visitation room. On the ledge was the purple frame with the poem

I had written about him in high school. I knew it was silly, but so much of Dave was wrapped up in those few lines. And I knew it had always made him happy.

I stood by the front of the room, where I was greeted with hugs and handshakes. Some visitors gave me confused looks and asked where Jesse was. I shrugged my shoulders as I looked at them sheepishly. "I don't know," I said.

Dave's coffin sat at the front of the room, adorned with a set of purple flowers that hung off the sides. I didn't remember picking that colour. There was not much I remembered from the past three days except for the fact that my cell phone wouldn't stop ringing with Dave's friends and co-workers, all of whom were in shock about what had happened.

I watched a steady row of visitors shuffle their way to the casket to pay their respects. Rona was among those waiting in line. She placed her hand briefly on Dave's coffin before she turned around to greet me with a hug. I put my arms around her, squeezing her shoulder blades; she was so much smaller than I'd remembered.

Eventually, we all made our way to our seats and waited until an older woman wearing a periwinkle dress took her place behind the organ. Despite her frail appearance, she banged on the instrument with immense force, triggering the pipes to erupt in a funeral dirge. It was the ugliest sound I'd ever heard, each chord synonymous with untimely death.

A man from the funeral home walked up to the front of the room once the hymn was over. He smoothed out the creases of his shirt before he spoke. His opening remarks were brief and generic as Dave was not a religious guy. He said something about the importance of having supportive friends and family and that's when I felt a hundred eyes staring at the back of my head. I looked toward my feet and noticed my pantyhose had a run. I crossed my legs and placed my finger at the start of the tear, tracing the line up and down until I heard my name being called. I walked up to the front, unsure where I had left the scrap piece of paper that contained the basis of my eulogy.

I stood for a moment and stared out at the faces. Half of the guests had to line up against the side and back walls, not lucky enough to have scored a seat in the tiny room. How many people were there. Fifty? Fifty-five? I wondered what Dave would have thought: a room full of half-strangers but his daughter nowhere in sight.

I didn't see Jesse or even Jason, but as I scanned the back row I noticed Fred, the man with the horseshoe hair-line who came into my room during Dave's backyard barbeque all those years ago. I stared at him for a few seconds, long enough to make the room uncomfortable by my silence. He was looking down and perhaps didn't notice he was the subject of my gaze. I stared until I started crying, the salt of my tears stinging my cheeks. But my tears were not ones of sadness. Instead, they were ones of rage at everyone who had fucked Dave over.

At the top of the list was God for ending Dave's life at the young age of fifty-eight when he hadn't even flown on an airplane, when he clearly deserved to become an old man. Number two was my mother, who took Dave away from his simple, happy days as a single man and then abandoned him with a baby and a stranger's child. Next up was Jesse, who never knew how lucky she was to have him as a father, who took advantage of his time and attention, and who couldn't even be bothered to show up to bury him. And then there was this asshole Fred, the pervert lurking at the back of the room, the backstabbing prick who tried to prey on Dave's stepdaughter and then had the nerve to show up at his funeral with his polyester suit and his ugly, shiny head. At least he was looking down in shame. I cried for two solid minutes, an eternity for everyone who had to sit there, shifting in their seats, growing increasingly uncomfortable.

Nobody approached me, but as I stood sobbing I noticed Becky with her husband and sons, all seated with their heads bowed. Feeling guilty, I pushed the anger down just enough so that I could start to speak.

"I'd like to say a few things about Dave—my father," I said. My voice was shaky at first but grew increasingly steady as I went on.

"As most of you know, Dave wasn't my biological dad. I'm not even sure if I can technically call him my stepfather. He was my mother's boyfriend for a short time, and that's all that really connected us. That—and the fact that he raised me and my sister after my mom left. By the way, Jesse isn't here today ... I know some of you were wondering."

I looked out the window for a second as I thought of what to say next. A child kicked the seat in front of him. Somebody coughed.

"I met Dave at the diner where my mom worked when I was a kid. In some ways, it feels like that happened last week. It's almost as if, were I to reach out my hand, I might be able to touch his face or feel his jean jacket on that day.

"By all appearances, Dave was a simple guy. He loved dogs. He liked to be outdoors. He listened to rock music full-blast and he was most comfortable behind the wheel of a truck.

"Yet Dave was also the most special person I've ever known. He took me in and raised me like a daughter and never in all of my life did he make me feel like we had anything less than any other father-daughter relationship. In fact, he always made me feel like we had something even more special. Because we were not linked by blood, our bond was even deeper. I don't know why it took me so long to realize that, and to acknowledge it. Maybe I was too afraid it wouldn't last, that one day he would change his mind and not want to be my dad anymore. I was too busy thinking about myself. And now I'm standing here and I'm wishing that I told him. I wish that I told him how much I loved him. And what a wonderful, selfless person he was.

"Dave taught me forgiveness. He taught me sacrifice. But above everything, he showed me what the true meaning of family really is."

I finished my eulogy by spending the next several minutes thanking some of the people who helped Dave along the way. I thanked Becky and her family. I thanked Mom for bringing Dave and me together. And, even though she really, really didn't deserve it, I thanked Jesse for bringing joy to Dave's life. I hadn't planned on being so generous, but Dave would have wanted me to do it. And so I did it. I did it for him.

CHAPTER TWENTY-SIX

EMMA

September 2011

THE DOORBELL RANG. I ignored it the first time, not wanting to be disturbed by some charity seeking a donation. But it rang again, the second time longer and more insistent.

I got up off the couch and went to the door, opening the safety latch and then the lock.

It was Jason with a girl. His daughter. My niece.

"Hi," he said.

I didn't say anything. I was frozen.

"This is Emma. Say hi, Emma."

The girl didn't say hi, but instead slid herself further behind her dad's leg. Her hair was dark blonde and she had a few freckles sprinkled on her nose and cheeks. I wasn't searching for any kind of resemblance, but it struck me immediately: she looked like Dave.

A few seconds of awkward silence, and then Jason asked: "Do you mind if we come in? I thought we could talk about a few things."

"Sure," I said, feeling my arms tingle from the shock and surprise of greeting them at my door. I didn't know what he wanted. I didn't know why he was there. I opened the door at a wider angle to welcome them in. Jason stepped in first; he held Emma's hand as she followed him.

"We can go in the kitchen and I can make tea ... or hot chocolate even."

"That'd be great," Jason said.

Jason followed my lead as if he'd never been in the house before. Both he and Emma sat down at the kitchen table as I pivoted to the stove. I put on some water to boil and joined them.

"So," I said. "How have you been?"

"Surviving," Jason said. "We're busy with work and school. Emma just started Senior Kindergarten."

"That's nice," I said. "Congratulations."

She didn't say anything.

"Melanie, could we turn on the TV for Emma so that she can watch it while we talk?"

"Sorry," I said. "I cut the cable. I didn't watch it much anymore."

The little girl looked at me.

"But I have crayons and paper?" I said. "I used to love doing art when I was your age. Would you like that?"

Emma nodded.

"Yes, please," Jason said.

"Yes, please," she said.

I opened one of the kitchen drawers, where I had a few sheets of loose-leaf paper and a box of crayons. The package was several years old, a holdover from a previous class I taught. I placed them in front of Emma and her face brightened at the blank canvas.

"Maybe the kitchen's not the best place for this," Jason said. "Do you have a desk or somewhere for her to colour?"

"I have a special place upstairs." It was the second bedroom. The spare room. "Emma, would you like to see what I mean?"

She nodded, but kept her gaze fixed on her dad, making sure it was okay. The three of us got up and Jason led her by the hand to the bedroom I'd converted to an office. He knelt down as she sat in the desk chair to make sure they were at eye level. "Have fun, sweetheart. You can colour here while me and Melanie talk downstairs. Call me if you need me, okay?"

"Okay," she said.

The two of us headed back downstairs. I turned off the boiling water and sat in front of him at the table.

"So, what did you want to talk about?" I asked. There was no sense in further pleasantries.

"I've been in touch with Jesse," he said, his hands clasped together in front of him on the table. "It wasn't easy to find her this time."

"That's nice. Did you ask her why she missed Dave's funeral?"

"Melanie . . ."

"But that'd be a silly question coming from you, right? Because you weren't there, either."

"You know you didn't want me there," Jason said. "Believe me, it was harder to stay away. I was hurting, too, when Dave died."

"Oh, please."

"Jesse's not coming back, Melanie. She's still out west and finished a stint in rehab a few months ago. It was some strange-sounding clinic, one of those places that puts a lot of emphasis on spirituality. She says she's started a new life."

"That's great," I said.

"She's changed her name. She doesn't want any part of her past."

"Good for her."

"She doesn't want to see me or Emma. She says she's clean now. She's moved on and hopes I understand."

"I'm happy for her … but what do you want from me?"

Jason bristled and looked down at the table for a moment. "Could you make me a cup of tea?"

The tea. I had forgotten about it. I got up from my seat and walked to the cupboard. We'd been talking for only a few minutes, and I already needed a break.

"Chamomile or orange pekoe?" I asked, even though I already knew the answer.

"Orange pekoe."

"Sugar or milk?" But I knew this answer, too.

I poured the tea and added the milk and sugar, placing the mug in front of him. Jason wrapped both hands around it and looked at me.

"Melanie, I spent three months looking for Jess before I finally found her … I guess I came here to let you know that she's okay. And that she says she doesn't want anyone to contact her anymore. I felt I should tell you … and also, I thought you'd want to know for Emma's sake."

"What do you mean?"

"I mean, I don't think there's really any hope of Jesse being in Emma's life. And I know … I know you know what that's like … for a child."

"In what sense? I don't know what you mean."

Jason sighed. "You know what I mean, Mel."

"Not really. My mother was around for my early years. Jesse was never a mother to Emma. The fact that she doesn't plan to come home means absolutely nothing."

"Do you think things have been easy for me?" Jason asked. "Or Emma?"

"I wouldn't know, Jason, but I didn't make these choices. I didn't ask you to do what you did."

"I know that, Mel." He sighed and took a sip of his tea. "But things haven't been easy. Emma's a beautiful little girl, but she needs a mom. She deserves better."

I didn't say anything.

"So," he said, slowing his speech, looking down at his mug, "if there's any chance that you wanted to play a part in any way, see her regularly, in spite of everything between us ... that might be ... that would be nice."

"You've got to be kidding."

"I'm not."

"It's a joke. You're joking."

"Who's laughing?" He looked at me.

"Jason, please go ... just please leave."

"Come on, Mel. Why do you have to be this way?"

"Be what way, Jason? Why are you here? Because you need help?"

"I don't need help," he said, his voice charged. "I've been doing this on my own for years now. This is about Emma. And what Emma doesn't have is a mother. I thought you'd maybe consider playing some kind of role in her life—the same way Dave did with you."

I stood up from my chair and slammed the table, Jason's tea rippling in his mug in front of him.

"Don't you dare! Don't you dare play on my emotions when it comes to Dave to try to get what you want. Don't do that to me."

Jason stood up to meet my gaze. "Why not? Why couldn't you step up to the plate the same way that Dave did with you when you were a kid? I'm not even asking for that much. I'm not asking you to take her in or anything. What I want is for her to have a female figure in her life. Someone to take her to soccer practice. Someone for her to talk to. Someone to look up to."

"No," I said. "The situation with me was different."

"And so what?" Jason said. "Dave didn't have to raise you—and yet he did. He took you on and you were a stranger."

"Dave was my father," I said. "We had a special relationship and I was a good daughter."

"Is that what you think? That you were so perfect?" Jason was still standing, still staring me in the eye. "The problem with you, Melanie, is that you always think you're right—you blame everyone else for everything."

"Stop it!" I yelled. "Stop trying to hurt me. You don't know anything." I was angry. I was shaking.

"I know what I know," Jason said. "I should probably leave."

"Please go now."

I stood in the kitchen and waited for him to get Emma. I didn't meet them at the door and I didn't say goodbye. Instead, I waited and listened as they put on their shoes and left the house, quietly shutting the door behind them.

CHAPTER TWENTY-SEVEN

MOTHERHOOD

October 2011

IT WASN'T EASY finding the cabin in the woods again. While I remembered the place well, I had no record of its address. I did my best rifling through Dave's old files. And then I did some sleuthing online. Finally, I called Becky to ask if she could remember anything. Turns out she was the one who helped Dave rent it in the first place.

"I can't believe it," I said. "Do you think I can go back for a visit?"

Becky hesitated. "I'm not sure, Mel. It's not as easy as you think."

"Please Beck, it's important. It's just for a couple of days."

"You bringing a lover boy or something?"

"No, just myself. Come on—what do you think?"

Becky stayed silent for a few seconds and then cleared her throat. "My uncle still owns the place, but he's been sick for a while now. Nobody's been there in years. From what I hear, the place is falling apart. It may not even be standing to tell you the truth."

"I'll take my chances."

She agreed to see what she could do and promised to call me later. It took a couple of weeks, but Becky finally reached out to say she had the keys. "I'll mail them to you if you still want to go," she said. "But be warned, I'm not sure you'll want to stay there."

The air and the leaves were already crisp, so I decided to head up before the weather turned any cooler. The keys arrived the next Thursday and I left Friday after work. It was Thanksgiving weekend with thousands of college and university students trying to leave town. I packed my car with a giant overnight bag with water, candles, dried food, blankets, clothes and toilet paper. I started my drive at the peak of Friday afternoon rush hour and inched my way east. The sky was dark and the air was cool, but I kept my window open so I could hang my arm outside the way Dave used to. Traffic intensified the closer I got to Toronto, so I pulled off the 401 and took the rural roads. I picked up speed as I passed by farmers' fields, feeling calm as I pushed through on my journey.

With the help of the car's navigation system, I rediscovered the route Dave took nearly twenty-five years before. After several hours of driving, I pulled up along the gravel path, put my car in park and surveyed what was ahead of me.

The outside of the tiny green cabin looked just as I'd remembered. I sat and stared at it, rubbing my fingers along the back of my head. I felt the small rough patch of skin that remained where a tuft of hair had once been.

Taking a deep breath, I turned off my car, the hum of the engine halting suddenly. I found the key to the door, grabbed my overnight bag, jumped out of the vehicle and raced toward the cabin. Guided by minimal moonlight, I climbed the uneven floorboards of the front porch, jamming the key inside the lock of the dilapidated door. I turned right and pushed forward. The stench of mildew hit me in the face as soon as I walked inside.

Trembling, I shut the door behind me and felt my way along the wall until I found a light switch. I flipped it on, but nothing happened. Prepared for this possibility, I crouched down and fished through my bag until I found the stubby bottom of one of the candles I'd packed. I pulled it out and, with the matches tucked away in the back pocket of my jeans, illuminated the room.

The lone candle provided enough light to see the outline of the simple square room and its limited contents: a floppy couch, a wooden dresser and a door to a toilet and sink. Even by candlelight I could see the thick layer of dust coating the floor.

I curled up on the sofa and wrapped myself in a blanket, worried I'd be up all night. Sleep came easily, but I woke up a short time later in the middle of the night to a fierce storm whose booms of thunder bounced off the lake. I got out of bed and tried looking out the windows, but they were so dirty I could only make out when lightning struck. I returned to the couch and a few minutes later heard a thud against the door. It wasn't aggressive, but something was on the other side, hitting it almost rhythmically. My heart pounding, I dragged the old wooden dresser a few feet over so that it was blocking the door, unsure if it was large or sturdy enough to hold back whatever was on the other side. I lay back down, the blood coursing through my veins and my adrenaline racing. I stayed like this for at least another hour until I finally drifted back to sleep.

I woke up several hours later to sunshine, a crisp autumn morning that bore no signs of the storm that raged the night before. Needing to pee, I opened the front door as slowly as possible, poking my head outside to see if there was any sign of whatever lurked last night. It seemed safe enough.

I walked out and found a place to go to the bathroom, close enough to run back inside if I saw a bear. The trees around me were still wet, the air fresh with the cooler season. As I headed back to the cabin, I noticed a loose cable hanging from the roof of the porch, something that was used to perhaps hold a light or a wind chime of some kind. That was what had been hitting the front of the cabin during the storm.

With the sun fully risen and the cabin bathed in light, I changed clothes and headed back outside to take a walk. Though the property had been neglected, it was as serene and beautiful as I'd remembered. The lake was still dark and grey, its stillness only briefly interrupted by the occasional autumn breeze.

At the side of the cabin, I found a shed that was padlocked. I took out the keychain Becky sent me—a plastic loon that had been slightly chewed either by a dog or a child—and tried one of the keys. I opened the doors and saw it right away: the orange paddleboat standing upright, its bottom up against the back wall. Tilted diagonally so that it could fit inside the shed was a green canoe. I started with its paddles, taking each one out carefully and placing them beside the shed. Then I took hold of the canoe, grabbing the bottom end to drag it outside. This was trickier than it looked. With both ends jammed up against each corner of the shed, I wriggled it to loosen things up, but it wouldn't budge. The paddleboat was up against the back wall, taking up space, so I slid my hands underneath it at the bottom and moved it a few inches. This gave the canoe some breathing room at the top where it was jammed. I pulled the canoe out of the shed and down toward the lake, leaving the paddleboat where it was.

With the ground slick from the rainstorm, I slid the canoe into the water so that the back end was still on land. I climbed in gingerly, careful not to tip it and spoil one of my few sets of clothes. Once I was settled in, I grabbed the oar and slowly eased my way further into the lake.

I decided to turn left, paddling awkwardly at first but finding my rhythm as I kept going. I let the boat glide as I picked up speed, taking a moment to notice the trees around me, the bright morning sky. Instead of hugging the shoreline, I stayed squarely in the centre of the lake so that I could keep my bearings and take in all of what was around me.

Besides the odd cabin or cottage, all of which appeared to be abandoned for the cooler season, I saw no one and heard nothing. Surrounded by solitude, my thoughts turned to my husband and sister, my mom, baby and dad.

I thought of Jason as I paddled through the same narrow terrain I passed the last time. I thought of Jesse as the lake widened and the weeping willows came into view. I thought of Mom as I noticed the cottage where that couple had helped us. I thought of my baby as I decided to keep going and see where the water took me. But, mostly, I thought of Dave and all the love he gave me. I paddled for so long that my cheeks became flush, my throat burned and my arms ached.

Eventually, I stopped the canoe and looked around. The crimson reds, golds and oranges of the trees that surrounded me glowed against the darkness of the lake. I took a deep breath and thought about my bond with Dave, the dotted lines that connected us, and why I came back here.

Did I want to help raise Emma, a girl who was not only not mine, but who was also alive only because my own daughter was not? I knew I had every right to run away, to reject Jason's offer and to move on. And yet, when I thought of her, and remembered everything Dave had given me, I no longer felt resentment. I felt gratitude.

I sat there for a while longer, then turned around to head back to the cabin. As I paddled those last few strokes, I wondered how we had ever managed to get lost. I knew where I was this time. I knew how to get back.

I wasn't sure what time it was when I finally returned. Seeing where the sun was and where the light hit the lake, I could tell it'd been hours. Once I was a few metres from shore, I stood up in the canoe, the boat rocking heavily and threatening to throw me overboard. I sat back down for a moment, taking a minute to kick off my pants, sweater and shoes. Then I stood up, closed my eyes, plugged my nose and jumped out of the canoe and into the dark lake.

My heart lunged in my throat as the cold water slapped the back of my arms, filled my ear canals, tingled

my toes. I emerged a few moments later, the canoe bobbing a few feet away. I squealed, then shrieked. And then
I laughed to myself, feeling calm and happy.

For the first time in a long time, I felt happy. I knew
I had better days ahead of me. I was going to help raise
Emma. I was going to be a mother.

Continuing to laugh to myself, I swam back to shore,
tugging the green canoe along with me. Once I was in
shallow water, I stood up on my feet, pulled the boat
back to land, grabbed my dry clothes and ran back into
the cabin.

ACKNOWLEDGEMENTS

I WOULD LIKE to express my gratitude to the University of Toronto School of Continuing Studies, where much of this book was produced during my completion of the creative writing program. Thanks in particular to the support of Michel Basilières, Lee Gowan, Ibi Kaslik, Alexandra Leggat and Ken Murray. My appreciation also goes to Terry Fallis, who was kind and generous enough to meet with a stranger to share his wisdom and guidance.

For their editorial help and encouragement, I would like to acknowledge my early readers: Paul Barbuto, Andrea Bernard, Edmund Fines, Maureen Mclafferty, Daniel Mueller, Matthew Pacchione and Anne-Marie Whittle. A second acknowledgment goes to Edmund for welcoming me into such a talented writing group.

Thank you to Michael Mirolla and the team at Guernica Editions for giving this story a wonderful home. Much gratitude goes to Julie Roorda, who edited with such attention to detail. And to David Moratto, who designed the beautiful cover.

For use of their lyrics from the song "Good Thing," I would like to acknowledge the Fine Young Cannibals (*The Raw & the Cooked*, London Records Ltd.)

Notably, I would like to extend my gratitude to the doctors, nurses and staff at the Princess Margaret Cancer Centre in Toronto who restored my good health during the editing process of this book. In particular, I would like to acknowledge Dr. Eitan Amir, Dr. Tulin Cil, Dr. Stefan Hofer, Dr. Anne Koch, Dr. Emma Mauti and the incredibly dedicated and compassionate teams who work with them. Thanks to Constance Lau and Rebecca Morier for allowing me to link my arms in theirs. And special recognition goes to Adina Isenberg, who swooped in from the skies above and stood by my side the entire time.

Many thanks to my big and beautiful family for surrounding me with lots of love and supporting me in every way possible. And to my friends for always cheering me on. Above all, thank you to Matthew Alexander for reading numerous drafts of this novel and for being the best partner one could have.

ABOUT THE AUTHOR

Stephanie Cesca was born and raised in Toronto, where she lives with her husband and three children. A former newspaper editor in both Canada and Europe, she holds an English degree from Western University, a journalism degree from Toronto Metropolitan University and a Certificate of Creative Writing from the University of Toronto School of Continuing Studies. Her work has been shortlisted for the Penguin Random House Canada Student Award for Fiction and The Marina Nemat Award for Creative Writing. *Dotted Lines* is her first novel.

Printed by Imprimerie Gauvin
Gatineau, Québec